W. M. L Jay, Phillips Brooks

Good Cheer for a Year

Selections from the Writings of Phillips Brooks

W. M. L Jay, Phillips Brooks

Good Cheer for a Year
Selections from the Writings of Phillips Brooks

ISBN/EAN: 9783337327262

Printed in Europe, USA, Canada, Australia, Japan

Cover: Foto ©Andreas Hilbeck / pixelio.de

More available books at **www.hansebooks.com**

FOR A YEAR

SELECTIONS FROM THE WRITINGS OF THE

Rt. Rev. PHILLIPS BROOKS, D.D.

BY

W. M. L. JAY

> All life which would not grow stale and monotonous must feed itself upon God. . . . All life which would make To-day the transmutation place where Yesterday shall give its power to Forever, must be full of the felt presence of Him in whom yesterday, to-day and forever are all one.— vi. 344.

NEW YORK

E. P. DUTTON AND COMPANY

31 WEST TWENTY-THIRD STREET

1896

Press of J. J. Little & Co.
Astor Place, New York

PREFACE.

IT is too soon to let the ministry of Bishop Brooks pass into the shadow of forgetfulness. He " yet speaketh " in a multitude of works which, in a remarkable degree, combine lofty spirituality and plain practicalness with rare human sympathy, and are therefore particularly well adapted to the sustenance and guidance of the daily Christian life. There are those who are so fortunate as to be able to study these works as a whole, but there are also many busy people who are glad to have one thought, suitable and sufficient unto the day, ready to their hands in a convenient form. To such a second year-book is offered, not by the same hand as the first, but compiled on the same plan, for the excellent reason that it cannot be bettered.

The labor of making the book has been increased by the abundance of the material. Many year-books might be quarried out of it without exhausting its richness and variety, or its wealth of helpful suggestion for those who are trying to live the life of faith in unison with the life of action, to "round every truth with its duty, and deepen every duty into its truth." Inevitably the thought comes that such a daily ministry to hearts thrilled and elated with life's duties and joys, or sore and weary with its burdens, must be deeply gratifying to him with whose rich and abundant life of faith and works it is impossible to associate any thought of death. The monks of Antioch were wont to say of a brother, not "He is dead," but "He is perfected."

For those who like to follow the Christian Year, and who may wish to use the book more than once, selections for the greater movable fasts and feasts are appended to the volume.

W. M. L. JAY.

[The Roman numerals at the end of the selections refer to the above list of books; the Arabic numerals to the pages where the selections may be found.]

*Be strong and of a good courage, . . . for the
Lord thy God is with thee wherever thou goest.*

JOSH. i. 9.

THE poetry of all growing life consists in
carrying an oldness into a newness, a past
into a future, always.   So only can our days
possibly be " bound each to each by natural
piety."   I would not for the world think that
twenty years hence I should have ceased to see
the things which I see now, and love them still.
It would make life wearisome beyond expression if I thought that twenty years hence I
should see them just as I see them now, and
love them with no deeper love because of other
visions of their lovableness.   And so there
comes this deep and simple rule for any man
as he crosses the line dividing one period of
his life from another: Make it a time in which
you shall realize your faith, and also in which
you shall expect of your faith new and greater
things.   Take what you believe and are and
hold it in your hand with new firmness as you
go forward; but as you go, holding it, look on
it with continual and confident expectation to
see it open into something greater and truer.

V. 296.

Go with the sun and the stars, and yet evermore in thy spirit
Say to thyself: It is good, yet there is better
than it:
This that I see is not all, and this that I do is
but little;
Nevertheless it is good, though there is better
than it.   ARTHUR HUGH CLOUGH.

I think that nothing made is lost,
   That not a moon has ever shone,
That not a cloud my eyes hath crossed,
   But to my soul is gone;

That all the lost years garnered lie
   In this Thy casket, my dim soul;
And Thou wilt, once, the key supply,
   And show the shining whole.

GEORGE MACDONALD.

WHILE we leave everything behind in time, it is no less true that nothing is wholly left behind. All that we ever have been or done is with us in some power and consequence of it until the end. . . . The unity of life is never lost. There must not be any waste. How great and gracious is the economy of life which it involves! Neither to dwell in any experience always, nor to count any experience as if it had not been, but to leave the forms of our experiences behind, and to go forth from them clothed in their spiritual power, which is infinitely free and capable of new activities,—this is what God is always teaching us is possible, and tempting us to do. To him who does it come the two great blessings of a growing life,—faithfulness and liberty: faithfulness in each moment's task, and liberty to enter through the gates beyond which lies the larger future. " Well done, good servant: thou hast been faithful over a few things. Enter thou into the joy of thy Lord."

VI. 57, 58.

And because ye are sons, God hath sent forth the Spirit of His Son into your hearts, crying, Abba, Father.—GAL. iv. 6.

WERE there ever verses that had a sublimer occupancy? God is there, and Jesus Christ, and the Holy Spirit. And in the midst of them all, as the being for whom they all are working, there is *man*. As the windows of these verses open, this is what we see: all the prevalent influence of heaven gathered around man, and by its united power bringing him into the perfect sympathy of God. The Father sees him and loves him; the Son comes and seeks him; the Spirit spreads through his heart the sense of all this love; and then he, loved, redeemed, and quickened, reconciled to God, is seen, at the last, lifting up his hands and claiming God, crying, " Abba, Father." What a vast chorus of sublimest life! How the soul stands amazed and awed! Here are all heaven and all that is capable of heavenliness upon earth met together, and the end of their meeting is complete accord. God is pouring His life into man. Man is sending back his tribute—rendering his life to God. It is the chorus of reconciled Divinity and humanity.   VII. 99.

O wonderful, oh, passing thought,
  The love that God hath had for thee,
Spending on thee no less a sum
  Than the undivided Trinity!

FABER.

From glory to glory.—2 COR. iii. 18.

WHEN Saint Paul wants to depict the vast variety of which the world is full, it was distinctly as a variety of glory that he conceived of it. Enough he knew of the variety of woe. Easily enough he might have depicted how man, the same man still, was tossed from suffering to suffering and remained the same identical miserable sufferer in all. It would have been the same truth taught upon its darker side. But Paul knew that the true side on which to teach it was its side of light. The real variety of life is a variety of glories. Such a choice of the side from which to draw his illustration is a noble characteristic of Saint Paul. It is a sign of how healthy he is. Change from glory into glory,—that was what life seemed to him. Remember, it is no rapturous and untired boy who is talking; it is a man all sore with sorrow, beaten and broken with disappointment and distress. Is it not a sign of what a true Christian he was that life seemed to him still to be only a variety and constant interchange of glories ?   V. 62.

" From glory unto glory ! " What great
    things He hath done ! . . .
But sweeter than the Christmas chimes rings
    out His promise clear—
That " greater things," far greater, our long-
    ing eyes shall see !
We can but wait and wonder what " greater
    things" shall be.

FRANCES R. HAVERGAL.

> " Comest thou as friend ?
>   Comest thou as foe ? "
>
> " Nay, 'tis thou wilt bend
>   Me to weal or woe.
>   As thou usest me,
>   Shall I be to thee
>   Friend or foe."
>
> J. L. M. W.

THINGS are what they are used for. . . .
The artist uses a stone, and it is a statue;
the mason uses a stone, and it is a doorstep.
And beyond mere nature.   See how we use
men.   We are each other's raw material.   I
make you up in some shape into my life, and
you in some way make me up into yours.   But
what man is of so fixed a character that he
can be made up only into one invariable thing ?
Each man makes of his neighbor that for which
he uses him. . . .

So of all influences and motives.   The same
educations wall and press upon two lives.   One
rises on them into greatness, the other drags
them down upon it and is crushed beneath
them into ruin. . . . How is it that the Phari-
see and the Publican came down the same
temple steps, one cold, and proud, and bitter,
and the other with his heart full of tenderness,
and gratitude, and humblest charity ?

VI. 25, 26.

Shine as lights in the world; Holding forth the word of life.—PHIL. ii. 15, 16.

A MAN'S place is made ready for him in the mind of God; the man's life is set here as a positive, clear fact; and what comes next? There is no doubt what ought to come. That life must *tell*. It must go out beyond itself. It must have *influence*. It must testify and supplement the mere fact of its existence by making other existences be something which they would not be without it. This seems so plain. This is so clearly set forth in the great typical life of Jesus. . . . Can you picture to yourself God coming into this world and then living a perfectly self-contained life —one that recognized no relations with and exercised no power over other lives about Him? No! The epiphany followed immediately on the advent and the nativity. . . . He let His life go forth on other lives. He let His great light shine before men. But how many there are who realize their advent and their nativity who have never conceived for themselves of an epiphany! . . . never have dreamed that they were put here *where* they are, and made to be *what* they are, in order that other men might be something else through them.

VII. 8, 9.

All are needed by each one:
Nothing is fair or good alone.

EMERSON.

The Son of Man came not to be ministered unto, but to minister, and to give His life a ransom for many.—MARK X. 45.

THERE are theories of self-culture which are printed in books, given as very gospels to our children as they grow up, which would be just exactly the same that they now are if no such dream as a possible duty of usefulness and influence from that child to other people had ever entered into the thought of God or man. . . . " Be strong, be rich, be wise, be good." What for ? " Why, so that you may be wise and rich and strong and good." The endless circle, with its bright monotonous round! No wonder that so many young men are asking in the bottom of their hearts questions of most terrible skepticism: " What is the use ? Is it worth while to be wise and strong and rich and good ? " Ah, you must find the use *outside yourself*. You must let your light shine *before men*, that they may see your good works, and glorify your Father which is in heaven. You must complete your advent and nativity with an epiphany of yourself. Then it will seem well worth while to light your human light most brilliantly and keep it trimmed most vigilantly.

Only shine *toward* your brethren's lives, only be your best in their direction.

VII. 9, 10.

What others claim from us is not our thirst and our hunger, but our bread and our gourd.

AMIEL.

He hath made everything beautiful in His time.
ECCLES. iii. 11.

FOR sin and holiness are not in things, but in souls; and all things are beautiful in the time when a soul uses them for holy uses with a loving, humble, and obedient life. . . . The human soul sits at the centre of everything, and Christ sits at the centre of the human soul. If HE changes us, then everything will be changed to us. "He that sitteth upon the throne saith, Behold I make all things new!" If the world is ugly and bitter and cruel to you: if circumstances taunt and persecute you: if everything you touch is a strain and a temptation, do not stand idly wishing that the world were changed. The change must be in you. To the new heart all things shall be new. The new man shall see already the new heaven and the new earth. If any man be in Christ, he is a new creature; and the new creature is immediately in the new creation. Some of you know already by daily experience what that means. And for all of you, it waits to be revealed, if you will let Christ do His work in you.   IV. 261.

There is a rest that deeper grows
  In midst of pain and strife;
A mighty, conscious, willed repose,
  The heart of deepest life.
To have and hold the precious prize,
  No need of jealous bars,
But windows open to the skies,
  And skill to read the stars.
GEORGE MACDONALD.

"O, TO be nothing, nothing!" cries the mystic singer in his revival hymn, desiring to lose himself in God. "Nay, not that; O, to be something, something," remonstrates the unmystical man, longing for work, ardent for personal life and character. Where is the meeting of the two? How shall self-surrender meet that high self-value without which no man can justify his living and honor himself in his humanity? Where can they meet but in this truth? Man must be something that he may be nothing. The something which he must be must consist in simple fitness to utter the divine life which is the only original power in the universe. And then man must be nothing that he may be something. He must submit himself in obedience to God, that so God may use him, in some way in which his special nature only could be used, to illuminate and help the world. Tell me, do not the two cries meet in that one aspiration of the Christian man to find his life by losing it in God, to be himself by being not his own but Christ's? II. 18.

I could not choose a larger bliss
  Than to be wholly Thine; and mine
A will whose highest joy is this,
  To ceaselessly unclasp in Thine.

.   .   .   .

We are not losers thus; we share
  The perfect gladness of the Son,—
Not conquered, for, behold, we reign,
  Conquered and Conqueror are one.

JEAN SOPHIA PIGOTT.

Son, why hast thou thus dealt with us?
LUKE ii. 48.

WHO is there of us that is not aware that his soul has had two educations? . . . Our own government of ourselves is most evident, is the one which we are most aware of, so that sometimes for a few moments we forget that there is any other; but very soon our plans for ourselves are so turned and altered and hindered that we cannot ignore the other greater, deeper force. We meant to do that, and look! we have been led on to this. We meant to be this, and lo! we are that. We never meant to believe this, and lo! we hold it with all our hearts. What does it mean? It is the everlasting discovery, the discovery which each thoughtful man makes for himself with almost as much surprise as if no other man had ever made it for himself before, that this soul, for which he is responsible, is not his soul only, but is God's soul too. The revelation which came of old to the Virgin Mother about her child—Not your child only, but God's child too; yours, genuinely, really yours, but behind yours, and over yours, God's.

IV. 36.

Why ever make man's good distinct from
    God's?
Or, finding they are one, why dare mistrust?
BROWNING.

I AM often struck by seeing how the loftiness of the life of Jesus altogether escaped the perplexity of many of the questions with which our lives are troubled, as the eagle flying through the sky is not worried how to cross the rivers. We debate whether self culture or our brethren's service is the true purpose of our life. We vacillate aimlessly. . . . We are so apt to live two lives. But Jesus knows but one. All culture of His soul is a part of our salvation. All doing of His work is ripening His nature. . . . And not until our brawling ceases and the champion of each side of the question rounds his truth with his adversary's truth which he has been denouncing, not until the apostle of self-culture knows that no man can come to his best by selfishness, and the apostle of usefulness knows that no man can do much for other men who is not much himself,—not until then shall men have fairly started on the broad road to the completeness of God their Father in the footsteps of the Son of Man.

VIII. 109.

Let Christ be thy Life;
Let Him be thy Meditation and thy Discourse;
Let Him be thy Desire, thy Gain, thy whole
    Hope, and thy Reward.
If thou seekest anything but God purely, thou
    wilt suffer loss;
Thou shalt labor and shalt find no rest.

THOMAS À KEMPIS.

Words divine, and prayers, and blessings,
Sorrows, sacraments, and alms,
Humble souls, with care o'erwearied,
Bended knees and folded palms,—
These are working wondrous changes,
Unperceived, except by faith.

CAROLINE M. NOEL.

THINK how with the successive generations of mankind, each leaving countless new monuments of divine love and human possibility upon the earth, the earth itself is growing richer every year. Every year some new valley gets its consecration from some new soul's struggle with sin. Every year some new mountain-top burns with another soul's rapture of salvation. We read of the promise of the new heavens and the new earth wherein righteousness shall dwell. Are not the heavens and the earth ever growing new, newer, and more full of righteousness every day? When the time shall come that every star in heaven and every stone on earth shall be vocal with some word of God which it has heard, and in their midst shall live the race of men, no longer deaf and obstinate, but quick-eared to hear and loving-hearted to obey those words as they come crowding in, making the air sacred on every side—when that shall come, shall not the promise then have been fulfilled, and the " New Heavens and the New Earth wherein dwelleth righteousness " be a sublime reality ?

VI. 275.

Faith is the sun of life; and her countenance
   shines like the Hebrew's,
For she has looked upon God.
LONGFELLOW.

GOD forbid that in trying to make faith
    seem glorious, I should make it seem
impossible! But it is true of God's gifts always that the most complete of them are the
most possibly universal. . . . To be loved is
better than to be admired; and admiration is
the privilege of a few brilliant natures, while
love is within the reach of any pure and loving
heart. Art is the privilege of the few, but
nature opens her treasures wide. . . . If this
be so, then how must it be with that blessing
which outgoes all others—the blessing of faith,
the blessing of living under the perpetually
recognized lordship of Christ? The finest of
all gifts of God—may we not look for it to be
the freest also ? Free as the air, which is the
most precious thing that the world contains,
and yet struggles as nothing else in all the
world struggles to give itself away.
VI. 104, 105.

At the devil's mart are all things sold,
Each ounce of dross costs its ounce of gold;
For a cap and bells our lives we pay:
   Bubbles we earn with our whole soul's task-
     ing;
'Tis only God that is given away,
   'Tis only heaven may be had for the asking.
JAMES RUSSELL LOWELL.

That ye might believe that Jesus is the Christ, the Son of God ; and that believing ye might have life through His name.—JOHN xx. 31.

SUPPOSE that this divinity of Jesus becomes part of a man's faith . . . suppose that a man really believes that, entering into our human life, God has been here upon earth. What will that belief be to him that holds it ? . . . The question answers itself. If to believe in God is a glory and delight, the nearer the God whom I believe in comes to me, the more glorious and delightful grows my life. To tread an earth which He has trodden, to think thoughts and to feel emotions which, just as I think and feel them, in their human shapes, He the eternal God has thought and felt—this is assuredly a marvellous enrichment of my living. I have gone out and up into a new world with this new faith—a new world, yet the old world still; the old world teeming and bursting with new meanings, radiant with new light, sacred and beautiful all through with the remembered presence of the Son of God. Surely no man who has once known what it is to live in that world can ever turn his back upon its richness.

VII. 329, 330.

No longer is our life
 A thing unused or vain;
To us, even here, to live is Christ,
 To us to die is gain.

HORATIUS BONAR.

The sun shall be no more thy light by day ; neither for brightness shall the moon give light unto thee ; but the Lord shall be to thee an ever-lasting light.—Is. lx. 19.

THE lives of men who have been always growing are strewed along their whole course with the things which they have learned to do without. As the track of an army marching deep into an enemy's country is scattered all along with the equipage which the men seemed to find necessary when they started, but which they have learned to do without as the exigencies of their march grew greater, and they found that these provisions and equipments were partly such as they did not need at all, and partly such as they could gather out of the land through which they marched; so from the time when the child casts his leading strings aside because his legs are strong enough to carry him alone, the growing man goes on forever leaving each help for a higher, until at last, in that great change to which Isaiah's words seem to apply, he can do without sun and moon as he enters into the immediate presence and essential life of God.

I. 283.

I say that man was made to grow, not stop;
That help, he needed once and needs no more,
Having grown but an inch by, is withdrawn;
For he hath new needs, and new helps to these.
This imports solely—man should mount on each
New height in view: the help whereby he mounts,
The ladder-rung his foot hath left, may fall,
Since all things suffer change save God, the
      Truth.   BROWNING.

HOLINESS does not make men monotonous. The dimmer the light the more things look alike. Increase the light and then you see how different they are. Childhood with its bright hopefulness, and manhood with its enterprise, and womanhood with its tenderness—each grows more specially itself at the touch of grace. The old man and the young man, the thinker, the artist, the worker, the merchant, the doctor, and the lawyer—out of each comes up to the surface a profounder individuality when they all begin to live to God. And the subtler differences which distinguish man from man and woman from woman, making each being a separate thought of God, unlike any other—these become clearer as the idea of God in the creation of each becomes more fully realized. The pebbles lie dull and dead and all gray alike in the dry bed of the brook till with the spring freshet the water comes pouring down and wets them all alike and brings out their beautiful variety of color and makes them all different.

VII. 40.

The sunlight takes the hue
Of whatsoever shade it shineth through,
    Crimson or blue;
    And thus we find
The One great Light, that lighteth all mankind,
Taketh a varied coloring from each mind.

ANNA E. HAMILTON.

Whatever He saith unto you, do it.

JOHN ii. 5.

YOU make a friend, you read a book, you take a journey, you buy a house, you write a letter, and so full is the great world of God, so is He waiting everywhere to make Himself known and to give Himself away, that through this act of yours, to men who are looking and listening, there comes some revelation of His nature and some working of His power. . . . For acts have their true meanings in the points of manifestation and operation which they give to God. It was not because she knew that somehow they would have wine or something better, it was because her Son would surely show Himself through their obedience, if they obeyed Him, that Mary cared what these servants did. It is strange to think what a dignity and interest our own actions might have for us if we constantly recognize this capacity in them which they have not now. We play with bits of glass, finding great pleasure in their pleasant shapes, but never knowing what glorious things they would be if we held them up and let the sun shine through them.

V. 346.

O Everlasting Light,
  Shine graciously within!
Brightest of all on earth that's bright,
  Come, shine away my sin!

HORATIUS BONAR.

Curse ye Meroz, said the angel of the Lord, . . . because they came not to the help of the Lord against the mighty.—JUDG. v. 23.

THE sin for which Meroz is cursed is pure inaction. There is no sign that its people gave any aid or comfort to the enemy. They merely did nothing. We hear so much about the danger of wrong thinking and the danger of wrong doing. There is the other danger, of not doing right and not thinking right, of not doing and not thinking at all. . . . Whenever men hide behind their conscious feebleness; whenever, because they can do so little, they content themselves with doing nothing; whenever the one-talented men stand with their napkins in their hands along the roadside of life,—there is Meroz over again. . . . Grant that you are as small as you think you are, you are the average size of moral and intellectual humanity. Let all the Merozes in the land be humble like you, and where shall be the army ? Only when men like you wake up and shake the paralysis of their humility away, shall we begin to see the dawn of that glorious millennium for which we sigh; which will consist not in the transformation of men into angels, nor in the coming forth of a few colossal men to be the patterns and the champions of life, but simply in each man, through the length and breadth of the great world, doing his best.   II. 291, 298, 299.

> When obstacles and trials seem
>   Like prison walls to be,
> I do the little I can do,
>   And leave the rest to Thee.   FABER.

And they said . . . Let not God speak with us, lest we die.—Ex. xx. 19.

IS it not almost as if the fish cried, " Cast me not into the water, lest I drown," or as if the eagle said, " Let not the sun shine on me, lest I be blind " ? It is man fearing his native element. He was made to talk with God. . . . We find a revelation of this in all the deepest and highest moments of our lives. Have you not often been surprised by seeing how men who seemed to have no capacity for such experiences passed into a sense of divine companionship when anything disturbed their lives with supreme joy or sorrow ? Once or twice, at least, in his own life, almost every one of us has found himself face to face with God, and felt how natural it was to be there. Then all interpreters and agencies of Him have passed away. He has looked in on us directly; we have looked immediately upon Him; and we have not died,—we have supremely lived. We have known that we never had so lived as then. We have been aware how natural was that direct sympathy and union and communication with God.

V. 82.

And blest are they
Who, in this fleshly world, the elect of Heaven,
Their strong eye darting through the deeds
    of men,
Adore with steadfast, unpresuming gaze
Him, Nature's essence, mind, and energy.

S. T. COLERIDGE.

Acquaint now thyself with Him, and be at peace ; thereby good shall come unto thee.

JOB xxii. 21.

THE more you come into communion with God, catch His spirit, understand His life; the more quick your eye becomes to detect the spiritual life of other men though it be hidden under the strangest forms, the more broad your heart grows to embrace it.   Coming to love God is like climbing a high mountain.   It takes you out of the low valley of formal life.   It sets you upon the open summit of spiritual sympathy, close to the sun. Thence you look out into unguessed regions of noble thought and living, with which you never dreamed that you had anything to do. . . . There never was a man who really tried to serve God who did not have his sympathy with his fellow men widened thereby.

VII. 314.

ON THE MOUNTAIN TOP.

Dear world, I behold but your largeness; I
   forget that aught evil or mean
Ever marred the vast sphere of your beauty,
   over which as a lover I lean.
And not by our flaws will God judge us; His
   love keeps our noblest in sight:
Dear world, our low life sinks behind us; we
   look up to His infinite height.

LUCY LARCOM.

M EN talk as if because Christ is the same loving, willing Christ for all of us, and all of us are nothing and can have nothing but Him, therefore the meagre, mercenary saint ought to shine with the same lustre as the pure spirit passionate for holiness, and ready for all the completed will of God. As if one said that because the sun is the same sun always, and because there is no light except from him, therefore the rose and the daisy ought to look alike. No! He in His love outgoes our prayers. He gives us more of what we ask than we know how to ask for; more beauty to the seeker after beauty, more wisdom to the student, more safety to the poor culprit asking forgiveness. And He is always trying to make the self which asks a larger self, that He may give it other things of higher kinds. But yet the truth remains, that at each moment He can give Himself to us only as at that moment we give ourselves to Him.

III. 285.

Higher, purer, deeper, surer,
Be my thought, O Christ, of Thee!
Stretch the narrow bounds that limit
All my earth-born, sin-bound spirit
　　To the breadth of Thy divine.
　　Be the image purely Thine,
Not my thought, but Thy creation;
　　Deep within my spirit's shrine
Make the secret revelation;
　　Reproduce Thy life in mine!

Mrs. Merrill E. Gates.

ONE man approaches the divine Redeemer asking no divine redemption, but touched and fascinated by the beauty of that perfect life.   He would feed his wonder, he would cultivate his taste, upon it. . . . Another man comes to Jesus with a self that is all alive with curiosity.   He takes Christ's revelations—for Christ does not refuse him either—and goes away content to know much of God and man, and what there is beyond this world. . . . Each gets from Jesus that which the nature he brings can take. . . . Only when at last there comes a man with his self all open, with door behind door all unclosed, ready to give himself entirely, wanting everything that Jesus has to give, wanting and ready to take the whole of Jesus into himself—only then are the last gates withdrawn, and as when the ocean gathers itself up and enters with its tide the open mouth of the river, . . . so does the Lord in all His richness, with His perfect standards, His mighty motives, His infinite hopes, give Himself to the soul which has been utterly given to Him.   III. 284, 285.

Lord, we are rivers running to Thy sea,
Our waves and ripples all derived from Thee;
A nothing we should have, a nothing be,
          Except for Thee.

Sweet are the waters of Thy shoreless sea,
Make sweet our waters that make haste to
      Thee;
Pour in Thy sweetness, that ourselves may be
          Sweetness to Thee!
                    CHRISTINA G. ROSSETTI.

*And the king said, Is there not yet any . . . .
that I may show the kindness of God unto him?*
                          2 SAM. ix. 3.

HOW shall you make man know that God
    loves him? In every way,—there is no
speech nor language in which that voice may
not be heard,—but most of all by loving the
man with a great love yourself, by a lofty and
generous affection of which he shall know that,
coming through you, it comes from beyond
you, and say, "It is my Father that my
brother utters," and so be led up to the
Father's heart. We talk about men's reaching
through Nature up to Nature's God. It is
nothing to the way in which they may reach
through manhood up to manhood's God, and
learn the divine love by the human. God
make us all such revelations of His love to
some of His children!

                          V. 50.

For by human lovings climb we
    (As to cause from consequence)
To some dim, imperfect vision,
    To some awed but precious sense
Of the Love of love whose loving
    We have surnamed "Providence."

Ah, what gladness in the glory
    Of the better land to know
That to some poor, doubting, fearing,
    Hungering, thirsting soul below,
All unknowing, in our loving,
    We the love of God did show.
                          J. L. M. W.

For our light affliction, which is but for a moment, worketh out for us a far more exceeding and eternal weight of glory ; while we look not at the things which are seen, but at the things which are not seen : for the things which are seen are temporal ; but the things which are not seen are eternal.—2 COR. iv. 17, 18.

OH, the next life seems all so vague to us! We reach out after it. We believe in it, but how hard it is for us to take hold of it! How can we ? Only by living here with Him who is to bring us there. Only by growing so familiar with Christ that when He outruns us and enters in behind the veil, when the strings of His influence outgo our mortal state and run into the darkness, we may still feel the tug upon them from beyond the darkness and know the reality of heaven because our Christ is there. By constant living with the Eternal, so only can you realize Eternity. . . .

To welcome all His leadings now so cordially that we shall know our Leader when He opens the last great door; to be always following Him so obediently that we shall have faith to follow Him when He leads us into the river and into darkness,—this, and only this, is readiness for death.   VI. 185, 186.

O Lord of Light, steep Thou our souls in Thee,
  That when the daylight trembles into shade,
And falls the silence of mortality,
  And all is done, we shall not be afraid,
But pass from light to light; from earth's dull
    gleam
Into the very heart and heaven of our dream.
                    RICHARD WATSON GILDER.

*And suddenly there shined round about him a
light from heaven: . . . And he trembling and
astonished said, Lord, what wilt Thou have me to
do?*—ACTS ix. 3, 6.

WE talk so much about confession and
forgiveness; we elaborate their theory
so much; we see such intricate relations of
the divine and human natures involved in the
transaction, that we almost unconsciously
transfer the long train of thought into a long
period of time. We feel as if that result
which implies so much spiritual action must
be reached only by a process of correspond-
ingly prolonged duration. "To confess and
be forgiven—that is the work of months and
years, of a whole lifetime," we declare. . . .
But the volcano that the chemistry of years
has been preparing breaks into eruption in an
hour. The blossom that the patient plant
has been designing for a century bursts into
flower in a single night. And so the reconciliation of a soul to God, which it has been the
labor of the ages to make possible, which
dates for its conception back to the dateless
time when the Lamb was slain from the foundation of the world, comes to its completion
in the sudden meeting of a soul filled with
penitence and a God filled with mercy.

VII. 184.

As to Thy last Apostle's heart
Thy lightning glance did then impart
   Zeal's never-dying fire,
So teach us on Thy shrine to lay
Our hearts, and let them day by day
   Intenser blaze and higher.   KEBLE.

*Man shall not live by bread alone, but by every
word that proceedeth out of the mouth of God.*

MATT. iv. 4.

MAN is represented as feeding on the words
of God, and every word of God must
come for nurture to the life that is made up
of many parts. How splendid the figure is!
God . . . speaks once: "Let the earth bring
forth grass, the herb yielding seed, and the
fruit-tree yielding fruit."   And as He spoke,
those words, "proceeding out of the mouth
of the Lord," were caught by the quick, obedient ground of Genesis, and became the power
by which the physical life of man in all his
generations has been nourished. . . . Again,
He speaks out of some Sinai mountain, or
out of that Sinai of the inner life, our conscience. "Do this," He says, "and live,"
laying down duty after duty, which the moral
nature takes to itself and feeds upon, and
grows by them into rectitude and strength.
And then, last of all, to the highest life of
all, He utters His sublimest voice. What shall
we say that last word is by which He utters
Himself to, on which He feeds, man's deep
religious nature ? What can it be but that
eternal " Word " which was in the beginning
with God, which was God, which was made
flesh, and dwelt among us; that bread of life
which came down from heaven, of which a man
may eat and never die; the fulness of divine
utterance in the world's Saviour, Jesus Christ ?

VII. 155, 156.

THE real life, what is it ? Is it the wretched, sordid details of earthly living, uninspired by a single suggestion that in their mud and mire there are the seeds of any spiritual, transcendent fruit or flower ? On the other hand, is the real life a vision of some experience beyond the stars which has no connection with the dreariness and degradation of many of the mortal conditions which it has passed through and left behind ? Not so. The real life of a man is his highest attainment kept in perpetual association with the meanest and commonest experience out of which it has been fed. When men shall so write and paint the lives of one another, then we shall have the true realism,—a realism in which, to use the Psalmist's words, " Truth shall flourish out of the earth and Righteousness look down from Heaven."

VI. 226.

Natural things
And spiritual;—who separates these two
In art, in morals, or the social drift,
Tears up the bond of nature, and brings
    death . . .
Leads vulgar days, deals ignorantly with men,
Is wrong, in short, at all points.

ELIZABETH BARRETT BROWNING.

For we can do nothing against the truth, but for the truth.—2 COR. xiii. 8.

THERE is an absolute truth about every-thing, something which is certainly the fact about that thing, entirely independent of what you or I or any man may think about it. No man on earth may know that fact correctly —but the fact exists. It lies behind all blunders and all partial knowledges, a calm, sure, un-found certainty, like the great sea beneath its waves, like the great sky behind its clouds. God knows it. It and the possession of it makes the eternal difference between God's knowledge and man's.

It is a beautiful and noble faith when a man thus believes in the absolute truth, unfound, unfindable perhaps by man, and yet surely ex-istent behind and at the heart of everything. It is a terrible thing when a man ceases to be-lieve in it, and ceases to seek for it.

VI. 210.

Seek, then, now, O my soul, so singular and
    so supereminent a Good.
As long as thou art in the flesh, cease not to
    seek;
Since that can never be sought enough, which
    can never be grasped to the full.

THOMAS À KEMPIS.

Jesus saith unto him, I am . . . the Truth.

JOHN xiv. 6.

CONSIDER what would be the idea of Christ and His relation to the world which we should get if this were all we knew of Him,—if He as yet had told us nothing of Himself but what is wrapped up in these rich and simple words, "I am the Light of the World," "I am the Light of Life." They send us instantly abroad into the world of Nature. They set us on the hill-top watching the sunrise as it fills the east with glory. They show us the great plain flooded and beaten and quivering with the noon-day sun. They hush and elevate us with the mystery and sweetness and suggestiveness of the evening's glow. There could be no image so abundant in its meaning; no fact plucked from the world of Nature could have such vast variety of truth to tell; and yet one meaning shines out from the depth of the figure and irradiates all its messages. They all are true by its truth. What is that meaning? It is the essential richness and possibility of the world and its essential belonging to the sun.

V. 2.

O only Lord God, Father of lights and Maker of darkness, send forth Thy light and Thy truth that they may lead us through dimness of things seen to clarity of things unseen : For our Lord Jesus Christ's sake, the Light of the world. Amen.

CHRISTINA ROSSETTI.

I am the Light of the world.—JOHN viii. 12.

A THOUSAND subtle, mystic miracles of deep and intricate relationship between Christ and humanity must be enfolded in those words; but over and behind and within all other meanings, it means this,—the essential richness and possibility of humanity and its essential belonging to Divinity. . . . The truth is that every higher life to which man comes, and especially the highest life in Christ, is in the true line of man's humanity; there is no transportation to a foreign region. There is the quickening and fulfilling of what man by the very essence of his nature is. The more man becomes irradiated with Divinity, the more, not the less, truly he is man. The fullest Christian experience is simply the fullest life. To enter into it therefore is nowise strange. The wonder and the unnaturalness is that any child of God should live outside of it, and so in all his life should never be himself.

V. 4, 6.

'Tis He, as none other can,
Makes free the spirit of man,
And speaks, in darkest night,
One word of awful light
That strikes through the dreadful pain
Of life a reason sane—
That word divine which brought
The universe from nought.

RICHARD WATSON GILDER.

There is no power but of God.—ROM. xiii. 1.

"WHERE does the power come from?" is the natural question always when we are watching any strong effect. "Where did it begin?" we curiously ask as we stand by the side of any process and watch its steady flow. . . . Such search for the seats of original power is among the first instincts and the keenest pleasures of the human mind. And when such a source of power is found, then the human soul bows down before it and pours out its reverence. All idolatry is merely the giving to some secondary cause that virtue and regard which can belong only to the Highest and First Cause: to worship the sun instead of the God who makes him shine; to deify a hero or sage into the place of the God who makes him brave or wise; to glorify an abstract virtue until it sits cloudily in the place of the distinct personal God in whose nature all virtue has its being—these are the great types in which idolatry has prevailed among mankind. And to-day the man who is looking to his money or his education or his good repute or his family for the satisfaction and the culture which God gives us through them all, but which neither of them gives us of and by itself, he is the modern idolater. He, like all the idolaters of old, has cut the channels of life off from the source of life, and sits with his thirsty lips pressed to their dry mouths, getting no real refreshment, however he may delude himself. VII. 35, 36.

These are wells without water.—2 PET. ii. 17.

To be spiritually minded is life and peace.
ROM. viii. 6.

"I HAVE no spiritual capacity," says one. "It is not in me to be a saint," another cries. "I have a covetous soul. I cannot live except in winning money." "I can make many sacrifices, but I cannot give up my drink." "I can do many things, but I cannot be reverent." So the man talks about himself. Poor creature, does he think that he knows, down to its centre, this wonderful humanity of his? It all sounds so plausible and is so untrue! . . . How can he know what lurking power lies packed away within the never-opened folds of this inactive life? Has he ever dared to call himself the child of God, and for one moment felt what that involves? Has he ever attacked the task which demands those powers whose existence he denies, or tried to press on into the region where those evil things cannot breathe which he complacently declares are an inseparable portion of his life?

VI. 69.

Oh, there are heavenly heights to reach
    In many a fearful place
Where the poor timid heir of God
    Lies blindly on his face,—

Lies languishing for light divine,
    That he shall never see
Till he go forward at Thy sign,
    And trust himself to Thee.

WHITTIER.

*And the Child grew, and waxed strong in spirit, filled with wisdom ; and the grace of God was upon him.—*LUKE ii. 40.

THE evident design of God's creation, the comprehensive form of the incarnation, the clear presence in children of the power of and the need of religion, these are the forces which, in spite of every tendency of the grown people to make children wait till they grow up, has always kept alive a hope, a trust, however blind, that a child's religion was a possible reality; that a child might serve and love and live for God. . . . His are the years when one can really believe in ideals. God can stand out before him, awful, yet dear. . . . No doubt of God's faithfulness, no questioning of His ways comes in to cloud the perfectly unspotted adoration.   How good it is that there are years at the beginning of every life when it is the most easy thing to believe in absolute right and goodness!

IV. 136, 137.

How good a thing is feeling—admiration ! It is the bread of angels, the eternal food of cherubim and seraphim.

AMIEL.

MAN never is sent into the world, and bidden to evolve out of his own being the conditions in which he is to live. Always there is something before him. . . . The food is before the hunger, and says, "I have waited for you to come." The river is before the thirst. Beauty was in the sky and on the hills before the eye was fashioned. Music was breathing on the winds before the ear was framed. Fragrance was in the violet and the forest before the nostrils came to catch its odor. The picture was before the imagination which discerned it; the sea before the ship that sailed it. Man finds the rocks waiting with their problems, frost and heat holding their inspiration and their comfort in expectation of his coming. And he never says, "Here I am," that the servants do not stand in ranks at the door of his great homestead to welcome the heir into his own, and to pledge him their obedient service. The material is background for the spiritual,—the earth, which is body, for man, who is soul.

V. 41.

For us the winds do blow;
The earth doth rest, heaven move, and fountains flow.
Nothing we see but means our good,
  As our delight, or as our treasure:
The whole is either our cupboard of food,
  Or cabinet of pleasure.

GEORGE HERBERT.

To whom shall we go?   Thou hast the words of eternal life.—JOHN vi. 68.

IF a soul has many doubts and bewilderments about Christ, and yet knows that there is a Saviour, and that that Saviour's home is in the land of righteousness and truth, then to that land of righteousness and truth that soul will go by any road that it can find, eager to get there, seeking a road, pressing through difficulties, that it may be in the same country with, and somewhere near, its unfound Lord. It may be that the clouds that for us mortals haunt that land of righteousness and truth may long hang so thick and low that living close to Him the soul may still fail to see Him, but some day certainly the fog shall rise, the cloud shall scatter, and in the perfect enlightenment of the other life the soul shall see its Lord, and be thankful for every darkest step that it took towards Him here.

VI. 150.

I felt like one upon his journey brought
By ways he knows not of; these pathways
    dim
Had ever seemed their promised end to cheat,
      Yet had they led to Him
In whom life's tangled, broken threads com-
    plete
Are gathered up, its wasted things made meet
For holier use, its roughness smoothed, its bit-
    ter turned to sweet.

DORA GREENWELL.

EVERYWHERE this invitation rings through the world. True, the sight which we send out in answer to the invitation must be the large use of all our faculties. Not merely the outward eye must see, the mind must see as well. It is not answering the whole invitation unless the whole man goes and sees with all his powers of vision. The eye sees phenomena; the soul sees causes underlying and connecting the phenomena. We must not stop merely with what the eye sees, and, having written down the facts we have discovered, call that the all of science, and brand all beyond as superstition. It is not superstition, not prejudice, but science still, spiritual science, when the mind sees a causal will, out of which all phenomena proceed, and the heart feels a mighty love beating through all the ordered system. It is not well to live and see only from the eyes and brain outward.

VI. 138.

Look down in pity, Lord, we pray,
  On eyes oppressed by moral night,
And touch the darkened lids, and say
  The gracious words, " Receive thy sight! "

Then in clear daylight, shall we see
  Where walks the sinless Son of God;
And, aided by new strength from Thee,
  Press onward in the path He trod.

BRYANT.

We love Him because He first loved us.
> 1 JOHN iv. 19.

TO know that long before I cared for Him, He cared for me; that while I wandered up and down in carelessness, perhaps while I was plunging deep in flagrant sin, God's eye was never off me for a moment, He was always watching for the instant when His hand might touch me and His voice might speak to me,—there is nothing which can appeal to a man like that. The man is stone whom that does not appeal to. When, touched by the knowledge of that untiring love, a man gives himself at last to God, every act of loving service which he does afterwards is fired and colored by the power of gratitude, surprised gratitude, out of which it springs. How shall he overtake this love which has so much the start of him? This is what makes his service eager and enthusiastic. It is a " reasonable service," justified by the sublime reason of the soul which loves its God because He first loved it.

V. 54.

Because Thy love hath sought me,
  All mine is Thine, and Thine is mine;
Because Thy love hath bought me,
  I will not be mine own, but Thine.

I lift my heart for Thy heart,—
  Thy heart sole resting-place for mine:
Shall Thy heart crave for my heart,
  And shall not mine crave back for Thine?

CHRISTINA ROSSETTI.

Let the peace of God rule in your hearts.

COL. iii. 15.

THAT peace cannot come in this life, you say. But I do not know. There have been men and women with lives so calm and high that they seemed to have reached it, even on this tumultuous earth. Hardly a flake of spray from the storm below them ever seemed to dash up and wet their steadfast and placid feet. But whether it can come in this life or not, the struggle for it makes the two lives one. Already to him who is working towards it, part of its peace is given. The rock runs out under the sea, and your feet may be firm upon it even while the waves are still breast high.

Such be the peace in Christ which shall make all of our lives strong through all their struggle, until at last we enter into that rest which remaineth for the people of God.

VI. 127.

No clouds of care that gather,
  No waves of sin that toss,
No blasts of desolation,
  No blight, no strife, no loss,
Shall break the mystic circle
  Of that enshrining peace
Which round the steadfast spirit
  Doth grow, and doth not cease.

J. L. M. W.

WHAT is it in the highest sense to do what all men try to do in some sense, to get a living? Those words are very lightly used, and narrowed down to very insignificant dimensions. . . .

Breathing is not life, thought is not life, duty is not life. The perfect life includes them all. No man is thoroughly, that is, through and through, alive unless from end to end of his capacity that capacity is full. Complete life involves the conception of a body with every power perfect, a mind with every ability active, a conscience that never swerves from purity, a spirit that reaches to and fastens itself on God. Everything short of that is stagnated, impeded, partial life. To complete that high result is what a man ought to mean when he talks about "getting a living." Is it not one of the mortifying things, dear friends, to take now and then these words that we are using every day so lightly and see how much they really mean; to wipe through the dust and rust that are on these coin-words, which constant friction has worn so smooth and unimpressive, and look upon the royal image and superscription that is on them? VII. 152, 154.

There is no end to the sky,
  And the stars are everywhere,
And time is eternity,
  And the here is over there;
For the common deeds of the common day
Are ringing bells in the far-away.

HENRY BURTON.

ALL history of man bears witness that man, though himself finite, demands infinity to deal with and to rest upon. What truly enthusiastically human man will tolerate the drawing of any line, however far away, outside of which he shall be bound to believe that human enterprise shall never go? Who will let any limit mark for him the certain boundary beyond which no yet more wonderful invention shall be devised, and no yet more beautiful miracle of art flower out of the rich ground of man's exhaustless fancy? What man ever truly loves and sets a limit, consciously and absolutely, to the loveliness of that which he is loving? The love that defines the limits of its idol's loveliness is not entire love; pure love lives in its power of idealizing, and loves the infinite in the finite type to which it gives its homage. So everywhere there comes the testimony of this endless reach of man after the infinite, and of his inability to rest upon anything less.

III. 120.

The saints' good days
Are good, because the good Lord lays
No bound of shore along the sea
Of beautiful Eternity.

HELEN HUNT JACKSON.

A peasant may believe as much
  As a great clerk, and reach the highest stat-
      ure:
Thus dost Thou make proud knowledge bend
      and crouch,
  While grace fills up uneven nature.
GEORGE HERBERT.

NO man grows good by mere increase of intellectual development.   Look at the
melancholy record of the private lives of
many of the most brilliant thinkers and scholars.   Look at the dissoluteness of the bad,
bright times of Greek or Roman culture. . . .
As powerless as is the mere training of the
body to educate the mind, or the culture of
the mind to reform the morals, so utterly hopeless is it that any man living under God's inevitable laws should grow by the mere struggle of moral rectitude into that condition of
resemblance and spiritual nearness to God
which we mean when we speak of a man's
being holy.   That high estate, the abiding of
the divine life in the human soul—you must
set it down as the first truth of your religion
—can be ever reached only by the personal
acceptance of that means by which it was first
and forever typified—the indwelling of the
Divine in the human in the great representative miracle of spiritual history, the Incarnation of Jesus Christ.   VII. 157.

I say, the acknowledgement of God in Christ,
Accepted by thy reason, solves for thee
All questions in the earth and out of it,
And has so far advanced thee to be wise.
BROWNING.

So speak ye, and so do, as they that shall be judged by the law of liberty.—JAMES ii. 12.

THE freeing of souls is the judging of souls. A liberated nature dictates its own destiny. . . . Look at Christ, and see [this truth] in perfection. His was the freest life man ever lived. Nothing could bind Him. He walked across old Jewish traditions and they snapped like cobwebs. He acted upon the divinity that was in Him up to the noblest ideal of liberty. But was there no compulsion in His working? Hear Him: "I must be about my Father's business." Was it no compulsion that drove Him those endless journeys, footsore and heartsore, through His ungrateful land? "I must work to-day." What slave of sin was ever driven to his wickedness as Christ was to holiness? What force ever drove a selfish man into his voluptuous indulgence with half the irresistibility that forced the Saviour to the cross? O my dear friends, who does not dream for himself of a freedom as complete and as inspiring as the Lord's? Who does not pray that he too may be ruled by such a sweet despotic law of liberty?   II. 197, 198.

O voice of Duty, still
  Speak forth: I hear with awe;
In thee I own the sovereign Will,
  Obey the sovereign law.

Thou higher voice of Love!
  Yet speak thy word in me;
Through Duty let me upward move
  To thy pure liberty!
                    SAMUEL LONGFELLOW.

Abraham Lincoln born, 1809.

GREAT men are in the world what the most enlightened and exalted experiences are in the life of any man. They are the mountain-tops on which the influences which are afterward to fertilize our whole humanity have birth. There stands out some great pattern of unselfishness; some martyr-life which totally forgets itself and lives in suffering self-sacrifice for fellow-men. About that man's life gathers an utterance, an exhibition, of the glory of self-sacrifice—of how it is the true life of mankind, of how in it alone man becomes truly man. Does all that abide in him, live and die in his single personality ? Does it disappear forever in the withering flames which consume him at the stake ? Does not that fire set it free, cast it forth into the atmosphere of the universal human nature, and make it the possession of all mankind ? Have not you and I the power to live more unselfishly to-day because of the unselfishness of the great monumental lives of devotion ?

VII: 344.

As thrills of long-hushed tone
Live in the viol, so our souls grow fine
With keen vibrations from the touch divine
Of noble natures gone.

JAMES RUSSELL LOWELL.

Heroes are the mortal pipes
  Thorough which God's breath doth blow;
Little care they how they strain
  If aright the tune doth go.   J. L. M. W.

IDEALITY, magnanimity, and bravery,— these are what make the heroes. These are what glorify certain lives that stand through history as the lights and beacons of mankind. The materialist, the sceptic, and the coward, he cannot be a hero. We talk sometimes about the unheroic character of modern life. We point to our luxurious living for the reason. But, oh, my friends, it is not in your costly houses and your sumptuous tables that your unheroic lives consist. It is in the absence of great inspiring ideas, of generous enthusiasms, and of the courage of self-forget-fulness. . . . Do not blame a mere accident for that which lies so much deeper. There are moments, when you bear your sorrows, when you resist a great temptation, when your faith or your country is in danger,—there are such moments with you all when you seize the idea of human living and are made generous and brave because of it. Then, for all your modern dress, for all your modern parlor where you stand, you are heroic like David, like Paul, like any of God's knights in any of the ages which are most remote and picturesque. Then you catch some glimpse of a region into which you might enter, and where, with no blast of trumpets or waving of banners, you might be heroic all the time.

II. 173.

Blessed are they which do hunger and thirst after righteousness, for they shall be filled.
MATT. v. 6.

THE essence of every beatitude is in the human heart, and yet the human heart loves to hear the utterance of the beatitudes from the mouth of God as if they were His arbitrary enactments. I know by that of the nature of God which is in me as His child, that they which hunger and thirst after right-eousness shall certainly be filled. I am sure, by that subtle knowledge of Him which the child must have of the Father, that He could not leave a really longing soul unsatisfied in all His world. That importunate happiness, ready to give itself away, must pour itself into every ready life.
VIII. 32.

There's not a craving in the mind
   Thou dost not meet and still;
There's not a wish the heart can have
   Which Thou dost not fulfil.
  .   .   .   .

All things that have been, all that are,
   All things that can be dreamed,
All possible creations, made,
   Kept faithful, or redeemed,—

All these may draw upon Thy power,
   Thy mercy may command;
And still outflows Thy silent sea,
   Immutable and grand.
FABER.

Behold, what manner of love the Father hath bestowed upon us, that we should be called the sons of God.—1 JOHN iii. 1.

THERE is a deeper nature which belongs to every one of us as a child of God. . . . The man who lives in that deeper nature, the man who believes himself the son of God, is not surprised at his best moments and his noblest inspirations. He is not amazed when he does a brave or an unselfish thing. He is amazed at himself when he is a coward or a liar. He accepts self-restraint only as a temporary condition, an immediate necessity of life. Not self-restraint, but self-indulgence, the free, unhindered utterance of the deepest nature, which is good—that is the only final picture of man's duty which he tolerates. And all the life is one; the specially and specifically religious part being but the point at which the diamond for the moment shines, with all the diamond nature waiting in reserve through the whole substance of the precious stone.

V. 20.

Take all in a word: the trust in God's breast
Lies trace for trace upon ours impressed;
Though He be so bright and we so dim,
We are made in His image to witness Him.

BROWNING.

A STRONG, unalterable persuasion that
God is merciful and kind has been poured
onto your life, into your mind. That fact itself, once known, absorbs your contemplation.
You would sit lonely in the empty world and fill
your soul with gazing on the brightness of that
truth. So you do sit to-day when there comes
some sort of appeal from fellow-men. . . .
Somehow the cry awakens you, and you go
down and put your truth into your brother's
hands. At first it seems almost a profanation.
The truth is so sacred and seems so thoroughly
your own. But as you give it to your brother,
new lights come out in it. For God to be good
means something more when the goodness
turns to new forms of blessing in the new need
of this new life. O you who think you know
that God is merciful because of the mercy
which He has shewed to you, be sure there is a
richness in your truth which you have not
reached yet, which you will never reach until
you let Him make your life the interpreter of
His goodness to some other soul!

IV. 15.

> A toil that gains with what it yields,
>   And scatters to its own increase,
> And hears, while sowing outward fields,
>   The harvest-song of inward peace.

WHITTIER.

The blessing of the Lord, it maketh rich.

PROV. x. 22.

YOU say, How can I believe in God? Only by coming close to God, and learning by deep and sweet experience that He has better things to give to His beloved than what men call prosperity,—the peace that passeth understanding, the calm rest of forgiven sin, and of a soul trusted away from itself into its Saviour's hands. To one who knows what those high blessings mean, how little does it seem that other hands should fill themselves with the shining trifles which its hands are too full to hold. Think how it will seem in heaven! Standing before the throne, filled with the unspeakable vision, conscious through all the glory of the culture that suffering has brought, hurrying with joy on the high missions of the Lord, who will look back then and be troubled an instant at the recollection of how a wicked man sat at a little richer table, or had a little higher seat in the market-place when we were here on earth?

VI. 126.

Lose the less joy that doth but blind;
Reach forth a larger bliss to find.
To-day is brief; the inclusive spheres
Rain raptures of a thousand years.

ADELINE D. T. WHITNEY.

CONSECRATIONS of our lives to others are often not less real and powerful because they are unconscious. . . . We have gone on with our work in life, thinking that the purpose of our work was centred in ourselves. . . . But some day a friend died—one who was very near to us, one in whom our life was bound up in many ways. Who has not known the dreadful going out of all the interest of living at the time of such a death? It seemed as if there were nothing left to live for. . . . It was terrible. But it was blessed if you did not stop there, but, with persistent love that would not be satisfied until it found the object it had lost, you traced the precious life on as it left you, till you followed it into the very bosom of the God who took it, and poured out there the treasures of devotion which had no longer any one dear enough to tempt them on the earth.

VI. 48, 49.

And, dearer than the living ones that dwell
   Beyond the throbbing sea,—
And dearer than the Dead, whose voices swell
   The heavenly melody,—
ONE visiteth His people in the night,
Who giveth songs, and makes the darkness
   bright.

B. M.

NOTHING is more sad than the way in which we comfort ourselves and one another for our sorrows, by vague, unrealized promises that sorrow cannot last forever.

We conceive of life as a great swinging sphere which must forever run a vast orbit, doomed to perpetual change, and so sure by and by to sweep into the sunlight, if we can only keep alive and wait.   It is a forlorn and miserable comfort.   It loses all the certainty and personal graciousness of Christianity. There is no *piety* about it. . . . David's pilgrims going through the vale of misery " use it " for a well. . . . It was not simply a sorrow that was succeeded by joy, not merely a peace promised and looked for and waited for, it was a peace found.   When they grew thirsty they looked, not merely farther on into the heart of the future, but deeper down into the bosom of the present.

VI. 23, 24.

Some narrow hearts there are
That suffer blight when that they fed upon
As something to complete their being fails;
And they retire into their holds and pine,
And, long restrained, grow stern.   But some there are
That in a sacred want and hunger rise,
And draw the misery home and live with it,
And excellent in honor wait, and will
That something good should yet be found in it,
Or wherefore were they born ?

JEAN INGELOW.

HOW to secure humility is one of the hard problems of all systems of duty. . . . It is the oneness of the soul's life with God's life that at once makes us try to be like Him and brings forth our unlikeness to Him. It is the source at once of aspiration and humility. The more aspiration, the more humility. Humility comes by aspiration. If, in all Christian history, it has been the souls which most looked up that were the humblest souls; if the Christian man keeps his soul full of the sense of littleness, even in all his hardest work for Christ, not by denying his own stature, but by standing up at his whole height, and then looking up in love and awe and seeing God tower in infinitude above him,—certainly all this stamps the morality which is wrought out with the idea of Jesus with this singular essence, that it has solved the problem of faithfulness and pride, and made possible humility by aspiration.

VIII. 66.

All service should be done for Thee
In meek humility
   And awe most sweet,
That Thou shouldst take,
E'en for Thy Son Christ Jesus' sake,
   Service from servants so unmeet.

ANNA E. HAMILTON.

Whatsoever a man soweth, that shall he also reap.—GAL. vi. 7.

He which soweth sparingly shall reap also sparingly ; and he which soweth bountifully shall reap also bountifully.—2 COR. ix. 6.

THE world seems to be a great field in which every man drops his seed, and which gives back to every man, not just the same thing which he dropped there, any more than the brown earth holds up to you in the autumn the same blackberry which you hid under its bosom in the spring, but something which has its true correspondence and proportion to the seed to which it is the legitimate and natural reply. Every gift has its return, every act has its consequence, every call has its answer in this great live, alert world, where man stands central, and all things have their eyes on Him and their ears open to His voice.   III. 265.

Sow truth if thou the truth wouldst reap;
  Who sows the false shall reap the vain;
Erect and sound thy conscience keep;
  From hollow deeds and words refrain.

Sow love, and taste its fruitage pure;
  Sow peace, and reap its harvest bright;
Sow sunbeams on the rock and moor,
  And find a harvest-home of light.
                    HORATIUS BONAR.

Great Truths are portions of the soul of man;
  Great souls are portions of eternity;
Each drop of blood that e'er through true
    heart ran
With lofty message, ran for thee and me.

IT is the great patriots that interpret the value of their country to the common citizen. The man absorbed in his own small affairs, or so restricted in his power of thought that he would never have taken in the national idea for himself abstractly, sees how Washington and Webster and Lincoln loved the land; and through their love for it, its worthiness of his own love becomes made known to him. Still his love for his country, when it is awakened, is his own, and may impel him to serve her in most peculiar personal ways, very different from theirs, but none the less it is true that but for the interpretation of these great men's honor for her, he would have honored his country less or not at all. They interpret to their fellow-men what God has first interpreted to them, till ultimately the fire which starts from the central heart of all runs through the world, and the blindest are enlightened *to* discern, and the most timid become bold enough to praise, the movement which at first had no friend but God.

V. 328, 338.

And shall we praise?   God's praise was his
    before;
And on our futile laurels he looks down,
    Himself our bravest crown!

JAMES RUSSELL LOWELL.

Great peace have they which love Thy law.
Ps. cxix. 165.

ARE you at peace with yourself? If your will is taking your powers, which were made to do noble and gentle and generous things, and forcing them to do sordid and brutal and mean things; if you are living a life of miserable drudgery, treating yourself like a machine; or if you are living a life of dissipation, treating yourself like a brute, then you are not at peace with yourself surely. Yourself is misusing, is abusing yourself. . . . A man is both harp and harper. The harp may not complain, but all the time the music it was meant to make sleeps in its strings; and it cannot be at peace with the cruel fingers that make it unmusical. And in your powers sleeps the nobleness that they were made to do, in everlasting protest against the wickedness to which you compel them. O my dear friends, to be at peace with ourselves is not to loosely approve ourselves in what we are. It is to work with ourselves, that we may be all that God made us for.

VI. 194.

> " Couldst thou in vision see
>   Thyself the man God meant,
>   Thou never more wouldst be
>   The man thou art—content."

Of these men which have companied with us, . . . must one be ordained to be a witness with us of His resurrection. . . . And the lot fell upon Matthias.—ACTS i. 22, 26.

HOWEVER the Gospel may be capable of statement in dogmatic form, its truest statement we know is not in dogma but in personal life. . . . So I think a man's best sermon is the best utterance of his life. . . . If it is really God's message through him, it brings him out in a way that no other experience of his life has power to do, as the quality of the trumpet declares itself more clearly when the strong man blows a blast for battle through it than when a child whispers into it in play. Remember this: . . . then, when you hear your brother preach, honor the work that he is doing and listen as reverently as you can to hear through him some voice of God. . . . He is the messenger of Christ to the soul of man always.

XI. 27, 135, 140.

O Almighty God, who didst choose Thy faithful servant Matthias to take part in the ministry and apostleship from which Judas by transgression fell ; Grant that Thy Church, preserved from false Apostles, may ever be blessed with faithful Ministers of Thy word and sacraments ; through Jesus Christ our Lord. Amen.

MEXICAN PROVISIONAL OFFICES.

As Thou, Father, art in Me, and I in Thee, that they also may be one in us.—JOHN xvii. 21.

WHO can read words like these and not catch sight of what it was that was to fill these disciples' lives with energy, and to be the atmosphere wherein their new goodness should get all its growth? God's fatherhood made visible to them in Christ, His Son; their sonship to God made visible in Christ, their brother. It was as if at the beginning of all ages down which their Christian life has run, they lay, like Jacob on the night when he went out to his new life from his father's home, and to them, as to him, a ladder seems to stretch up into heaven, and the angels of God ascended and descended on it,—the angels of duty bringing God's strength to men, and carrying men's obedience to God, on the ladder of the fatherhood and sonship that bound the heavens to the earth, set up in the new Beth-el, the new House of God, which was the life of Jesus.

VIII. 60.

By eyes that are pure and hearts that are clean,
At morn and at eve is a Ladder still seen:
And the angels still come, and the angels still
    go
To the hands lifted up, from the heads bended
    low,
With the blessings He gives and the thanks
    that we say,
With the grace that we need and the worship
    we pay.

J. L. M. W.

O YOUNG disciples, whatever other kind of falseness to your faith you may fall into, may you be saved at least from ever being ashamed of it. It is the noblest, the divinest, thing on earth. You may have only got hold of the very borders of it, but if in any true sense you can say, " Jesus is the Lord," you have set foot into the region wherein man lives his completest life. Go on, without one thought or dream of turning back, and with no shamefaced hiding of the new mastery under which you are trying to live. If your Christian service is too small in its degree for you to boast of, it is too precious in its kind for you to be ashamed of. Go on forever craving and forever winning more faith and obedience, and so learning more and more forever that faith and obedience are the glory and crown of human life.

VI. 100.

Life may be given in many ways,
And loyalty to Truth be sealed
As bravely in the closet as the field,
So bountiful is fate;
But then to stand beside her,
When craven churls deride her,
To front a lie in arms and not to yield,
This shows, methinks, God's plan
And measure of a stalwart man.

JAMES RUSSELL LOWELL.

HOW in a time like this can a man live and get the best out of it, and at the same time shun its worst?   Here in this time of uncertainties, here in this wandering transition age, we are to live, whether we will or no. . . . And what can one do with his own personal life to keep it from complete confusion, and, if it be possible, to make it grow strong and rich and true, out of these very circumstances which, perhaps, we hopelessly deplore? . . . Above all things, there is the strength and permanence of religion.   Never was there such a time for a man to cling to that.   " Ah, but," you say, " that is the most uncertain of all things !   What is more unsettled than religion?"   But no, my friends. . . .   The knowledge that love is at the root of everything; the answer of the human soul to the appealing nature and life of Jesus Christ; the value of the soul above the body, of the character above the circumstances; and the eternal life,—these are what men may cling to.   If any man does cling to these, he is really upon a rock, and whatever else which he thought was rock may prove to be ice and melt away, here he is safe.   Here is the great, last certainty.   Be sure of God.   With simple, loving worship, by continual obedience, by purifying yourself even as He is pure, creep close, keep close to Him.   I. 172, 173.

> With Thee our souls in peace abide;
> In Thee heaven's childhood we begin;
> Thy kingdom we shall enter in,
>   Not pure, but purified.
>
> LUCY LARCOM.

Then Jesus took unto Him the twelve, and said unto them, Behold, we go up to Jerusalem, and all things that are written concerning the Son of man shall be accomplished.—LUKE xviii. 30.

AND so every true life has its Jerusalem to which it is always going up. At first far off and dimly seen, laying but light hold upon our purpose and our will, then gradually taking us more and more into its power, compelling our study, directing the current of our thoughts, arranging our friendships for us, deciding for us what powers we shall bring out into use, deciding for us what we shall be. . . . You stop the student at his books, the philanthropist at his committee, the saint at his prayers. You say to each of them, "What does it all mean ? What are you doing ? What is it all for ?" And the answer is everywhere the same : "Behold, we go up to Jerusalem." We draw back the vail of history, and everywhere it is the same picture that we see. Companies, great and small, climbing mountains to where sacred cities stand awaiting them with open gates upon the top. The man who is going up to no Jerusalem is but the ghost and relic of a man. He has in him no genuine and healthy human life.

IV. 317.

Yea, very vain
The greatest speed of all these souls of men,
Unless they travel upward to Thy throne !

ELIZABETH BARRETT BROWNING.

Whose high endeavors are an inward light
That makes the path before him always
        bright; . . .
Who, doomed to go in company with pain,
Turns his necessity to glorious gain.

WORDSWORTH.

IF the life which you have chosen to be your
  life is really worthy of you, it involves
self-sacrifice and pain.   If your Jerusalem
really is your sacred city, there is certainly
a cross in it.   What then?   Shall you flinch
and draw back?   Shall you ask for yourself
another life?   O no, not another life, but
another self.   Ask to be born again.   Ask
God to fill you with Himself, and then calmly
look up and go on.   Go up to Jerusalem ex-
pecting all things that are written concerning
you to be fulfilled.   Disappointment, mortifi-
cation, misconception, enmity, pain, death,
these may come to you, but if they come to
you in doing your duty it is all right.   "It
cannot be that a prophet perish out of Jerusalem," said Jesus.   "It is dreadful to suffer
except in doing duty.   To suffer there is glorious."   That is our translation of his words
into our own life.

IV. 331.

One endless living story!
  One poem spread abroad!
And the sum of all our glory
  Is the countenance of God.

GEORGE MACDONALD.

The time is short.—1 COR. vii. 29.

THE shortness of life is closely associated, not merely with the great hopes of the future, but with the real vitality of the present. What then? If you and I complain how short life is, how quickly it flies through the grasp with which we try to hold it, we are complaining of that which is the necessary consequence of our vitality. You can make life long only by making it slow; and if you want to make it slow, I should think there were men enough in town who could tell you how,—men with idle hands and brains, who seem to have so much trouble to get through life as it is that we cannot imagine that they really wish that there were more of it. . . . The shortness of life is bound up with its fulness. It is to him who is most active, always thinking, feeling, working, caring for people and for things, that life seems short. Strip a life empty and it will seem long enough.

I. 318, 319.

He liveth long who liveth well,—
   All other life is short and vain;
He liveth longest who can tell
   Of living most for heavenly gain.

Waste not thy being; back to Him
   Who freely gave it, freely give;
Else is that being but a dream—
   'Tis but to be, and not to live.

HORATIUS BONAR.

THE more we watch the lives of men, the
more we see that one of the reasons why
men are not occupied with great thoughts and
interests is the way in which their lives are
overfilled with little things. It is not that
you deliberately dislike thought and study
and benevolence. It is mainly that you are
so busy with amusement and society and idleness that you are living such an unprofitable
life. It is not that you despise the highest
hopes and interests of your immortal nature
that you neglect them so. It is that your
passions crowd so thick about you that you
are entirely occupied with them. . . . You
have got to say to these crowding passions of
yours: "Stand aside. Leave my soul open,
that it and God, it and duty, may come together;"—making an emptiness about the soul
that the higher fulness may fill it. It may be
temporary. Once more the lower needs may
fasten on us, the lower pleasures try to satisfy
us; but they never can be quite so arbitrary
and arrogant as they were, after they have
once had to yield to their superiors. . . .
Perhaps some day they may themselves become, and dignify themselves by becoming,
the meek interpreters and ministers of those
very powers which they once shut out from
the soul. II. 206, 209, 212.

For when thou seekest not altogether visible things to
 enjoy them,
But beholdest them to bless the name of thy Creator—
Fashioning to thyself out of the highest and lowest of His
 works a sort of ladder,
On which thou mayest lean to get upwards—
Thou shalt be delivered from the baneful snares of this
 world. THOMAS À KEMPIS.

THE purpose of God's government, the one design on which it all proceeds, is that the whole world, through obedience to Him, should be wrought into His likeness, and made the utterance of His character. . . . With wills harmonized with His will; with souls that love and hate in truest unison of sympathy with His; with no purposes left in us but His purposes,—then we have come to what He wants the world to come to. We have taken our places in the slowly rising temple of His will. To whatever worlds He carries our souls when they shall pass out of these imprisoning bodies, in those worlds these souls of ours shall find themselves part of the same great temple; for it belongs not to this earth alone. There can be no end of the universe where God is to which that growing temple does not reach, the temple of a creation to be wrought at last into a perfect utterance of God by a perfect obedience to God. II. 69, 71.

Thy wonderful grand will, my God;
  Triumphantly I make it mine;
And faith shall breathe her glad " Amen "
  To every dear command of Thine.

Beneath the splendor of Thy choice,
  Thy perfect choice for me, I rest;
Outside it now I dare not live,
  Within it I must needs be blest.

Then may Thy perfect, glorious Will
  Be evermore fulfilled in me,
And make my life an answering chord
  Of glad, responsive harmony.
JEAN SOPHIA PIGOTT.

HE who has lived in the form of an experience looks back, while he who has entered into the substance and soul of an experience looks forward. "The outward man perishes," as Paul says, "but the inward man is renewed day by day." The perishing of a form and method in which we have lived may naturally bring a pensive sadness like that which always comes to us as we watch a setting of the sun, but he who is in the true spirit of the sunset turns instantly from the westward to the eastern look. The things the day has given him,—its knowledge, and its inspirations, and its friendship, and its faith, —these the departing sun is powerless to carry with it. They claim the new day in which to show their power and to do their work. Live deeply and you must live hopefully. That is the law of life.

VI. 329.

Though this very day
Casts but a dull stone on Time's heaped-up
    cairn,
A morning light will break once more and
    draw
The hidden glories of a thousand hues
Out from its crystal depths and ruby-spots
And sapphire-veins, unseen, unknown before.
   .   .   .   .   Time
Is God's, and all his miracles are His;
And in the Future he overtakes the Past,
Which was a prophecy of times to come.

GEORGE MACDONALD.

Men see not the bright light which is in the clouds.—JOB xxxvii. 21.

THE sense of human pain grows stronger all the time. And it sometimes seems as if the sense of purpose and education grew weaker in a multitude of souls. It is the heart of man taken, Balaam-like, to a place whence it can see the part and not the whole; and who that listens does not hear the muttering of the curse? Where is the help, first for your soul, then for the whole great world? Not in saying that pain is not pain, not in shutting the eyes to the part which is so awfully manifest, but in seeing, in insisting upon seeing, the whole.

> " To feel, although no tongue can prove,
> That every cloud that spreads above,
> And veileth love, itself is love."

That is the only help. He who lets his heart bear witness, he who lets the experience of countless sufferers bear witness, he who lets Christ bear witness, that no suffering ever yet came to any human creature by which it was not possible that that human creature should be made better and purer and greater,—he has caught sight of the whole; and though he walks in silence and perplexity and suspense, he does not curse.

VI. 222.

Knowing that here we live but in a tent,
And that our house is yonder, without fail.
GEORGE MACDONALD.

*Then was Jesus led up of the Spirit into the
wilderness to be tempted of the devil.*

MATT. iv. 1.

THE temptation of Jesus is certainly a very
wonderful event. There is no incident
in all His history on which the imagination
may expend itself with a more lavish speculation; and, on the other hand, there is
none that comes nearer to practical life with
stimulus and comfort. . . . The man who has
seen Christ tempted will not deny temptation
thenceforth. He will not be found explaining
it away. He will not delude himself with
vain hopes of escaping it and living a smooth,
untempted life. He will read in the temptation of the perfect Life that that is impossible
forever for any man. When he is depressed
and hungry and exhausted, he will look for the
devil as his Lord did, and when he sees him
coming, when he hears his words and feels
the desire of sin stirring in his heart, he will not
say, " Oh, this is nothing but one stage of my
growth." He will recognize the old enemy
of his Master coming for the old battle, and
gather up his strength and pray for his Master's strength in the hour of terrible, inevitable struggle.   VII. 130, 133.

> Distrust thyself, but trust His grace,
>   It is enough for thee :
> In every trial thou shalt trace
>   Its all-sufficiency.
>
> Distrust thyself, but trust His strength :
>   In Him thou shalt be strong :
> His weakest ones may learn at length
>   A daily triumph-song.

FRANCES R. HAVERGAL.

S URELY it always must be full of meaning,
    that Christ Himself, before He began His
struggles with the Pharisees and Scribes, went
out into the desert and struggled with Himself. . . .   Many a time the wilfulness, and
narrowness, and selfishness which He saw in
the faces which surrounded Him in some
crowd in the temple must have been clearer to
Him and easier to understand, because they
were just the passions which had tried to take
possession of His own heart, and failed, during those long terrible days in the dark wilderness.   And oh! my friends, there is no way in
which whatever personal struggles with faith-
lessness and sin we may have gone through
can be made to keep their freshness and power,
and at the same time be kept from becoming
a source of morbid wretchedness, no way that
is half so efficient as that they should constantly be called on to light up for us the
same sort of struggles in other men, and give
us the power to help them with intelligence
and sympathy.   Demand that lofty service
of every deep experience through which you
pass.   Demand that it shall help you understand and aid the battles of your brethren.

VI. 84, 85.

So thou wilt be sterner foe,
    So thou wilt be dearer friend;
So the saints thy name shall know,
    And Christ own thee at the end.

CANTICA SPIRITUALIS.

Command that these stones be made bread.
MATT. iv. 3.

IF we had stood there and heard the Satanic demand made we should have waited, stopping our breath to hear some supreme assertion of the Godhead that repelled so low an insult. "Go to men," we should have listened for the Lord to say—"go to men with arguments like those. Their natures are built to answer such appeals. All that a man hath will he give for that life which bread must feed." . . .

I love Christ all the more when I see how different His answer was from that. I love Him when I see Him declare Himself a man, and from the human standpoint fling aside the tempter's plea. I reverence and cling to the true human nature that there was in Him when I hear Him go back and take up the words that had been on human lips, that declared the resources of human nature, that asserted the higher life in Man: "It is written, Man shall not live by bread alone, but by every word that proceedeth out of the mouth of God." The danger is to us who hold so much to the divinity of Christ that His humanity will mean too little. Let us remember that in times such as this of the temptation there is a strength for us in the thought that it was a Man who fought and conquered, which no simple assurance of His being God could give.
VII. 151, 152.

For in that He himself hath suffered, being tempted, He is able to succor them that are tempted.
HEB. ii. 18.

YOU cannot be man and live a man's life without coming into this world where sin is and where you must be tried. That great temptation that comes swaggering up and frightening you so has got the best part of your character held under his brawny arm. You cannot get it without wrestling with him and forcing it away from him. That mountain that towers up and defies you has got your spiritual health away up on its snowy summit. That is what shines there in the sun. You cannot reach it except by the terrible climb. Ask yourself what you would have been if you had never been tempted, and own what a blessed thing the educating power of temptation is. And then . . . as Christ's temptation was vicarious, and when. He conquered He conquered for others besides Himself, so it was with us. There are men and women all around us who have got to meet the same temptations · that we are meeting. Will it help them or not to know that we have met them and conquered them? Will it help us or not to know that if we conquer the temptation we conquer not for ourselves only, but for them? The vicariousness of all life! There is not one of us who has not some one more or less remotely fastened to his acts, concerning whom he may say, as Christ said, " For their sakes I sanctify myself."

VII. 140, 141.

Nor knowest thou what argument
Thy life to thy neighbor's creed has lent.
EMERSON.

Count it all joy that ye fall into divers tempta-tions.—JAMES i. 2.

HOW strange it seems to us that there should be such a thing as temptation in the world at all! God sends us into the world and hangs in the great distance before us certain lofty prizes—goodness, truth, purity—which He has made our hearts capable of desiring. . . . But we have not really started towards them before the presence of another power begins to show itself. Hands pluck at us to draw us out of the straight way. Voices call to us with enticements or with threats to make us turn aside. . . . No adoption of any strict rule of life, no separation of ourselves from a certain region of dangerous occupations, sets us free from the persecution of temptation. We are tempted to sin everywhere. It is pathetic, almost terrible, to think how long this has been going on. Through all those weary years which it tires us to think of, they have been so many; through all those monotonous generations that we hear flowing on endlessly through the cavernous depths of history, as one listens to a stream dropping down monotonously forever underground; through all the years and generations of human life men have been tempted—not one that ever lived that did not meet this persistent, intrusive enticement to sin.   VII. 130.

Now, the training, strange and lowly,
    Unexplained and trying now :
Afterward, the service holy,
    And the Master's " Enter thou ! "
                FRANCES R. HAVERGAL.

*Will He plead against me with His great power?
No ; but He would put strength into me.*

JOB xxiii. 6.

FOR years you have lived, it may be, a se-
cluded and protected life. " Lead me
not into temptation," so you have prayed
every morning, and every day has brought
the answer to your prayer. But some day all
that breaks and goes to pieces. A great
temptation comes and is not hindered. Then
you cry out for the old mercy and it is not
given. . . . And then, behold what comes! A
new mercy! You go into the temptation. Your
old security perishes, but by and by out of its
death comes a new strength. Not to be saved
from dying but to die and then to live again
in a new security, a strong and trusty character, educated by trial, purified by fire,—that
is what comes as the issue of the whole. Not
a victory for you, preserving you from danger,
but a victory in you, strengthening you by
danger,—that is the experience from which
you go forth, strong with a strength which
nothing can subdue.

V. 35.

Oh, may we follow undismayed
　Where'er our God shall call!
And may His spirit's present aid
　Uphold us lest we fall!
Till in the end of days we stand
As victors in a deathless land.

JOHN HENRY NEWMAN.

The mind shall banquet, though the body pine.
SHAKESPEARE.

HEALTH, companionship, life itself, these are no longer indispensable when Christ has shown us God. A resignation that is not despair, but aspiration; a looser grasp on time, that means how strongly we are holding to eternity; this must come to us when, after all our doing of little temporary things, we have at last begun in Christ the life and work that is to go on forever and forever. Then even the most essential things of this world we can do without, if need be. We have passed from the lower to the higher necessities. We walk by faith, and not by sight. Already, even while we are yet in the flesh, before we cross the river, the promise finds its fulfilment. We live in the world, but we do not live by the world. Already the sun is no more our light by day; neither for brightness does the moon give light unto us; but the Lord is unto us an everlasting light, and our God our glory.
I. 298.

Light of the world! for ever, ever shining;
  There is no change in Thee;
True Light of life, all joy and health enshrin-
    ing,
  Thou canst not fade nor flee.

Thou hast arisen, but Thou descendest never;
  To-day shines as the past;
All that Thou wast Thou art, and shalt be
    ever,—
  Brightness from first to last!
HORATIUS BONAR.

*Then Jesus answered and said unto her, O wo-
man, great is thy faith : be it unto thee even as thou
wilt.—MATT. xv. 25.*

FAITH is the necessary power that the
weaker has over the stronger, the lower
over the higher. . . . This power comes to
perfection in Jesus. Could there be a more
complete picture of it than shines out in His
own story of the shepherd and the sheep?
The shepherd has folded his ninety-and-nine;
everything is safe and strong and prosperous;
he stands with his hand upon the sheepfold
gate; and then, just as he seems all wrapped
up in the satisfaction and completeness of the
sight, there comes, so light that no ear except
his can hear it, the cry of one poor lost sheep
off in the mountains, and it summons him with
an irresistible challenge, and his staff is in his
hand instantly, and he turns his back on
everything else to be the slave of that one
lost sheep till it is found. What a wonderful
and everlasting and universal story that parable is!   III. 174, 175.

He bendeth low from His holy hill
Searching the shadows gray and chill,—
And clear through the angel-singing—
    What time the sons of God
Shout loud, for joy upspringing,
    Till all the heavens are bowed—
He hears the faintest sighing
    Of some poor, far-off soul,
Who turns to look to the holy place
    While the billows round him roll.
                           B. M.

I seek not mine own will, but the will of the Father who hath sent me.—JOHN v. 30.

IT was in His sonship to God that the secret of the holiness of Jesus lay. His Father's business was the sum of all His life. . . . The model and the impulse of all duty He carried in His own filial heart, which was forever bearing witness to Him of His Father's perfectness. His incarnate days, with all their common duties held and illuminated in that high consciousness of sonship, must have been one with the eternity of the past and the eternity that was to be. Duty must have been its own revealer and its own reward. Liberty must have been sublimely consistent with the most scrupulous obedience. The doing right and the being right must have been like the sunshine and the sun. And what duty was to our Master it shall be to us just as soon as we are filled with His idea,—just as soon as His spirit bears witness with our spirits that we are the sons of God.

VIII. 70.

For what is freedom but the unfettered use
Of all the powers that God for use had given?
But chiefly this, Him first, Him last to view
Through meaner powers and secondary things
Effulgent, as through clouds that veil His
    blaze. S. T. COLERIDGE,

No man cometh unto the Father but by Me.

JOHN xv. 6.

BY the power of Christ we may all come near to God too, and have from out the open door of His sanctuary, to which we have fled, His view of mortal life and all its interests. For us, too, this world's existence may subside into its clearly marked circles, and we may see as God sees where each circle ends; see how the selfishnesses soon die out; see how the affections sweep out into wider lines; see how nothing but the highest loves reach out into infinity and send life forward into eternity. These times, when we are nearest to God, are the times when this world's things show their true values to us. Do you not know that? Do you remember how it all looked to you when you came home from the funeral, not morbid with hopeless sorrow, but seeming to be above the world, and to be standing with the friend who had gone, in the presence of the throne of God? Do you remember how things changed their relative importance to you then, how the last were first and the first were last, as they shall be on the judgment day? . . . You were above complaints and small trials. You had entered into the sanctuary of God, and you saw the end of these things.

VI. 121.

The Almighty's shadow is a starlit night;
His cloud is ever full of hidden light.

SAMUEL LONGFELLOW.

THE great truth of Christianity, the great
truth of Christ, is that sin is unnatural. . . . And that which is unnatural is not
by any necessity permanent. The struggle of
all nature is against the unnatural—to dislodge
it and cast it out. That beautiful struggle
pervades the world. It is going on in every
clod of earth, in every tree, in every star, and
in the soul of man. First to declare and then
to strengthen that struggle in the soul of man
was the work of Christ. That work still lingers and fails of full completion, but its power
is present in the world. When He takes possession of a nature He quickens that struggle
into life. No longer can that nature think
itself doomed to evil. . . . The wonder is
not that it should some day be cast out; the
wonder is that it should ever have come in.
The victory promised in a sinless Son of man
is already potentially attained in the intense
conception of its naturalness.

VI. 65.

Courage!—we travel through a darksome cave;
But still, as nearer to the light we draw,
Fresh gales will reach us from the upper air,
And wholesome dews of heaven our forehead
　　lave,
The darkness lighten more, till full of awe,
We stand in the open sunshine—unaware.

R. G. TRENCH.

YOU never did a sin that did not give its warning to you before you did it. . . . Perhaps you did not hear, but it was not that the warning bell did not ring. Perhaps you called that first sign of weakness a mere accident, and tried to believe that it meant nothing, but if you gave your thought to it you knew . . . it was the house's feeble timbers creaking before their fall. There are such warnings of coming sins that every one of us has received—sins yet undone; sins which, it may be, are to make our whole life dark some day, whose threatening we can read, if we are wise enough, in something that has come to us already. . . .

Life is full of such warnings. No man grows to be more than a mere boy without learning on what side of his moral nature he will fall if he falls at all. Every one of us knows, who is in the least thoughtful, what sort of villain he would be if he grew villainous. Thank God, these warnings may save us from the things they warn us of. These blessed bells that ring out in the darkness may turn us resolutely off from the cruel surf that roars behind them.

VII. 121, 122.

Man is no star, but a quick coal
    Of mortal fire:
Who blows it not, nor doth control
    A faint desire,
Lets his own ashes choke his soul.
GEORGE HERBERT.

The mystery of iniquity.—2 THESS. ii. 7.

THERE is something oppressive, something terrible, in this great mysterious presence of sin right in our midst, so that nothing goes on save in its shadow,—no state is formed, no family grows up, no social compact is organized, no character matures without its blighting mixture. Right in our midst, and yet no voice of man or God is opened to tell us how it came here. . . . [Yet] there was a time when it was not, there was a moment when it began to be. . . . There is no other way of explaining the strange fact that amid all the personal badness, and social corruption that is in the world, the human mind has been able to preserve the ideal of a pure society and a perfect life, to dream of it, sometimes to strive after it, except by acknowledging the reality of an entrance of iniquity into the world, and looking back to a time before that invasion when the world was sinless.

VI. 9, 4.

My own hope is, a sun will pierce
  The thickest cloud earth ever stretched;
That after Last returns the First,
  Though a wide compass round be fetched;
That what began best can't end worst,
  Nor what God blest once, prove accurst.

BROWNING.

That whosoever believeth in Him should not perish, but have everlasting life.—JOHN iii. 16.

WE have spoken of the mysteriousness of sin in its origin and operations. It would be cruel, false, and unchristian if I closed without telling you of the diviner mystery in which human iniquity finds its cure. The first thought round which the grand wonder of the atonement grows into shape is this thought of sin as a real live thing standing forth to be fought with, to be conquered, to be killed. . . . To meet that enmity, to slay that giant, Christ comes forth with his wonderful nature. He undertakes a distinct and dreadful struggle. We see its outward manifestation in the agony of the cross. All the deeper battle goes on out of our sight. We know not how it fares till the word of God comes to tell us that the victory is won by our Redeemer, and that Satan is trodden into death by the dying Christ. Of all the Mystery of Iniquity, where is the Mystery like this? You see how true a mystery it is. Nothing but the fact we know. . . . That shining, splendid fact, that gracious, glorious fact—the fact of the Lord's victory and of Satan's fall—stands forth so clear that none can doubt it. It takes its place as the one certain, central fact of hope. By it the living live, by it the dying die; in it the glorified rejoice forever.

VI. 14, 15.

Then came the disciples to Jesus apart, and said, Why could not we cast him out?

MATT. xvii. 9.

HE tells them that the reason of their failure is that they have been trying to do by themselves what they can only do when He is behind them, when their natures are so open that His strength can freely flow out through them. . . . Look at the artist's chisel. "Why cannot I carve?" it cries. And then the artist comes and seizes it. The chisel lays itself into his hand, and is obedient to him. That obedience is faith. It opens the channels between the sculptor's brain and the hard steel. Thought, feeling, imagination, skill flow down from the deep chambers of the artist's soul to the chisel's edge. The sculptor and the chisel are not two, but one. It is the unit which they make that carves the statue.

This is our principle, then. The unit of power for moral victory—in other words, for goodness—on the earth is not man and is not God. It is God and man, not two, but one, not meeting accidentally, not running together in emergencies only to separate again when the emergency is over; it is God and man belonging essentially together, God filling man, man opening his life by faith to be a part of God's, as the gulf opens itself and is part of the great ocean.

III. 181, 185.

When I am weak, then I am strong.

2 COR. xii. 10.

IF the condition for which man was made was a related, a bound up, a dependent condition, then the highest human happiness must always come with the most complete conformity to that first idea of human life. If dependence, then, be happiness, . . . independence of God, self-sufficiency, must be unhappiness. And since suffering, in all its various departments, is the breaking up of self-sufficiency, of self-confidence, is it not evident that, rightly used, it may be the setting free of the human soul from an unnatural and forced condition, into its natural, intended, and so happiest life? . . . Anything in body, brain, or heart that gets that idea of insufficiency home to us, may set us to digging beneath the self-surface of our vale of misery to find the God below for which the thirsty soul was made. . . . Prosperity is unconscious of God. Suffering, whether we will or no, has to be conscious of him.

VI. 29, 30.

Submit thy sorrow and thy soul to God,
And learn what peace it is to kiss His rod,
Who answers wishes ere they turn to prayers,
And with His blessings takes us unawares.

ABRAHAM PERCY MILLER.

No man can say that Jesus is the Lord but by the Holy Ghost.—1 COR. xii. 3.

NO soul is too low to be brought by the Holy Spirit to the place where, answering back by the divine within it to the divine above it, it may say that " Jesus is the Lord." No soul is too high to find in that announcement of its faith the consummation of its life. Here, then, is where the highest and the lowest meet.   Here is where they have met through all the ages.   Glorious thinkers, great strong workers, sufferers whose lives were miracles of patience, all of these singing as they went their ways, " Jesus is Lord, Jesus is Lord."   And all around them, and in among them, dull, plodding souls, and minds whose thought was all confused and bewildered with emotion, and little children, with their crude clear pictures in their simple brains, all these too singing, in their several tones and with their several clearness, " Jesus is Lord, Jesus is Lord." . . .

And oh, my friends, remember that the owning of Christ's mastery here is but the beginning of the participation in Christ's glory in heaven.   VI. 106, 107.

> Oh, let Christ and sunshine in,
> Let His Love its sweet way win!
> Nothing human is too mean
> To receive the King unseen;
> Not a pleasure or a care
> But celestial robes may wear:
> Impulse, thought, and action may
> Live immortally to-day.   LUCY LARCOM.

If ye have faith, and doubt not.

MATT. xxi. 21.

GET rid of the awful assumption that it [sin] is bound up in your constitution; cease to be a weak fatalist about it. . . . There are few things more constantly marvellous about our human nature than its power of acclimating itself in moral and spiritual regions where it once seemed impossible that it should live at all. The tree upon the hillside says: "Here and here alone can I live. Here my fathers lived in all their generations. . . . Take me down to the plain and I shall die." The gardener knows better. He takes the doubting and despairing plant and carries it, even against its will, to the broad valley, and sets it where the cold winds shall not smite it, and where the rich ground feeds it with luxuriance. And almost as they touch each other the ground and the root claim one another, and rich revelations of its own possibility flood the poor plant and fill it full of marvel with itself.

VI. 68.

For all grows sweet in Thee
Since Thou didst gather us in One, and bring
This fad'ng flower of our humanity
To perfect blossoming.

DORA GREENWELL.

Blessed are the pure in heart, for they shall see God.—MATT. v. 8.

THROUGH the mists of long and devout tradition which have obscured her character and made her very person almost mythical, we are surprised sometimes in reading the Gospels at the clearness and simplicity with which Mary the mother of our Lord stands out before us there. She speaks only on three occasions, but . . . those three utterances of hers are like three clear notes of a bell, that show how sound and rich its metal is. Think what they were. In the presence of the messenger who comes to tell her of her great privilege she bows her head and says, " Behold the handmaid of the Lord. Be it unto me according to thy word." When she finds her Son in the temple she cries out to Him, " Son, why hast Thou thus dealt with us ? Thy father and I have sought Thee sorrowing." When she stands with Him before the puzzled guests at Cana she turns to the servants and says, " Whatsoever He saith unto you, do it." The young soul's consecration! The mother's overrunning love! The disciple's perfect loyalty! What can be clearer than the simple, true, brave, loving woman that those words reveal?

V. 340.

Still to the lowly soul
  He doth himself impart,
And for His cradle and His throne
  Chooseth the pure in heart.
KEBLE.

In Thy light shall we see light.

Ps. xxxvi. 9.

STAND where you cannot see man's greatness, and the Incarnation seems a wild,
inexplicable dream.   Stand where no music
reaches you from the deep harmonies of man's
present spiritual life, and it is out of your
power to believe in heaven.   Lose sight of
sin, and the darker possibilities of eternity are
hideous impossibilities.   The religious truth
which you see by itself, out of its position in
the great whole which ought to hold it, fails
to bear witness of its truth.   Strive then for
wholes, and let the parts reveal themselves
within them.   Strive for God, who is the
whole. . . .   By obedience, by communion,
climb to the height where you shall be with
God, and then the truths about God shall open
their reasonableness, their richness, and their
harmony.

VI. 220.

For no man by himself is able to investi-
    gate this mystery;
Nor is it grasped by human wisdom;
But rather by the strength of faith,
And the intuition of a pure mind,
Enlightened from above.

THOMAS À KEMPIS.

THE age of real faith does not covet again the chains of superstition. The world at peace does not ask to be shaken once more by the earthquakes of war. But faith does feel the beauty of complete surrender which superstition kept for its sole spiritual virtue; and peace, with its diffused responsibility, is kindled at thought of heroic and unquestioning obedience which the education of war produced. Still let superstition and war lie dead. We will not call them back to life; but we will borrow their jewels of silver and jewels of gold as we go forth into the wilderness to worship our God with larger worship. Do you not feel this is in all the best progress? Do you not see it in the eyes of mankind, in the depths of the eyes of mankind always, as·it turns away from the dead forms of its old masters and goes forth into the years to be; the hoarded power of the past glowing beneath the satisfaction of the present and the fiery hope of the unknown future?

VI. 62.

Out of the years bloom the eternities!

.   .   .   .

And nothing dies that ever was alive;
    All that endears
And sanctifies the human must survive;
Of God they are, and in His smile they thrive—
    The immortal years!

LUCY LARCOM.

They say unto Him, We have here but five loaves, and two fishes. He said, Bring them hither to me.—MATT. xiv. 17, 18.

SURELY, the act is a very striking one. . . . Our first notions of a Deity are of One who is above all law and order and economy. Let the poor be niggardly, a slave to rules, counting over his little stock, squeezing every penny that he pays; but let the All-Powerful be open-handed, counting as nothing what other beings must save, originating life whenever life is needed, full of an easy spontaneity, flinging the miracles of creation everywhere. But it is striking to see how, as men go on and learn more of God, these ideas which were at first cast almost indignantly out of their conception of Him, gradually come back and are set in the place of highest honor. It is God's highest glory that He is a God of Law. Continuousness is the crown of His government. That He brings every future out of some past is the charm of all His government. That He lets nothing go to waste is the highest perfection of His boundless resource. Continuity and economy are His solemn foot-prints by which we trace His presence in our world. The need of evolution, the necessity that everything which is to be should come out of something which has been before, and the abhorrence of waste,—continuity and economy,—these are the proof-marks of Divinity.

II. 129, 130.

Earth holds heaven in the bud : our perfection there has to be developed out of our imperfection here.
CHRISTINA G. ROSSETTI.

THERE is the surface sight of life, which is bright and enthusiastic.   There is the sight of life which is deeper than this, which is sad and puzzled.   There is the deepest sight of all, which is bright again with a truer light, and enthusiastic again with a soberer but a more genuine happiness. . . .   There come forth adaptations for the higher work in things which have seemed wholly unfitted to produce the lower.   Things which never could have made a man happy, develop a power to make him strong.   Strength and not happiness, or rather only that happiness which comes by strength, is recognized as the end of human living.   II. 151, 153.

" Give me the wine of happiness," I cried,
" The bread of life!—Oh ye benign, unknown,
Immortal powers!—I crave them for mine own;
I am athirst, I will not be denied
Though hell were up in arms!"—No sound
        replied;
But turning back to my rude board and lone,
My soul, confounded, there beheld—a stone,
Pale water in a shallow cup beside!
With gushing tears, in utter hopelessness,
I stood and gazed.   Then rose a voice that
        spoke:
" God gave thee this, and what He gives will
        bless."
And 'neath the hands that trembling took and
        broke,
Lo, truly, a sweet miracle divine—
The stone turned bread, the water ruby wine!
                               Stuart Sterne.

If He should make my web a blight
Of life's fair picture of delight,
My heart's content would find it right.
EMERSON.

AMONG the tests of men there stands very
high this power to do without. . . .
But then this power of doing without some
things is, at its bottom, a power of not doing
without some other things. We are rescued
from the abject slavery of the lower by entering into the absolute servantship of the higher.
He to whom honor is necessary can do without money. He who must have goodness can
get along without praise. He who must have
God's communion can do without the sweet
companionships of fellow-men. He who cannot lose his eternity can easily cast aside time
and the body which belongs to it, and by the
martyr's slow or sudden death exchange
the visible for the invisible, the symbol for
the reality. Nay, he who values most intensely
his friend's or his child's eternal life can, not
easily but still not grudgingly, let go the joy
and daily comfort of his friend's or his child's
hourly presence, and see him die that he may
enter into life. On these two ladders, as it
were, by these two scales, the order of human
character mounts up,—the power to do without and the power not to do without.
I. 292.

Not for ourselves alone we strive,
Since thy perfection manifest
Bids self resign what self desired,
Postponing good for best.
BLISS CARMAN.

We wrestle . . . against powers.

EPHES. vi. 12.

ST. PAUL believed in spirits good and bad. The beauty of his belief in them was that, different as they might be from us in the conditions of their life, they still belonged to the same great moral system to which he belonged. The good spirits were not to be propitiated, and the evil spirits were not to be disarmed by magic and incantations. He who did righteousness called to himself the most mysterious strength of the unseen worlds. . . . For him all good beings fought; against his simple righteousness all evil beings would beat themselves in vain, and ultimately must go down and fail, here or beyond the stars. That is a noble faith. In the simplicity and grandeur of a faith like that, man will some day come once more to the now almost lost belief in the connection of his life with unseen spiritual powers.

VI. 75.

While we discern it not, and least believe,
On stairs invisible betwixt His heaven
And our unholy, sinful, toilsome earth
Celestial messengers of loftiest good
Upward and downward pass continually.
ARTHUR HUGH CLOUGH.

MEN talk—very religious men—as if God were a sort of reserve force, to be called in when He was needed, a sort of last resort when man's strength failed. . . . The thought of God which Christ came to reveal, the thought of God of which all Christ's own life was full, is something totally different from that. To Christ's thought God and man are part of one system—one structure, one working-force. To separate them is not simply to deny man a power that he needs : it is to break a unity, and to set a part of the power to the attempt to do what the whole power ought to do as one. . . . It is engine and steam that are to make the running power. It is artist and chisel that are to carve the statue. It is God and you that live your life. For you to try to live it alone is to try to do all the work with one part of the power. God is not a crutch coming in to help your lameness, unnecessary to you if you had all your strength. He is the breath in your lungs. The stronger you are, the more thoroughly you are yourself, the more you need of it, the more you need of Him.

VI. 102, 103.

He breathed forth His spirit
Into the slumbering dust, and upright standing, it laid its
Hand on its heart, and felt it was warm with
a flame out of heaven.
Quench, oh, quench not that flame! It is the
breath of your being.

LONGFELLOW.

IN a picture by Domenichino at Bologna, an angel stands at the foot of the empty cross, and tries with his finger one of the sharp points in the crown of thorns which the Saviour had worn during His passion. It is all a sad inexplicable wonder to him. It appeals to no experience of wickedness and woe in his pure and angelic nature. But when you or I take the crown of thorns into our hands we know in our own hearts the meanness, the jealousy, the hatred which it represents. . . . With simple wonder an angel might walk through our State Prison halls; but a man must walk there full of humbleness and charity; for, as the best man that ever lived finds something of common humanity in us which makes his goodness seem not impossible to us, so the worst of men stirs by the sight of his human sin some sense of what human power of sinfulness we too possess.

I. 251.

How much, preventing God, how much I owe
  To the defences Thou hast round me set,—
Example, custom, fear, occasion slow,—
  These scornèd bondsmen were my parapet.
  I dare not peep over this parapet
To gauge with glance the roaring gulf below,
  The depths of sin to which I had descended,
  Had not these me against myself defended.

EMERSON.

MEN cry to-day, "Christianity is the religion of the rich and comfortable," and
while they speak their cry is drowned in the
rush of the poor, the hungry, and the wretched
to some common men's revival. They cry
again, "The Christian belief belongs to the
ignorant," and lo, the wisest thought of the
world comes back again, as it is ever coming,
to the mystery of Christ and of His treatment
of the soul of man. It is not that they have
mistaken the class to which they should assign
the Christian faith. Their mistake is in giving
it to any class. It belongs to the individual.
It always has its eyes fastened on him. One
of the noblest functions of Christianity in the
world is to lie behind the class crystallizations
of mankind, like a solvent into which they
shall return and blend with one another,—to
crystallize, no doubt, again, but always to be
reminded that the classes into which they crystallize are lesser facts than the manhood into
which they are repeatedly dissolved.

VIII. 114.

For the love of God is broader
   Than the measures of man's mind;
And the heart of the Eternal
   Is most wonderfully kind.

But we make His love too narrow
   By false limits of our own;
And we magnify His strictness
   With a zeal He will not own.

There is plentiful redemption
   In the blood that has been shed;
There is joy for all the members
   In the sorrows of the Head.   FABER.

Through Jesus Christ.—ROM. vi. 23.

IN Jesus of Nazareth appeared the Mediator by whom was to be the Atonement. His was the life and nature which, standing between the Godhood and the manhood, was to bridge the gulf and make the firm, bright road over which blessing and prayer might pass and repass with confident, golden feet for ever. . . . But from which side did the bridge spring? Who moved toward the reconciliation? It is the most precious part of our belief that it was with God that the activity began. It is the very soul of the Gospel, as I read it, that the Father's heart, sitting above us in His holiness, yearned for us as we lay down here in our sin. And when there was no man to make an intercession, He sent His Son to tell us of His love, to live with us, to die for us, to lay His life like a strong bridge out from the divine side of existence, over which we might walk, fearfully but safely, back into the divinity where we belonged. Through Him we have access to the Father. As the end was divine so the method is divine. As it is to God that we come, so it is God who brings us there. I can think nothing else without dishonoring the tireless, quenchless love of God.   I. 237.

The exhibition of so great a love and mercy is
    a very deep abyss,
And as it were a divine sea which can not be
    swum over,
Yet in which the spiritual fishes, small and great,
Whom Thou hast inclosed in the net of faith,
Swim to and fro.   THOMAS À KEMPIS.

THERE comes no real content to the seeker
after goodness until, behind all the patterns which hold themselves up to him with
pride and boasting in their practicalness, at
last he hears the voice of the sublime imprac-
ticable standard, far out beyond them all, calling to him, "Be ye perfect as your Father in
heaven is perfect." Then the finite has heard
the voice of the infinite to which it belongs, to
which it always will respond, and straightway
it settles down to its endless journey and goes
on content.

III. 121.

I toil, but I must also climb;
What soul was ever quite at ease
Shut in by earthly boundaries?

I am not glad till I have known
Life that can lift me from my own:
A loftier level must be won,
A mightier strength to lean upon.

And heaven draws near as I ascend;
The breeze invites, the stars befriend:
All things are beckoning towards the Best:
I climb to Thee, my God, for rest.

LUCY LARCOM.

IS it not wonderful to see how few sins in this world are done flatly, fairly, blankly, as sins? We carry our consciences by side attacks, by elaborate strategies and artifices. We almost never charge up in the face of our sense of right and take it by assault. It is a very rare thing, I think much rarer than we are often ready to suppose, for a man to say to himself, this thing is bad, bad and not good, certainly and necessarily nothing but bad, and yet I will do it. . . . Covetousness dresses itself in the decent robes of prudence, idleness calls itself innocence, prodigality goes garbed as generosity, they all masquerade through society and trap the souls of men. . . . We have our sins here all decently labelled, all decently clad. What if He came, the Spirit of all truth, and wiped out every false name and wrote up every true one! We tremble to think of what these walls must see. We should not dare look upon one another's shame, bowed down each with the supreme shamefulness of his own.

VI. 11, 13.

Into the truth of things,
Out of their falseness rise, and reach thou, and
    remain.

BROWNING.

If any man will do His will, he shall know of the doctrine, whether it be of God, or whether I speak of myself.—JOHN vii. 17.

I HAVE been struck by seeing how favorite a text that has become in our day. . . . Many and many a soul has found that that was indeed the message that it needed. Turning away from vain disputes of words, leaving theological subtleties alone, just trying to turn what it knew of Christ into a life, it has found that it has become assured of His divinity, sure that His doctrine was of God. Such souls have not found that the thousand curious questions of theology were answered, and all the mystery rolled away out of the sky of truth. Christ did not promise that. But they have found what He did promise: that coming near to Him in obedience, they have been made sure of the true divinity that was in Him and in the teachings that he gave. . . .

It is like all Christ's teachings,—one utterance of an essential universal truth. Everywhere the flower of obedience is intelligence. . . . Obey Jesus with cordial loyalty and you will understand Jesus. Not by studying Him, but by doing His will, shall you learn how divine He is. Obedience completes itself in understanding.

I. 32.

For meek Obedience, too, is Light,
And following that is following Him.
JAMES RUSSELL LOWELL.

7

In the wilderness shall waters break out, and streams in the desert.—Is. xxxv. 6.

A MAN loses his friend and he is sorry; he loses his property and he is crushed; he loses his health and he almost gives up; but there is a yet untasted woe of which that man knows nothing. . . . Let him find himself a sinner, let him stand guilty, guilty, without a plea, without a hope, just with his frightened and naked soul before the eye of God, and then in the conviction of sin, then he has found what suffering is. . . . He walks the valley of his misery and all is dark. And can this valley break forth into wells? Can these dry pools be filled with water? . . . Tell me, all ye who, bowed down in the dust in the humiliation of your worthlessness, have heard there, with your face close to the ground, what you could never hear while you stood upright, the streams of pardon running sweet music down below,—tell me, is not the well of richest joy right here in the midst of the valley of completest sorrow?—where sin abounded does not grace much more abound?

VI. 31.

Yea, though I sin, my sin is not to death;
In my repentance I have joy, such joy
That I could almost sin to seek for it—
Yes, if I did not hate it and abhor,
And know that Thou abhorr'st and hatest it,
And will'st, for an example to the rest,
That Thine elect should keep themselves from
    it.

ARTHUR HUGH CLOUGH.

THE truth which God gives us is like the wheat that a bounteous country sends into the city. It is all the same wheat; but men go and buy it and eat it, and this same identical wheat is turned into different sorts of force in different men. It is turned into bartering force in one, and thinking force in another, and singing force in another, and governing force in another. It is made manifold as soon as it passes into men. So I think every minister finds that, as his disciples grow older, if he has really succeeded in getting the truth to be their truth, they grow into more various forms of Christian charity and usefulness. Each grows more evidently to be not merely a Christian, but the Christian that God intended him to be. They think more. They think differently. The pure white light breaks itself to each in different colors.

Let us rejoice in the clear individuality of maturing Christian life. Its one principle is still identical; and so it already prophesies heaven, where we are sure we shall be all different illustrations of the one same grace, showing different characters, set to different works, but all moved by one spirit—all illustrations of the one same grace still.   II. 44, 45.

Lord, make me one with Thine own faithful ones,
Thy Saints who love Thee, and are loved by
     Thee,
Till the day break and till the shadows flee,—
At one with them in alms and orisons;
At one with him who toils and him who runs,
And him who yearns for union yet to be.
                    CHRISTINA G. ROSSETTI.

One star differeth from another star in glory.
1 Cor. xv. 41.

EVERY man who is a Christian must live a Christian life that is peculiarly his own. Every candle of the Lord must utter its peculiar light; only the true individuality of faith is marked by these characteristics which rescue it from bigotry: first, that it does not add something to the universal light, but only brings out most strongly some aspect of it which is specially its own; second, that it always cares more about the essential light than about the peculiar way in which it utters it; and third, that it easily blends with other special utterances of the universal light, in cordial sympathy and recognition of the value which it finds in them. Let these characteristics be in every man's religion, and then the individuality of faith is an inestimable gain. Then the different candles of the Lord burn in long rows down His great palace-halls of the world; and all together, each complementing all the rest, they light the whole vast space with Him.

II. 14.

"Slender the streams of good
  That flow from the lives of men,
But united they swell to a gracious flood
  That blesseth again and again."

And the multitudes that went before, and that followed, cried, saying, Hosanna to the Son of David ; Blessed is He that cometh in the name of the Lord. . . . And when He was come into Jerusalem, all the city was moved, saying, Who is this ?

MATT. ix. 10.

SO Jesus came into Jerusalem. He came at once as an Intruder and a King. There were men . . . who made the old streets ring with shouts of welcome. There were other men who . . . with muttered curses saw Him go by in His triumph. But through it all Jesus held on His way, claiming the town for His town because it was His Father's.

And so he claims our hearts. An Intruder and a King at once He seems to those hearts as He stands there on the threshold. There is something in every one of them that says to Him, "Come in, come in!" There is something, too, in every one of them that rises up at His coming and says, "Begone, begone! We will not have this Man to rule over us." But through their tumult, their struggle, Christ, whether He be King or Intruder, whether He be welcomed or rejected, goes on His way, pressing on into each heart's most secret places, claiming always that He and He alone is the heart's King. VII. 220.

Lord, we would fain some little palm-branch lay
    Upon Thy way . . .
If but the foldings of Thy garment's hem
    Shall shadow them,
These worthless leaves which we have brought and strewed
    Along Thy road
Shall be raised up and made divinely sweet,
    And fit to lie beneath Thy feet.

SUSAN COOLIDGE.

He goeth before you into Galilee.

MATT. xxviii. 7.

THIS is Christ's way. Wherever He would have His disciples go, He goes first Himself, and through the door which He has opened He draws them by His love. That is the whole philosophy of Christian culture. And that is the meaning of the Incarnation. God entered into human life; made Himself one with it as He only could have done with a nature that was originally one with His own. He became man as He could not have become brute or stone. Then in that human nature He outwent humanity. He opened yet unopened gates of human possibility. He showed what man might be, how great, how god-like! And by the love and oneness He has always been claiming man for the greatness whose possibility He showed. As we think of the Incarnation deeply, these three stages come in one thought. First, the God in Christ seems very near to us as we think of His love. Then He seems very far above us as we think of His holiness, and then again He seems to bring us very near to Himself as we feel His power. He is one with us. He goes beyond us, and He comes again and receives us unto Himself.   VI. 179.

Ah, the dear message that He gave her then,
Said for the sake of all bruised hearts of men !
" Go, tell those friends who have believed on Me,
I go before them into Galilee :

" Into the life so poor, and hard, and plain,
That for a while they must take up again,
My presence passes. Where their feet toil slow,
Mine, shining-swift with love, still foremost go."
                              ADELINE D. T. WHITNEY.

Who is among you that feareth the Lord, . . . that walketh in darkness, and hath no light? let him trust in the name of the Lord, and stay upon his God.—Is. i. 10.

"WHAT shall I do with this sorrow that God has sent me?" "Take it up and bear it, and get a strength and blessing out of it." "Ah, if I only knew what blessing there was in it, if I saw how it would help me, then I could bear it like a plume!" "What shall I do with this hard, hateful duty which Christ has laid right in my way?" "Do it, and grow by doing it." "Ah, yes; if I could only see that it would make me grow!" In both these cases do you not see that what you are begging for is not more faith, although you think it is, but sight? You want to see for yourself the blessing in the sorrow, the strength in the hard and hateful task. Faith says not, "I see that it is good for me, and so God must have sent it," but "God sent it, and so it must be good for me."

V. 351.

Hast thou forgotten that we walk by faith?
For keenest sight but multiplies the shows.
Lift up thine eyelids; take a valiant breath;
Fearful, dare yet the terror in God's name;
Step wider, trust the Invisible.

GEORGE MACDONALD.

Father, save me from this hour : But for this hour came I into the world. Father, glorify Thy name.—JOHN xii. 27, 28.

NO duty of doing frightens and dismays the human soul like the duty of mere suffering. I know nothing that will so cow and crush a strong, well man, with the red blood riotous in his full veins, as a certain conviction coming suddenly upon him that he is to be a poor, miserable, dependent invalid all the rest of his days until he dies. Nothing makes a man cry out to die like that. It is the most terrible sight one ever sees. . . . And then it is the most beautiful sight one ever sees. As the man lies there in his misery, out of the darkness comes his past and reads itself to him. Each bright old year of health comes with its message of God's unforgetting love. . . . He slowly sees that all the past of active duty was stocking his life with the graces that should fit him for these slow years of suffering duty. This bed of wretchedness was the result to which every path of education led. Slowly his soul accepts the lesson. "Father, save me from this hour. Nay, for this purpose came I unto this hour. Father, glorify Thy name." Then the hands drop patiently from their resistance. The meek lips are put up to taste the bitter cup. The life grows happy in its new enlightenment of pain.

> " ' Glory to God, to God ! ' he saith ;
> ' Knowledge by suffering entereth,
> - And life is perfected by death.' "

VII. 228.

I am the bread of life.
He that eateth Me, even he shall live by Me.
JOHN vi. 35, 57.

TO feed on Christ is to get His strength into us to be our strength. You feed on the cornfield and then go and build your house, and it is the cornfield in your strong arm that builds the house, that cuts down the trees and piles the stone and lifts the roof into its place. You feed on Christ and then go and live your life, and it is Christ in you that lives your life, that helps the poor, that tells the truth, that fights the battle, and that wins the crown.

But what is this strength of Christ that comes to us? It is His character,—His strength, His purity, His truth, His mercifulness,—in one word, His holiness, the perfectness of His moral life. That is the inner strength. That is the strength of food.

And notice how this last alone is vital. It alone makes life. It lives. The buttress keeps the dead wall standing, but the sap makes the live tree still more alive with growth. So compulsion and fear keep us true to duty, but love makes us larger and fit for greater duty every day. Every vital strength must be the strength which incorporates itself with the very being of the thing that it supports. Except we eat we can have no life in us. II. 246, 242.

*Lord, evermore give us this bread.—*JOHN vi. 34.

> Lord, leave us not athirst, unfed, . . .
> Until, these mortal needs all past,
> We sit at Thy full feast at last,
> The bread of angels broken by Thee,
> The wine of joy poured constantly.
>   SUSAN COOLIDGE.

Pilate saith unto them, Behold the man.

JOHN xix. 5.

THINK of Christ's life and death, not with reference to the mysterious redemptive efficacy that was in it, but as the great human life, the representative life that set forth the ideal experience and culture of a human soul. And surely it does not fail us here. Whatever else comes to a life, there is a final grace and greatness which it cannot have until it has been touched by pain. I do not speak it sentimentally. I do not mean the mere pathetic romance which gives a charm to the story of the unfortunate. I mean the very stuff and qualities of our manhood—those things which make us really and completely men. . . . Maturity of character is as sure a sign of some healthy experience of pain, however secret, as the brilliancy and clearness of a bit of glass is of the fire through which it has passed.

We do not dishonor the humanity of Jesus when we thus make it the type of what ours may be. He wanted and He loves to have us use it so. "As I am, so are ye in this world," He declared. Only remember He is not only pattern, but power. We must be like Him, but we cannot be, save as He makes us. We must come to Him, but we can only come to Him by His grace and help.   VII. 11, 12.

Thou art our Pattern to the end of time,
  Oh Crucified! and perfect is Thy will:
The workers follow Thee in doing good;
  The helpless think of Calvary, and are still.

CAROLINE M. NOEL.

THE broken edges everywhere! The half-finished tasks that men have to leave and go into the darkness! The young careers so full of promise that suddenly stop! The great ideas and wishes, growing legitimately out of earthly life, yet evidently too large for it, finding no satisfaction here! And most of all the unfinished characters! I can think that it is no great thing for a man to die with his fortune half made, or his barn half built; but that he should die just as his character is rounding into shape, and from a crude study becoming a picture of beauty and an engine of power, this is what most bewilders us. This is what most of all, I think, has made men guess that this earthly life we see is a part and not a whole, and set their eyes pathetically searching for that other world they thought must be beyond the waters.

XI. 15.

Still must we hope what we believe,
And what is given us receive;
Must still believe, for still we hope
That in a world of larger scope
What here is faithfully begun
Will be completed, not undone.
ARTHUR HUGH CLOUGH.

If after the manner of men I have fought with beasts at Ephesus, what advantageth it me, if the dead rise not?—1 COR. xv. 32.

YOU can test the work that you are engaged in in the world by seeing whether it needs, whether it is restless and cramped without the truth of, an immortality. If it is not, if you can do your little fight just as well without any hope of an eternity, be sure the fight that you are at is a poor one, is not worthy of your highest powers—is too small a fight for a man, a child of God, to spend his life in fighting.

The world's poor heart knows very well what it wants. For years and years it longed to see one man rise from the dead. If it could only have that! It could let many other questions go unanswered, but, oh, for some light on that darkness—oh, for some sound out of that silence! If it could have that, then its bonds would be broken, its whole pale life flooded with color, its best truths verified completely, and a hope lighted upon every grave. No longer should spiritual philosophy labor under the burden of materialism; no longer should the dying die in terrible doubt, and the mourners go hopelessly about the streets. My friends, the world's prayer is answered. A true man has risen from the grave. Life and immortality are brought to light.

XII. 29.

Most human and yet most divine,
The flower of man and God!
WHITTIER.

HOW this "power of the resurrection" transfigures and changes not merely all internal, but all external things! . . . The world itself, even material nature—trees and fields and skies, noontimes and mornings, sunsets and midnights—cannot be the same when they are found to be the education-place of a being with a destiny such as the resurrection of Jesus Christ makes known for man. They must bring moral meanings to that soul which this new truth of immortality exalts to be the monarch of the world. You say that this is poetry. There is no poetry on the earth like the Christian's faith, that most noble of all creative powers, "the substance of things hoped for, the evidence of things not seen." And so it is the commonest Christian consciousness, belonging to all Christian minds in their several degrees, that to them, with their new life, the whole world of nature became new too, had new words to speak to them of God and of eternity, and that all through their lives there are times when the enlightened universe becomes vocal, and its visible realities impart to them

> " Authentic tidings of invisible things,
> Of ebb and flow, and ever-during power,
> And central peace subsisting at the heart
> Of endless agitation."

VII. 283.

Handle me and see, for a spirit hath not flesh and bones as ye see me have.—LUKE xxiv. 39.

IN these words Christ after His resurrection appeals to His disciples to bear witness that He is a true living man, and not a disembodied spirit. He bids them use their human senses to discover that He is truly human like themselves. The words therefore may represent to us the perpetual appeal which Christ makes to our human consciousness and to the perceptions of mankind to recognize His true humanity. As He then offered His human body for the inspection of His disciples, and bade them own that it was truly a man's body, so He is always offering His whole human nature and calling on men to witness that He is truly human in thought and feeling and character, the pattern and fulfilment of humanity.

There are two knowledges of Christ, one lower and one higher. The first knowledge brings us to obedience. The second knowledge is the power of spiritual growth.

Into that higher knowledge may we all advance; making Christ ours first, that in the end He may make us His. With reverent hands may we handle Him and see that He is truly manly, that He really wears our humanity, that so we may through His humanity come to the Father God whom He reveals.

II. 253, 269.

*In your patience possess ye your souls. . . . Your
redemption draweth nigh.*—LUKE xxi. 19, 28.

THE world is growing better—I know it. A
great unceasing movement toward truth
and goodness is carrying slowly forward ever
the character of this great, mighty, mysterious
humanity. How slow it is, but oh, how real
it is, the study of the ages tells. And yet
behold how the good causes fail. Behold how
selfishness comes in to paralyze each great
endeavor for the good of man. Alas for him
who only sees this surface fact; who does not
feel beneath it all the heave and movement of
the whole race forward toward goodness,
toward God! To him who hears at once the
tumult of moral failures all around him and
the steady progress of the great moral success
beneath him—to him the world becomes
solemn and beautiful, pathetic and full of
hope. For him despairing pessimism and silly
optimism both become impossible. A divine
optimism, which, while it dares not say,
"Whatever is is best," devoutly says, "The
best is strongest and shall ultimately conquer
and use even the worst," becomes the habit
of his life. Such was the optimism of Jesus.
Such is the optimism of His disciples if they
catch His spirit.   VII. 206.

Then life is—to wake, not sleep;
    Rise, and not rest; but press
From earth's level, where blindly creep
    Things perfected more or less,
To the heaven's height, far and steep.
                              BROWNING.

THERE is a religion which finds the world unsatisfying, and so turns longingly, wistfully, pathetically, wearily to God. There is another religion which finds the world wondrously beautiful and good, yet always suggesting something more beautiful and better than itself, and this religion too turns to God, but glowingly, springingly, hopefully. The first religion starts from a sense of sin and comes to God for forgiveness. The second religion starts in a thankful joy, a sense of promise, and comes to God for fulfilment. The first starts with disgust at self, and so comes to love for God. The second starts in admiration of God, and so comes to forgetfulness of self.

IV. 136.

Happy ! Yes; and wherefore
  Should I not be so ?
Love Divine o'erhangeth
  All the way I go.

Darkest shadow showeth
  Smiling sun behind;
Where the sickle goeth,
  There the reapers bind.

Happy ! Yes; and wherefore
  Should I not be so,
Since by ways appointed
  Unto heaven I go ?

J. L. M. W.

THERE are many great and exultant moments in our lives; moments in which some new, heretofore unfelt motive takes us into its power, when some new work for us and some new power in us starts forth and makes life seem fresh and green, like a spring morning that forgets all the stains and storms that have gone before it. But among all such moments there is none that can compare with that in which duty passes into love—when morality, reaching itself out into eternity, asserts its sameness of nature with the service that the glorified nature is to render to God in the heavenly city, so that the obligation of honesty in our bargains is seen to rest on the same sanctions and to be lustrous with the same beauty now that will belong to the singing of the everlasting songs and the casting of the crowns before the Saviour's feet—the moment when our life thus knows Christ and the power of His resurrection.

VII. 285.

Something that leaps life's narrow bars,
   To claim its birthright with the hosts of
      heaven;
   A seed of sunshine that doth leaven
Our earthly dulness with the beams of stars,
   And glorify our clay
   With light from fountains elder than the Day.

JAMES RUSSELL LOWELL.

Father, I will that they also, whom Thou hast given me, be with me where I am ; that they may behold my glory.—JOHN xvii. 24.

BEFORE the words can soar into the high, pure meaning which belongs to them, we must remember what Christ's glory is which He wants us to see. Its essence, the heart and soul of it, must be His goodness. . . . And here the truth comes in, that in moral things only the like can see its like; only the good can really discern, appreciate, and understand goodness. That needs no proof. We see it every day. Men live alongside of the best saints the world possesses, do business with them, pass their whole lives with them, and never know that they are good. If we have ever made any advance in purity and unselfishness, has not the best of all its satisfaction been in this, that it has let us see something new of the self-sacrifice and purity in other men which have been hidden from us? The higher we climb, the more the peaks open around us. Now apply all this to the Saviour's prayer that we may see His glory. His glory is His goodness. Only by growth in goodness can His goodness open itself to us. What is He praying for then ? Is it not that we might be like Him ? So only can we see Him. It is His glory that He wants us to see, but, back of that, He wants us to be such men and women that we *can* see His glory.   I. 308, 309.

Walk with Him now ; so shall thy way be bright,
And all thy soul be filled with His most glorious light.
                    HORATIUS BONAR.

That we henceforth be no more children, tossed to and fro, but . . . may grow up into Him in all things.—EPHES. iv. 14, 15.

THE true faith which a man has kept up to the end of his life must be one that has opened with his growth and constantly won new reality and color from his changing experience. . . . It is the field that once held the seed, now waving and rustling under the autumn wind with the harvest that it holds, yet all the time it has kept the corn. The joy of his life has richened his belief. His sorrow has deepened it. His doubts have sobered it. His enthusiasms have fired it. His labor has purified it. His doctrines are like the house that he has lived in, rich with associations which make it certain that he will never move out of it. His doctrines have been illustrated and strengthened and endeared by the good help they have given to his life. And no doctrine that has not done this can be really held up to the end with any such vital grasp as will enable us to carry it with us through the river and enter with it into the new life beyond.

I. 62.

O Almighty God, who hast instructed Thy holy Church with the heavenly doctrine of Thy Evangelist Saint Mark ; Give us grace that, being not like children carried away with every blast of strange doctrine, we may be established in the truth of Thy holy Gospel ; through Jesus Christ our Lord. Amen.

BOOK OF COMMON PRAYER.

DESPERATION and bitterness come with the sight of pain without the sight of the higher consequences and results of pain. . . . "Curse God and die," seems sometimes to be the only outcome of it all. . . . It *is* the only outcome of it all, if the pain you see or feel is all. But if the whole of a man's life from its beginning to its endless end, from its surface to its inmost heart, is capable of being taken into account, then the desperate outcome is not the only one. There is a blessing and a thankfulness which may overcome and drown the curse. . . . Suppose that, looking at pain, and with the curse just growing into shape upon your lips, a great hand takes you up and lifts you. And as you rise your vision widens. And slowly education grows into your view, surrounding pain, and drawing out its sense of cruelty, and crowding in upon it its own sense of love and purpose. Then, in the larger vision, must not the curse perish? And if the lips are not strong enough to open into thankfulness, at least the eyes, still full of pity, may wait in peace.

VI. 221.

The Way of the Just is made strait, and the journey of the Saints is prepared.

After what manner?

By sorrow and labor; for this is the way to the Kingdom of Heaven.

Is there no other way to the Life Eternal?

None. The only straight way is that of the Cross.

It is so. Christ hath taught this in His Word.

THOMAS À KEMPIS.

We live by admiration, hope and love:
And even as these are well and wisely fixed,
In dignity of being we ascend.
WORDSWORTH.

WHAT does it mean when men as they grow older become narrow, sordid, and machine-like, when a vulgar self-content comes over them, and all the limitations of a finished life that hopes for and expects no more than what it is makes the sad picture which we see in hosts of men's middle life? Is it not certainly that those men have ceased to admire and trust? . . . The blight that falls upon their natures is the token of what a lofty and life-giving faculty it is which they have put out of use. It was this faculty which made them at every moment greater than themselves, which kept them in communion with the riches of a higher life, which preserved all the enthusiasm of active energy, and yet preserved humility which held all the other faculties to do their best work. This is the faculty whose disuse makes the mature life of so many men barren and dreary, and whose regeneration, when the man is lifted up into the new admiration and the new trust, the admiration for and trust in God, makes a large part of the glory of the full-grown life of faith. VI. 95, 96.

EVERY now and then there are flashes of light upon the Gospel page which let us see what a bright, sunny, and sympathetic life the Saviour lived,—how perfectly free from harshness and asceticism was that character which, at the same time, carries a sweet and gentle seriousness and a robust earnestness with it wherever it went. " The Son of man came eating and drinking, and they say, Behold, a man gluttonous and a wine-bibber, a friend of publicans and sinners,"—so Jesus himself described one day the current impression that His life made on the people of Jerusalem. The words are like an instantaneous photograph of that far distant time. . . . In those words we can see friends and enemies alike busied with the strange life of Jesus, and only gradually finding out that it was they who were strange, and not He,—gradually coming first to feel and then to understand that this life of His, so bright and yet so serious, so individual and yet so social, had reached completely what their lives were only crudely struggling after.   VIII. 86.

We would see Jesus! not alone in sorrow,
    But we would have Him with us in our
        mirth;
He at whose right hand there are joys for ever,
    Doth not disdain to bless the joys of earth.
                        ANNA E. HAMILTON.

Let us never be afraid of innocent joy. God is good, and what He does is well done. We must dare to be happy . . . regarding ourselves always as the depositaries, and not as the authors of our joy.   AMIEL.

He giveth power to the faint, and to them that have no might He increaseth strength.—Is. xl. 29.

DO you know what it is to be failing every day, and yet to be sure—humbly but deeply sure—that your life is, as a whole, in its great movement and meaning, not failing, but succeeding? You want to do that best work that a man can do—to make life brighter and nobler for your fellow-men. Not a day passes in which you do not somehow try to do that blessed work; but every time you turn away after one of those attempts to give sympathy or inspiration to your brethren, how your heart sinks, so cold and so ignoble are the words which you meant to be so generous and warm! And yet all the while you know that the whole life does not fail. Still there is the purpose! It does not die. It is not given up. It presses forward, wounded and bleeding, but more and more determined every day. Every day it grows clearer and clearer to you that without that wish and hope and resolution life would not be worth living.

VII. 40.

That Thy full glory may abound, increase,
And so Thy glory shall be formed in me,
I pray: the answer is not rest or peace,
But charges, wants, anxieties; . . .
But all my life is blossoming inwardly,
And every breath is like a litany,
While through each labor, like a thread of gold,
Is woven the sweet consciousness of Thee.

SUSAN COOLIDGE.

Some falls are means the happier to rise.
SHAKESPEARE.

THERE is a verse of one of the subtlest and truest of the English poets of our time which expresses so perfectly this idea of the relation between final success and the failures which precede it that I quote it to you: . . .

> " For while the tired waves, vainly breaking,
>   Seem here no painful inch to gain,
> Far back, through creeks and inlets making,
>   Comes silent, flooding in, the main."

The noisy waves are failures, but the great silent tide is a success. The waves are borne upon the bosom of the tide; they share its motion; nay, the failure of each of them in some degree is a reaction of the tide's motion as it is cast back from the beach. But all the time the tide is succeeding while the waves are failing. The failures are carried on the bosom of a success which is present underneath them all the time. A life might be succeeding in the struggle after goodness even while every effort of the man who lived that life to be good fell so far short of what he wanted it to be that he could call it nothing but a failure. The purpose, the consecration, of the life to God and goodness is its tide. The special struggles to do good things are the waves. The deep, persistent, and unchanging hate of the peculiar sin, which is determined never to be reconciled to it and to fight against it till it dies—that is the soul's success, which does not falter or stop, and which carries along upon it all the partial failures of which the life is full.

VII. 197, 198, 201.

Philip saith unto him, Come and see.
JOHN i. 46.

THIS was the admirable wisdom of Philip. What had converted him was the personal sight of Jesus. He has no other religion but that. . . . Jesus was His own evidence. To get his friend face to face with Jesus—this was his object. . . .

Christianity offers to the world her historic Christ. . . . Back in the centuries, yet set so clearly in the light of authentic history that all attempts to melt His life into a cloudy myth have always failed, there stands this figure. She claims that this Being to whom she points is the power and wisdom of God present upon the earth. You hesitate and doubt. Then "Come and see," she says. Put yourself in the presence of this Being. . . . Ennoble humanity as completely as you will, and it will not explain this phenomenal character and life. . . . She says it is God manifest in the flesh. Come, and find another explanation, if you can. Come, and if there is no other to be found, take this and own the divine Christ.
VI. 139, 144.

Behold Him now where He comes !
  Not the Christ of our subtile creeds,
But the Lord of our hearts, our homes,
  Of our hopes, our prayers, our needs;
The Brother of want and blame,
  The Lover of women and men,—
With a love that puts to shame
  All passions of mortal ken.
RICHARD WATSON GILDER.

As the Father knoweth me, even so know I the Father.—JOHN X. 15.

THE words are full of that idea of mutualness which gives so much of warmth and richness to all life. Any relation which is all one-sided is unsatisfactory and dull. It is not vividly interesting. We love to think of any two objects, any two beings which have to do with one another as ministering each to each, each sending to the other something in answer to that which it receives. That fills the relationship with motion, and with motion come light and heat. The sun and the earth, the insect and the plant, the nation and the citizen, the teacher and the pupil, the parent and the child, the air which, filled with light, gives to the light its substance and its swiftness,—in every relationship there is this principle of reciprocity. Nothing alone is thoroughly alive; all complete life subsists in the reaction of mutuality. To give is never perfect life; it needs the complement, the fulfilment of taking. To take is never perfect life; it needs the complement, the fulfilment of giving.

IV. 283.

O Jesus, who lovest us all, stoop low from
    Thy glory above:
Where sin hath abounded make grace to abound
    and to superabound,
Till we gaze on Thee face unto Face, and re-
    spond to Thee love unto Love.

CHRISTINA G. ROSSETTI.

Shall we serve Heaven
With less respect than we do minister
To our gross selves ?

SHAKESPEARE.

YOUR Christian duties, the prayers you pray, the self-denials that you practise, the charities you give,—what is the matter with them ? . . . You serve yourself, and how clear you are to yourself, and so, what life there is in every act of your own service; but you serve Christ and how dim He has grown ! and so, how listlessly the hands move at His labor ! Now if the Holy Spirit can indeed bring Him clearly to you, is not the Holy Spirit what you need ?   And this is just exactly what He does. I find a Christian who has really " received the Holy Ghost," and what is it that strikes and delights me in him ?   It is the intense and intimate reality of Christ. . . .   His whole life is light and elastic with this buoyant desire of doing everything for Jesus, just as Jesus would wish it done.   So simple, but so powerful!   So childlike, but so heroic!   Duty has been transfigured.   The weariness, the drudgery, the whole task-nature, has been taken away. Love has poured like a new life-blood along the dry veins, and the soul that used to toil and groan and struggle goes now singing along its way, *"The life that I now live in the flesh, I live by the faith of the Son of God who loved me and gave Himself for me."*

II. 228.

CHRIST saw all life in God. That means that He saw life in its completeness. No being ever saw the evil and misery as He beheld it. He saw sin with all the intensity of holiness. But nobody ever has dared call Jesus Christ a pessimist. He saw the end from the beginning. He saw the depth from the surface. He saw the light from the darkness. He saw the whole from the parts. Therefore He could not despair. There was no curse of life upon His lips, but infinite pity ! A pity that has folded itself around the world's torn and bleeding heart ever since—but no curse ! And who are we, with our little feeble rage and petulance, flinging our testy curses where the Lord's blessing descended like the love of God ?

VI. 214.

There is one Mind, one omnipresent Mind
Omnific.   His most holy name is Love.
Truth of subliming import !—with the which
Who feeds and saturates his constant soul,
He from His small particular orbit flies
With blest outstarting.   From himself he flies,
Stands in the sun, and with no partial gaze
Views all creation, and He loves it all,
And blesses it, and calls it very good !

S. T. COLERIDGE.

I came not to send peace, but a sword.
MATT. x. 34.

WE must think of Jesus as a soul undergo-
ing experiences, living a life all through
those years, or else the Gospels are a very
dead and barren book.   And if we have known
what it is to look forward and see, with a terror which yet is glorified by hope, that the
great purpose on which our heart is set is to
be won only by first casting it, with seeming
recklessness, away,— . . . then we can understand how the Rebuilder of human life about
the fatherhood of God dwelt with pathetic certainty upon the destruction that must come
before that construction could begin.   The
more intensely He knew the preciousness of
the end, the more necessary and the more terrible became the seeming sacrifice of that end
before He must go to reach it.   The more He
gloried, with His heart full of the memories
of heaven, in the prospect of the re-estab-
lished family of God where each child should
find his own distinctive childhood in the common filial life of all, so much the more He
saw with sadness, but with certainty, that the
merely human groupings of men, in which
each man lost his true self among his brethren,
must be broken up.   VIII. 102.

Old things shall pass away ;
The new shall come in abundance,
The holy desires shall overflow,
And rise up on every side where the cherishing spirit
    bloweth :
There shall be no more fear, but love shall fill all ;
For this change is from the right hand of God.
THOMAS À KEMPIS.

THERE are those who seem to be doomed to most earthly toil; just to be conscientious, and upright, and thorough, and true. It seems as if that were everything for them. There are other men whose souls leap to triumphant thoughts, and whose eyes are open to ecstatic visions. . . . These two sorts of men belong together, make one world, are serving the purposes of one God, and making ready one celestial kingdom, and deserve each the other's whole-souled respect. It is not that the lesser man is making his life successful by making possible a higher life which some other man may live, though that is much. It is that in this universe, where natural and spiritual succeed and minister to one another, he who at any spot is doing good work of any kind is serving the Universal Master and contributing to the universal success.

VI. 257.

Morning, evening, noon, and night,
"Praise God!" sang Theodite.
Then to his poor trade he turned,
Whereby the daily bread was earned.

.   .   .   .

But ever at each period,
He stopped and sang, "Praise God!"

.   .   .   .

Said Blaise, the listening monk, "Well done;
I doubt not thou art heard, my son,
As well as if thy voice to-day
Were praising God the Pope's great way."

BROWNING.

*There is one glory of the moon, and another glory
of the sun, and another glory of the stars.*

1 COR. xv. 41.

SAINT PAUL builds his argument for immortality upon the richness and the splendor of this mortal life. Often enough have
men made heaven a compensation for the woes
of earth. . . . Paul makes heaven not a compensation, but a development. Because this
world is so glorious, therefore the glory of
heaven must be surpassing and unspeakable.
How much nobler is Paul's way ! How much
fuller of inspiration and of genuine faith! . . .
For he who finds in the manifold glories of
this mortal life a symbol and witness of the
glories which belong to immortality will always be led to live this life as intensely and
profoundly as he can, in order that the higher
life may become real and attractive to him.
Men have thought that they must separate
themselves from earth in order that they
might believe in heaven. Paul's doctrine
says emphatically, "No! " He says, "The
deeper that you go in life, the more life must
spread itself out around you and become
eternity. He who gets to the centre feels the
sphere."

V. 59.

Deep love lieth under
  These pictures of time;
They fade in the light of
  Their meaning sublime.

EMERSON.

Your joy no man taketh from you.—JOHN xvi. 22.

IN these words Christ declared that there was a joy which no man could disturb. There is a limit to our power over one another; there is a chamber of our inner selves where we may turn the key and no one can come in. . . . The very fact that there is such a limit interests us. We can see how good it is for a man's life that, while there should be great regions of his happiness which are involved with what other men are and do, there should be also other regions which no man but himself can touch.

As I watch the growing life of the disciples, I see them coming to the best picture of what a human life ought to be, open and sensitive and sympathetic, and yet all the while self-respectful and independent; feeling other men and yet living their own life; as responsive as the ocean's surface to the winds of the living humanity which blew across them; and yet keeping, like the ocean, a calm and hidden depth which no storm upon the surface could disturb.　　　　　　III. 290, 293.

> O weary ways of earth and men !
> 　O self more weary still !
> How vainly do you vex the heart
> 　That none but God can fill !
>
> 　.　.　.　.　.　.　.　.
>
> These surface-troubles come and go
> 　Like rufflings of the sea;
> The deeper depth is out of reach
> 　To all, my God, but Thee.
>
> 　　　　　　　　FABER.

Your heart shall rejoice, and your joy no man taketh from you.—JOHN xvi. 22.

IT was a special joy, the inmost, the most secret and sacred of all joys which their Master promised. . . . And Jesus tells His disciples just what the power of this secret joy is to be. It is to be His presence with them: " I will see you again, and your heart shall rejoice, and your joy no man taketh from you." Everything is based upon the association which they are to have with Christ their Master. There is nothing at all of self-sufficiency in what is promised. It is not that these men are to develop some interior strength, or to drift into some region of calm indifference where the influences of their fellow-men shall not touch them any longer. It is that they are to come to a new life with Him. The new joy which is to enter into them, which they are to enter into, is to be distinctly a joy of relationship and not of self-containment, a joy which is to escape the invasion of the men who disturb all other joys by being held in the hand of a stronger being, out of which no earthly power shall be able to pluck it.

III. 292, 294.

He who has a relish for Thee, will he not find sweetness in everything ?

And he that has no relish for Thee, what can be sweet to him ?

THOMAS À KEMPIS.

Could not this man, which opened the eyes of the blind, have caused that even this man should not have died?—JOHN xi. 37.

COULD not Christ have saved Lazarus from dying? Could not Christ have saved you or me from perplexity or temptation or doubt? He could, because the power of life and death was in Him. . . . But if it were best for Lazarus to die, then Christ could not have caused that he should not have died. That is a sublime incapacity; to stand with the gift of life in the all-powerful hands, to see the cry for life in the eager eyes, to hear it in the dumb appeal of the terrified lips, and yet to say, '' No, not life but death is best,'' and so to be unable to give life,—that is a sublime, a divine incapacity. Could not Christ have answered your prayer? No, He could not; not because the thing you asked for was not in His treasury, but because behind the question of His giving or refusing it there lay the fundamental necessity of His nature and His love, that He should do for you only the absolutely best. The thing you asked for was not absolutely best, therefore He could not give it. Back of how many unanswered prayers lies that divine impossibility !

V. 38.

If He turn His face away,
  Never answering a word,
When for some ill boon we pray, . . .
Blessed be His name for aye
  For the prayers He hath not heard.
KATHERINE TYNAN HINKSON.

*Ye shall be sorrowful, but your sorrow shall be
turned into joy.*—JOHN xvi. 20.

IT must be somewhere in the grief that the
help of the grief is hidden. It must be in
some discovery of the divine side of the sorrow that the consolation of the sorrow will be
found. It is a wondrous change when a man
stops asking of his distress, "How can I throw
this off?" and asks instead, "What did God
mean by sending this?" Then, he may well
believe that time and work will help him.
Time, with its necessary calming of the first
wild surface-tumult, will let him look deeper
and ever deeper into the divine purpose of the
sorrow, will let its deepest and most precious
meanings gradually come forth so that he may
see them. Work, done in the sorrow, will
bring him into ever new relations to the God in
whom alone the full interpretation and relief
of the sorrow lies. Time and work, not as
means of escape from distress, but as the hands
in which distress shall be turned hither and
thither that the light of God may freely play
upon it; time and work, so acting as servants
of God, not as substitutes for God, are full of
unspeakably precious ministries to the suffering soul. But the real relief, the only final
comfort, is God; and He relieves the soul always in its suffering, not from its suffering;
nay, he relieves the soul by its suffering, by
the new knowledge and possession of Himself
which could come only through that atmosphere of pain.

II. 279.

THERE is something very beautiful to me in the truth that suffering, rightly used, is not a cramping, binding, restricting of the human soul, but a setting of it free. It is not a violation of the natural order, it is only a more or less violent breaking open of some abnormal state that the natural order may be resumed. It is the opening of a cage door. It is the breaking in of a prison wall. This is the thought of those fine old lines of an early English poet:

" The soul's dark cottage, battered and decayed,
  Lets in new light through chinks that time has made.
  Stronger by weakness, wiser men become
  As they draw near to their eternal home."

Oh, how many battered cottages have thus let in the light ! How many broken bodies have set their souls free, and how many shattered homes have let the men and women who sat in darkness in them see the great light of a present God! "Stronger by weakness !" " Who passing through the vale of misery use it for a well."

VI. 30.

Cast into the pit
Of lonely sorrow,
The suffering soul,
Looking aloft,
Sees with amaze
In the daytime sky
The light of stars.

RICHARD WATSON GILDER.

WE paint our heroes fighting their battles in the clouds or in the depths. Types of power which can only be developed in supreme joy or supreme sorrow enthrall our imagination; and then some plain man comes who knows not either rapture or despair, who simply has his daily work to do, his friends to help, . . . his trials to bear, his temptations to conquer, his soul to save; and what a healthiness he brings into our standards, with what a genuine refreshment he fills our hearts. Behold how great are these primary eternal qualities—patience, hope, kindness, intelligence, trust, self-sacrifice.

The arctic frost ! The torrid heat ! Behold the true strength, the real life of the planet is not in these. It is in the temperate lands that the grape ripens and the wheat turns calmly yellow in the constant sun. Blessed is the life which grows itself into the consciousness of how strong a man is who with the average powers of a man keeps his integrity and purity, becomes ever more upright and pure, and also encourages the lives of other men.

IV. 204.

All service ranks the same with God:
If now, as formerly He trod
Paradise, His presence fills
Our earth, each only as God wills
Can work. God's puppets, best and worst,
Are we; there is no last or first.

BROWNING.

To another he gave two talents.

MATT. xxv. 15.

THIS quiet, common-place, unnoticed man, going his faithful way in his dull dress which makes no mark and draws no eye, doing his duty insignificantly and thoroughly, winning so unobtrusively at last his master's praise, ought to be interesting to us all.

He ought to be interesting because he represents so much the largest element in universal human life. The average man is by far the most numerous man. The man who goes beyond the average, the man who falls short of the average, both of them, by their very definition, are exceptions. They are the outskirts and fringes, the capes and promontories of humanity. The great continent of human life is made up of the average existences, the mass of two-talented capacity and action.

IV. 194.

God sows June fields with clover, and the
    world
Broadcasts with common kindnesses,
With plain, good souls that cheerfully fulfil
Their homely duties in the common field
Of daily life, ambitious of no more
Than to supply the needs of friend or kin,
Yet serve God's higher will to human hearts.

SAMUEL LONGFELLOW.

Ignorance is the curse of God,
Knowledge the wing wherewith we fly to
   heaven.

SHAKESPEARE.

THOUGHT and the struggle after truth are the best joys of the best men. To follow out the lines of speculation and of revelation until they lead us near the heart of things, which yet we know that we can never perfectly reach; to make some few steps forward on the journey which stretches out before us, endlessly tempting and interesting, into eternity; to add each day some new stone to the structure whose lines already as they leave the earth prophesy an infinite height for the far topstone,—he has not lived who has not felt this pleasure. He is not really living, however full he may be of warmth of feeling and of energy in action, who does not in some degree know what it is to crave ideas and knowledge, to seek for truth, and to delight in finding it.

III. 302.

The sequences of law
   We learn through mind alone;
'Tis only through the soul
   That aught we know is known :
With equal voice she tells
   Of what we touch and see
Within these bounds of life,
   And of a life to be :
Proclaiming One who brought us hither,
And holds the keys of Whence and Whither.

FRANCIS TURNER PALGRAVE.

When the Spirit of truth shall come He shall guide you into all truth.—JOHN xvi. 13.

WE live in a redeemed world,—a world full of the Holy Ghost forever doing His work, forever taking of the things of Christ and showing them to us. That Christ so shown is the most real, most present power in this new Christian world. Men see Him, men talk with Him continually. They do not recognize Him ; they do not know what lofty converse they are holding ; but some day when, in some way, a man has become really earnest and wants to believe in the Son of God, and is asking, "Who is He that I may believe on Him ?" then that Son of God comes to him, —not as a new guest from the lofty heaven, but as the familiar and slighted friend who has waited and watched at the doorstep, who has already from the very first filled the soul's house with such measure of His influence as the soul's obstinacy of indifference would allow, and who now, as He steps in at the soul's eager call to take complete and final possession of its life, does not proclaim His coming in awful, new, unfamiliar words, but says in tones which the soul recognizes and wonders that it has not known long before, "Thou hast seen me. I have talked with thee."   V. 211.

Thrice Holy Faith! whatever thorns I meet,
As on I totter with unpractised feet,
Still let me stretch my arms and cling to Thee,
Meek nurse of souls through their long infancy.
S. T. COLERIDGE.

THERE is a large healthy hunger after belief which is as different from the morbid
appetite of superstition, as health always is
different from disease. There are men who
want to believe,—who would rather believe
than not,—when some great spiritual theory
of the universe is offered them to account for
its bewilderments and to help its troubles.
The secret of their life seems to be this, that
they are men deeply impressed with the infiniteness of life. Does that seem vague and
transcendental? They are men who are always conscious of the spiritual and unseen
underneath the visible and material,—men
who are always sure that there is a great region of unknown truth which they ought to
know, and who are restless after it. To such
men all that they see presupposes things
which they do not see.
V. 207.

Every natural flower which grows on earth
Implies a flower upon the spiritual side,
Substantial, archetypal, all aglow
With blossoming causes,—not so far away
But we whose spirit-sense is somewhat cleared
May catch at something of the bloom and
      breath,
Too vaguely apprehended.
ELIZABETH BARRETT BROWNING.

---

*Again, the devil taketh Him up into an exceed-
ing high mountain and showeth Him all the kingdoms of this world, and the glory of them.*
MATT. iv. 8.

SO does the young man in some moment or
some period of his life come in sight of
the great world. . . . It is all very vague—
it must be. The traveler upon the road to
London, all aglow with its vision, does not
trace how every street and alley runs in the
great city, nor see how the bricks are laid
in every man's back yard. It is the "light
of London," not the lamp in this or that
shop-window, that he sees. And so it is
the world, all vague, mysterious, and wonderful, which the spirit of the young man sees
from his mountain, not this or that which is
happening in the world. It is the world all
together, the world of tumultuous, roaring,
awful, fascinating human life, the kingdoms
of the world, and the glory of them—this is
what he sees. There is a special value, a
special contribution to the total experience
and character of a man, in the years which
hold that vision—the years when the narrowness of childhood is broken, but the absorption
in the details of life has not yet begun; these
years wherein the young man is catching sight
of the world. Blessed is he who keeps those
years pure and lofty.
VII. 168, 169.

Watch and pray that ye enter not into temptation.—MATT. xxvi. 14.

OUR Lord's temptation makes us see that temptation is not sin, nor does it necessarily involve sin. Christ was sinless and yet tempted; therefore it is possible for man to be tempted and yet sinless. Now so many of us, the moment we are strongly tempted, seem to fall into a sort of demoralized condition, as if our innocence were over, as if the charm were broken and we were already sinners; and so we too often give ourselves up easily to the sin. . . . To any soul in such a state what could we say but this : "Look up and see the truth in Jesus ; do you not see it there? To be tempted is not wicked, is not shameful, is not unworthy even of Him. It is the lot, in one view it is even the glory, of humanity. Sin does not begin and shame does not begin until the will gives way, until you yield to temptation. Stand guard over that will, resist temptation, and then to have been tempted shall be to you what it was to your Saviour— a glory and a crown, a part of your history worthy to be written with thanksgiving in the Book of Life, as His is written in His book of life." Is not this the strength and courage that many a soul needs ? VII. 133, 134.

Pray

"Lead us into no such temptations, Lord."
Yea, but, O Thou whose servants are the bold,
Lead such temptations by the head and hair,
Reluctant dragons, up to who dares fight,
That so he may do battle and have praise.

BROWNING.

IT is good to multiply experiences. It is good to do many things and to have manifold relations with the world. It is good to touch many people and to see many sights; but it is good, it is necessary, to be content with no experience which remains simply as experience and does not pass on and into character. Events are great if they make dispositions. The Natural is precious if " afterward," out of it, comes the Spiritual. The experienced man is happy, if he has really drunk the rain and sunshine of the experiences which have come to him into his heart and is the ripened man, otherwise he is only like the rock on which every passer-by has scrawled his name.

VI. 254.

And so shall bright patience
   And trustfulness teach
Some wonderful alchemy,
   Turning to gold
All things whatsoever
   That come in its reach—
The dull and the narrow,
   The new and the old,—
Till each shall be bright
   With the grace and the glow
Of the goodness of God,
   Who loveth us so !

J. L. M. W.

*Be strong, . . . and work ; for I am with you,
saith the Lord of hosts.*—HAG. ii. 4.

I THINK we want to urge most strenuously upon young men the need, the absolute necessity, that in the appointed and demanded work of their life they should look for and should find the joy of their life. To do your work because you must ; to do your work as a slavery ; and then, having got it done as speedily and easily as possible, to look somewhere else for enjoyment,—that makes a very dreary life. No man who works so does the best work. No man who works so lingers lovingly over his work and asks himself if there is not something he can do to make it more perfect. " My meat is to do the will of Him that sent me, and to finish His work," said Jesus.

II. 32.

Go from the east to the west, as the sun and
    the stars direct thee,
Go with the girdle of man, go and encompass
    the earth;
Not for the gain of the gold, the getting, the
    hoarding, the having,
But for the joy of the deed, but for the duty
    to do.
ARTHUR HUGH CLOUGH.

Man, if he do but live within the light
Of high endeavors, daily spreads abroad
His being armed with strength that cannot fail.
WORDSWORTH.

THERE are many among us who feel the need to have the labor of our life redeemed,—merchants, clerks, lawyers, laborers, teachers, housekeepers, one thing or another,—the chosen or fated task of our life so often seems to be mere drudgery, crowding us down, pressing the life out of us. . . . What you need is some purpose beyond. What shall it be? . . . If you can do your work for a friend or for a family as well as for yourself, you have already redeemed much of its sordidness. If you can do it for a cause, for the progress of society and the improvement of business, for your country, for your church, then you have lifted it still more. If you can do it for God, in perfect, childlike, loving desire for His glory, then your work, be it as heavy in its nature as it may, leaps of itself from the low ground, and, instead of crushing you with it to the earth, carries you up every day into the presence of the God for whom you did it.

VI. 52, 53.

Ye know that your labor is not in vain in the Lord.—1 COR. xv. 58.

I shall shew you plainly of the Father.
JOHN XVI. 25.

WHEN we want to gather into one great comprehensive statement the purpose for which Jesus lived, and the power which His life has had over the lives of men, we must seize His great idea and find His power there. . . . His power is not in the miracles that He did, not even in the marvellous nature that He bore, but in the great truth, the primal and final fact of the universe, so far as man has any part in it, which the whole nature of the Saviour uttered. . . . That idea is the relation of childhood and fatherhood between man and God. Man is the child of God by nature. He is ignorant and rebellious,—the prodigal child of God; but his ignorance and rebellion never break that first relationship. It is always a child ignorant of his Father; always a child rebellious against his Father. That is what makes the tragedy of human history, and always prevents sin from becoming an insignificant and squalid thing. To reassert the fatherhood and childhood as an unlost truth, and to reëstablish its power as the central fact of life; to tell men that they were, and to make them actually be, the sons of God,—that was the purpose of the coming of Jesus, and the shaping power of His life.
VIII. 12, 13, 14.

Who knows God's fatherhood
Knows he rides safe, however tempest-tossed:
There is no darkness ; in love's light 'tis lost.
S. W. WEITZEL.

Ask, and ye shall receive.—JOHN xvi. 24.

We kneel how weak, we rise how full of power !
Why, therefore, should we do ourselves this wrong,
Or others, that we are not always strong,
That we are ever overborne with care,
That we should ever weak and heartless be,
Anxious or troubled, when with us is prayer,
And joy, and strength, and courage are with thee?

R. G. TRENCH.

PURE humanitarianism and pure fatalism can neither of them pray. But let us have a world where the Creator's glory and the creature's good are like sound and echo, like sunlight and reflection to each other ; where every advance in one chronicles and repeats itself in the other ; let man by sovereign mercy be admitted into such an intimacy with his God, and then prayer—what is it ? What but the answer of the echo to the sound, the uttered sympathy of the one common life, man responding to God's " Be happy, O my child ! " with an ever grateful and reverent " Be glorious, O my Father ! " As we go up higher in the new life prayer becomes less servile and so becomes more true. When the new life is finished, the sympathy complete in heaven, who can say what prayer will be ? It will be what Christ's was, in His perfect humanity talking with the perfect Divinity to which it stood so near. There will be no wandering eyes, no listless thoughts, no formal words, no hearts that pray because they must; but souls alight with a new likeness shall leap into a new nearness to their God, and prayer be heaven to the perfected human life. God's glory and man's good—who will divide them there?

VII. 233.

Remember how short my time is.

Ps. lxxxix. 47.

IF a man is able to conceive of immortality; if he can picture to himself a being who can live forever; if he recognizes in himself any powers which can outlast and laugh at death,—then any limit of life must seem narrow; against the broad background of the whole, any part must seem small. On the blue sky the almost million miles of the sun's breadth seem narrow. It is here that the truth about the matter lies. It is only by the dim sense of his immortality, only by the divine sight of himself as a being capable of long, long life, that man thinks his life on earth is short. Only by losing that divine sight of himself, and looking at himself as the beasts look at themselves, can he come to think his life long. The beast's life never seems short to him. Think of yourself as a beast and your life will never seem short to you. It is the divine consciousness in man, the consciousness that he is a child of God, that makes him know he is short-lived. Feel this, and is not the shortness of life the crown and glory of the race?

I. 318, 319.

Courage! for life is hasting
  To endless life away:
The inner life unwasting
  Transfigures thy dull clay!

GEORGE MACDONALD.

A MEMORY which is not also a prophecy is terrible. . . . You recall the happy days of an old friendship. Unless it is a perpetual revelation to you of the perfect friendship of the perfect life it comes to be a torture.

> " Tis better to have loved and lost
>   Than never to have loved at all ; "

but the true blessedness is reached only when you know that that which you have seen plunged into the fiery furnace is to come out again, the same, but finer, purer, holier, more worthy of the child of God !

When we have really grasped this truth, then how interesting and impressive becomes the sight of the life of our fellow-men ! Many and many of these men whom we see plodding on in their dusty ways are travelling with visions in their souls. Nobody knows it but themselves and God. Once, years ago, they saw a light. They knew, if only for a moment, what companionships, what attainments, they were made for. That light has never faded. It is the soul of good things which they are doing in the world to-day. It makes them sure when other men think their faith is gone. It will be with them till the end, until they come to all it prophesies.

VII. 341, 342.

The vision is yet for an appointed time, but at the end it shall speak, and not lie ; though it tarry, wait for it.—HAB. ii. 3.

"A CLOUD received Him out of their sight." Into mystery and a darkness to which His going there alone gives any true light our Saviour goes. But oh, my friends, when by and by our way leads also into mystery and darkness, when truth becomes covered with doubt, and joy with sadness, and life begins to feel the waiting death, what can help us like the faith of the ascended Jesus? The way into the cloud may be a way up and not a way down, a way toward Him and not a way from Him. Doubt, sorrow, death—these may be, these to the true soul must be, like the clouds over the Mount of Olives through which the Son of God went up to the right hand of His Father. "We which remain shall be caught up in the clouds, to meet the Lord in the air: and so shall we ever be with the Lord. Wherefore comfort one another"—comfort yourselves too, comfort and strengthen yourselves and one another—"with these words."

VII. 301.

Out to the earthward brink
Of that great tideless sea
Light from Christ's garments streams.
Cowards that fear to tread such beams
The angels can but pity when they sink.
Believing thus, I joy although I lie in dust. . . .
Long as God ceases not, I cannot cease:
I must arise.

HELEN HUNT JACKSON.

*I go to prepare a place for you, . . . that where
I am, there ye may be also.*—JOHN xiv. 2, 3.

IF on some hitherto unexplored and unin-
habited island far away in the seas a man
goes to live, . . . he clothes the island with
intelligibleness.   I can understand and realize
its existence when I know that a human foot
has been pressed upon its sandy beach.   If he
is a great, strong, notably manly man who
goes there, carrying with him a large share of
our humanity, then he gives the island more
than intelligibleness.   He gives it dignity.   It
is full of interest. . . .   But if the man who
goes there is my friend, and if he tells me that
he is going to make it ready for my coming,
that he will come back again and take me to
it by and by, then how that island burns for
me—the one live, real, shining spot in all the
world !   It is the goal of all my thoughts, the
lodestone of my hopes.   I think of it until the
familiar house in which I was born, and where
I am living still, seems strange to me com-
pared with that one shining spot that has become so real.   My friend's love makes it all
glow and burn before me as if I myself already
saw the sun shining on its mountain-tops and
flashing on the surface of its rippling streams.

VII. 300.

So, when the times of restitution come—
The sweet times of refreshing come at last—
My God shall fill my longings to the brim ;
Therefore I look and wait and long for Him :
Not wearied, though the work be wearisome,
Nor fainting, though the time be almost past.

CHRISTINA G. ROSSETTI.

LET us try, if we are really Christians who believe that Christ our Lord has "ascended into heaven," to enter into His heavenly life by the largeness and loftiness of the prayers that we bring to Him. God forbid that we should so misread His exaltation that we should hesitate to ask Him for the very smallest things; but the things that belong to our peace are what He wants to give us. The things that make this world and its interests seem small when we think of them : the forgiveness of sin, the perfect purification of our souls, the driving out of selfishness, the disregard of comfort in pursuit of duty, the care for brethren more than for ourselves; not comfort, not spiritual rest, not freedom from pain here or hereafter—not these, but the chance, the power, the will to glorify God our Father in our lives as He, the perfect Son, did in His—this we may ask if we believe in the Ascension and have understood the heavenly life of Him who is still our Brother and Saviour.

VII. 294.

Beyond this shadow and this turbulent sea,
  Shadow of death and turbulent sea of death,
Lies all we long to have or long to be.
  Take heart, tired man, toil on with lessening breath,
Lay violent hands on heaven's high treasury,
  Be what you long to be through life's long scathe.

CHRISTINA G. ROSSETTI.

*When the burnt offering began, the song of the
Lord also began with the trumpets.*

2 CHRON. xxix. 27.

THE act of sacrifice was done with a chorus
of delight. . . . Self-sacrifice, which is
what these burnt offerings picturesquely represented, is universally and perpetually necessary. . . . Can the life, too, be offered as
the beast was of old, with song and trumpet? . . . There are always glimpses of
man's highest life which show us, like the first
streaks of light before the dawn, what it would
be if all the sky were filled with glory; and so
there are always exalted lives, and exalted moments in the lives, I hope, of all of us, in
which we do catch sight of the joy and glory
of self-sacrifice. Not many years ago, when
the young men went to the war, was it not
true that the fact of sacrifice intensified the
joy? It was a joy to save their country, to
feel sure, as it is not often given to men vividly to feel, that they were doing a real and
valuable part of her salvation. No safe and
easy task could ever have filled the heart with
such a sober and deep delight.

II. 23, 25.

'Tis no Man we celebrate,
By his country's victories great? . . .
But the pith and marrow of a Nation
Drawing force from all her men,
Highest, humblest, weakest, all,
For her time of need, and then
Pulsing it through them again.

JAMES RUSSELL LOWELL.

I saw the dead, small and great, stand before God.—REV. xx. 12.

[ST. JOHN] saw what souls go to. We are so apt to see only what souls go from. When our friend dies we think of all the warm delights of life, all the sweet friendships, all the interesting occupations, all the splendor of the sunlight which he leaves behind. If we could only know, somewhat as John must have known after his vision, the presence of God into which our friend enters on the other side, the higher standards, the larger fellowship with all his race, and the new assurance of personal immortality in God; if we- could know all this, how our poor comfortless efforts of comfort when our friends depart, our feeble raking-over of the ashes of memory, our desperate struggles to think that the inevitable must be all right; how this would all give way to something almost like a burst of triumph, as the soul which we loved went forth to such vast enlargement, to such glorious consummation of its life !

IV. 72.

Where chill or change can never rise,
Deep in the depth of Paradise
They rest world-wearied heart and eyes—
Jubilate.

Safe as a hidden brooding dove,
With perfect peace within, above,
They love, and look for perfect love—
Hallelujah.

CHRISTINA G. ROSSETTI.

Only the anointed eye
    Sees in common things—
Gleam of wave and tint of sky—
    Heavenly blossomings.
To the hearts where light was birth
    Nothing can be drear;
Budding through the gloom of earth,
    Heaven is always near.
Lucy Larcom.

I BELIEVE our lives are too prosaic. I think we might all live up in a purer air. . . . I think the strange beauty of the nature all around us might be more fully grasped. I think that, made pure and strong by thoughts like these, we might all make our lives to poems:

" Be good, be true, and let who will be clever ;
    Do noble things, not dream them, all day long ;
And so make life, death, and that vast forever,
    One grand, sweet song."

If it be poetry, as I think it is, to go out to-morrow morning with all our closets open and all our moral enginery in play, ready to see the miracle that the sun will bring up over the river and the hills once more, ready to learn the lesson of the earth—a work to do and manly strength to do it,—ready to sympathize with and worship all that is worthy of our sympathy and homage, ready to grow more godlike in our reverence for God—if this be poetry, then fifty poems may begin to-morrow, with earth's grand music for them all to sing to, and heaven at last to crown the victor with a sweet " Well done."
X. 245, 246.

Still are we saying, " Teach us how to pray " ?
    Oh, teach us how to love! and then our
        prayer
Through other lives will find its upward way.

HE best finds God and is God's who finds
    Him and becomes His, not in separation
from his brethren but in the certainty of God's
love to all and of the belonging of all souls to
God. . . . If I prayed all alone,—my prayer
the only prayer which pierced the darkness because mine was the only soul which stood in
need,—then I can possibly imagine that as I
stood and looked I should behold the answer
come like a white dove out of the distance
until it laid itself upon my soul and gave it
peace.   But now I cannot help seeing what a
far greater richness there will be if my petition blends with a million others, and the answer comes in some great ·outpouring of the
divine light and love which addresses itself to
all the world.

                                        V. 128.

Nor nursing each our own distress,
        To Thee we press;
Prayer's overflow drowns selfishness;
        Soul within soul,
One voice to Thee our linked petitions roll;
Healer of the world's hurt, oh, make us whole!

                            LUCY LARCOM.

But He answered her not a word.

MATT. xv. 23.

SOME prayers Christ does not answer, we may say, because they ask Him to do our work for us. . . . Tell me, is there a kinder thing that you can do for your pupil who comes up to you with his slate, asking you to work out for him his problem, than to bid him go back to his seat and do his task himself, and get that discipline and learning which is really the object of his having his task set to him at all? You ask Christ to show you with a flash of lightning what your sorrow means. You ask him to reveal to you by some supernatural illumination which path of life you ought to take, which friendship you shall cultivate, what profession you can most successfully pursue. There comes no answer to those prayers. . . . And why? Those are your problems. It is by hard work of yours, by watchful vigilance, by careful weighing of consideration against consideration, that you must settle those things for yourself.

V. 133.

Not for thy neighbor nor for thee,
Be sure, was life designed to be
A draught of dull complacency.
One Power too is it who doth give
The food without us, and within
The strength that makes it nutritive. . . .
So thou but strive, thou soon shalt see
Defeat itself is victory.

ARTHUR HUGH CLOUGH.

If Thou be the Son of God, command that these stones be made bread.—MATT. iv. 3.

DO you not see what the temptation was and what it is forever? O my dear friend, God made these things, and made you to live by them, but not by them alone. Go on; gather the joy out of the earth and sky, out of the bread He gives you power to win, out of the water that He makes to gush at your feet; only, when the time comes—as it is sure to come some time, as perhaps it is to come now—when, in order to speak some word out of His mouth to you, some word of duty or charity or holiness, He takes these things away, and you are tempted to shut your ear to His word in order that you may keep these pleasant things, then you are just where Jesus was—the devil is at your ear. May God help you to see what Jesus saw—what He said afterward, perhaps remembering His own temptation: " The life is more than meat." May he help you to say, " No! Nothing—not even His gifts—shall blind or deafen me to Him. Man shall not live by bread alone, but by every word out of the mouth of God "—the blessed sacrifice of sense to spirit.

VII. 143.

To sacrifice, to share ;
   To give even as He gave ;
For others' wants to care ;
   Not our own lives to save—

The hidden manna this,
   Whereof who eateth, he
Grows up in perfectness
   Of Christ-like symmetry.

LUCY LARCOM.

If any man thirst, let him come to me and drink.
JOHN vii. 37.

REMEMBER, it is not just compensation, but transformation that you are to seek. Not Heaven yet. That looms before us always, tempting us on; but now the earth, with all its duties, sorrows, difficulties, doubts, and dangers. We want a faith, a truth, a grace to help us *now*, right here, where we are stumbling about, dizzied and fainting with our thirst. And we can have it. One who was man, yet mightier than man, has walked the vale before us. When He walked it, he turned it all into a well of living water. To them who are willing to walk in His footsteps, to keep in His light, the well He opened shall be forever flowing. Nay, it shall pass into them and fulfil there Christ's own words: "Whosoever drinketh of the water that I shall give him shall never thirst, but the water that I shall give him shall be in him a well of water springing up into everlasting life."

VI. 34.

I am the Fountain of Life, that cannot be exhausted.

Whosoever is sorrowful, let him come to me that he may be comforted;

Whosoever is dry, let him come that he may be filled with the richness and fulness of the Spirit;

Whosoever is wearied, let him come that he may be refreshed with joy.

THOMAS À KEMPIS.

The communion of the Holy Ghost be with you all.—2 COR. xiii. 14.

THE doctrine of the Holy Ghost is a continual protest against every constantly recurring tendency to separate God from the current world. A God who made the world and then left it to run its course under the tyranny of force and law; a God who redeemed the world eighteen centuries ago and left it to be blessed by or to miss the blessing of the redemption which He had provided—neither of these ideas of Deity can comprehend the truth of God the Holy Ghost. A present God, an ever-living God, an ever-pleading, ever-helping, ever-saving God—this is the God whom Christ told of and promised, the God who came in the miracle of Pentecost and is forever here. . . . Wherever men's dealings with each other, or men's value of each other, is colored with the influence of the truth that we live in a world full of God; wherever our communion with each other takes place through Him, the sacredness and usefulness of what we are to each other resulting from what He is to all of us, then our communion is a communion of the Holy Ghost.   VII. 307.

We faintly hear, we dimly see,
  In differing phrase we pray;
But, dim or clear, we own in Thee
  The Light, the Truth, the Way.

.   .   .   .   .

Thy litanies, sweet offices
  Of love and gratitude;
Thy sacramental liturgies
  The joy of doing good.   WHITTIER.

A friend,—it is another name for God,
  Whose love inspires all love, is all in all;
  Profane it not, lest lowest shame befall!
Worship no idol, whether star or clod;
  Nor think that any friend is truly thine,
Save as life's closest link with Love Divine.

Lucy Larcom.

ONE of the most valuable changes which comes to a human friendship when it is deepened into a communion of the Holy Ghost is the assurance of permanence which it acquires. There is always a lurking distrust and suspicion of instability in friendship which has not the deepest basis. No present certainty answers for the future. Present kindness only bears witness of present regard, and each new moment needs its new proof. How we have all felt this!

> " Alas that neither bonds nor vows
>   Can certify possession !
> Torments me still the fear that love
>   Died in its last expression."

This must be so to some degree with an affection where each is held to each only by the continuance of personal liking. But when friendship enters into God, and men are bound together through their common union with Him, all the strength of that higher union authenticates and assures the faithfulness and perseverance of the love that is bound up with it. The souls that meet in God may well believe that they shall hold each other as eternally as He holds each and each holds Him.

VII. 312.

My peace I give unto you.—JOHN xiv. 27.

I KNOW that there is such a thing as *peace* to seek and find. But here is my work to do, to worry over whether I am doing it right, to keep myself restless over how it will turn out. "*My work*," I say; but if I can know that it is not my work, but God's, should I not cast away my restlessness, even while I worked on more faithfully and untiringly than ever? . . . If I could pour through all the good plan over which I am laboring the certainty that all that is good in it is God's and must succeed, how that certainty would drive the darkness out of it! and while I worked harder than ever, my work would have something of the calmness with which He labors always. . . .

To every poor sufferer, to every discouraged worker, to every man who cannot think much of himself and yet is too brave to despair, this is the courage that the gospel gives. Not what you can do, but what He can do in you; not what you are, but what you can help men to see that He is—that is the power by which you are to work.

VII. 49, 53.

Lord, Thou wilt ordain peace for us ; for Thou also hast wrought all our works in us.
Is. xxvi. 12.

We see but half the causes of our deeds,
Seeking them wholly in the outer life,
And heedless of the encircling spirit-world,
Which, though unseen, is felt, and sows in us
All germs of pure and world-wide purposes.
                    JAMES RUSSELL LOWELL.

OH, there are households among you where some son or daughter who is dead is stronger in the shaping of the daily life than any of the men and women who are still alive. His character is at once a standard and an inspiration. . . . To say that he is not *with you* is to make companionship altogether a physical, not at all a spiritual thing. To say that he is absent from you, and that the neighbor of whom you know nothing, for whom you care nothing and who cares nothing for you, is present with you, is to confuse all thoughts of neighborhood, to put the false for the true, the superficial for the deep.

This is the difference of men—those whose power stops with their death, and those whose power really opens into its true richness when they die. The first sort of men have mechanical power. The second sort of men have spiritual power. And the final test and witness of spiritual force is seen in the ability to cast the bodily life away and yet continue to give help and courage and wisdom to those who see us no longer; to be, like Christ, the helper of **men's souls even from beyond the grave.**
                    VII. 14, 15.

Thou shalt hide them in the secret of Thy presence from the strife of tongues.—Ps. xxi. 20.

WE believe in Jesus and try to live with Him. How is it that a flippant toss of skeptical smartness about Him, or a sneer at our folly in making Him our Master, lays hold of and stings us so, sends us home anxious, puzzled, and worried? We are not wholly hidden from the strife of tongues. It must be that we are not completely in the secret of His presence. We are not there constantly enough. There are moments, times when we are praying, times when in sorrow His sympathy is like life to us, when there is not the tongue so rude and bitter that it could ruffle the rest of our souls in Him; times when nothing that man could say would frighten or depress us. At such times we learn what it is to be thoroughly with Him, and understand what a guarded and safe life it must be to be hidden there always.

I. 88.

Wisest of spirits that spirit which dwelleth
    apart
  Hid in the presence of God for a chapel and
    nest,
Sending a wish and a will and a passionate
    heart
  Over the eddy of life to that Presence in
    rest:
Seated alone and in peace till God bids it
    arise.

CHRISTINA G. ROSSETTI.

And they sent forth Barnabas, . . . Who, when he came, . . . exhorted them all, that with purpose of heart they should cleave unto the Lord.
ACTS xi. 22, 23.

WHEN a man gathers up his life and goes out simply to spend it all in telling the children of God who never heard it from any other lips than his that their Father is their Father; when all that he has known of Christ is simply turned into so much force by which the tidings of their sonship is to be driven home to hearts that do not easily receive so vast a truth; to that man certainly the idea has become a master and a king, as it has not to us. Belief is power. By the quantity of power I may know the quantity of belief. He is the true idealist, not who possesses ideas, but whom ideas possess; not the man whose life wears its ideas as ornamental jewels, but the man whose ideas shape his life like plastic clay. And so the true Christian idealist is he whose conception of man as the redeemed child of God has taken all his life and moulded it in new shapes, planted it in new places, so filled and inspired it that, like the Spirit of God in Elijah, it has taken it up and carried it where it never would have chosen to go of its own lower will.
II. 176.

Should He need a goodly tree
　For the healing of the nations,
He will make it grow; if not,
Never yet His love forgot
　Human love and faith and patience.
DINAH MULOCH CRAIK.

Serving the Lord with all humility.
ACTS xx. 19.

HOW very rare it is to find an exceedingly useful and hard-working man whose energy and devotion are not tainted by self-satisfaction! But here, if all we do is but to make ourselves channels through which the power of God shall flow; if when a man stands up and calls a whole city out of corruptness, or a whole race out of slavery, he is deeply and genuinely conscious that it is not he that speaks, but God (as Jesus, you remember, told His disciples it should be with them), then that is won which is so rare in the great workers (or in little ones either): all self-satisfaction disappears. The man is lost in the cause; nay, the cause itself is lost in joy that God, whom to know is life, has made Himself hereby a little more known to men.

VII. 49.

Lord, give me light to do Thy work;
  For only, Lord, from Thee
Can come the light by which these eyes
  The way of work can see

  .   .   .   .   .

The work is Thine, not mine, O Lord,
  It is Thy race we run;
Give light! and then shall all I do
  Be well and truly done.

HORATIUS BONAR.

Awful in unity,
O God, we worship Thee,
More simply One, because supremely Three!

FABER.

WHEN we preach the Fatherhood of God we preach His divinity; when we point to Christ the perfect Saviour, it is a Divine Redeemer that we declare; and when we plead with men to hear the voice and yield to the persuasions of the Holy Spirit, the Comforter into whose comfort we invite them is Divine. The divinity of Father, Son, and Holy Ghost, this is our Gospel. By this Gospel we look for salvation. It is a Gospel to be used, to be believed in, and to be lived by; not merely to be kept and admired and discussed and explained.

I. 228.

If a man does believe the doctrine of the Trinity, he ought to rejoice and glory in his faith as the enrichment of his life. Not as a burden on his back, but as wings on his shoulders, he ought to carry his belief. To cease to believe it would be, not welcome liberty, but incalculable loss. For a new soul to come to believe it is not, as men have often foolishly talked, the putting out into a sea all dark with mists and fogs. It is the entrance into a luxuriant land where all life lives at its fullest, where nature opens her most lavish bounty, and where man has the consummate opportunity to be and do his best.

VII. 334.

NOTHING could be more misleading than ... to talk about the doctrine of the Trinity as if it claimed to be the solution, the dissipation, of the mystery of God. I say "God" to the heathen who has gone so far as to believe that there is one God and not many gods in the universe; and he gazes into the darkness of the great idea and says: "I do not know what God is. A million questions come buffeting me like bats out of the darkness the moment that I dare even to turn my face that way. Let me hear His commandments and go and do them. For Himself I dare not even ask what He is." That is the mystery of darkness. . . . Then I say "God" to the Christian and he looks up and says: "Yes, I know; Father, Son, and Spirit; my Father, my Brother, my inspiring Friend. I know Him, what He is, for He has shown Himself to me." But with each word, Father, Brother, Friend, there come flocking new questions, not like bats out of the darkness, but like sunbeams out of the light, bewildering the believing soul with guesses and insoluble suggestions and intangible visions of the love, the truth, the glory of God, which were impossible until this clothing by God of Himself with radiance in Christ had come. That is the mystery of light.

II. 312.

O Blessed Trinity!
In the deep darkness of prayer's stillest night
We worship Thee blinded with light!

FABER.

---

*Who coverest Thyself with light as with a gar-
ment.*—Ps. civ. 2.

WITH all deep things the deeper light
brings new mysteriousness. The mystery of light is the privilege and prerogative
of the profoundest things. The shallow things
are capable only.of the mystery of darkness.
Of that all things are capable. Nothing is so
thin, so light, so small, that if you cover it
with clouds and hide it in half-lights it will not
seem mysterious. But the most genuine and
profound things you may bring forth into the
fullest light, and let the sunshine bathe them
through and through, and in them there will
open ever new wonders of mysteriousness. The
mystery of light belongs to them. And how
then must it be with God, the Being of all
beings, the Being who is Himself essential
Being, out of whom all other beings spring and
from whom they are continually fed? Surely
in Him the law which we have been tracing
must find its consummation. Surely of Him
it must be supremely true that the more we
know of Him, the more He shows Himself to
us, the more mysterious He must forever be.
The mystery of light must be complete in Him.

II. 309.

The subtlest and profoundest of men cannot explain mysteries; the simplest person
can appropriate and exult in them.

CHRISTINA G. ROSSETTI.

And the four and twenty elders fall down before him that sat on the throne, and worship Him that liveth for ever and ever, and cast their crowns before the throne.—REV. iv. 10.

ONLY those who have crowns to cast can do true homage before His throne. . . . Only those who are kingly themselves can properly honor the kingliest. . . . Men are measured by their reverences.   All human life is like the annual procession of the Jews, marching up to Jerusalem, to the Holy City. The nearer we are to that place of supreme adoration, the nearer the purpose of our life is fulfilled.   What do you adore, what do you really reverence and respect ? is the real test question of your life.   In an age which makes too little‘ of reverence, let us not dare to let drop the truth that only that which is high can worship the highest, and so covet as the best crown of our existence the power so to know and feel that we can genuinely worship God.

VI. 38, 44, 45.

It is life
From self-enfranchised, opening every vein
To let in glory from above, and give
What we receive in fragrance, color, fruit,—
Life, which is Heaven's: ourselves dead matter, else.

LUCY LARCOM.

So long as a man is living for himself and honoring himself, there is an association, however remote it may be, with all the lowest forms of selfishness in which men have lived; but the moment a man begins to live in genuine adoration of the absolute good, and worship God, he parts company from all these lower orders of human life. . . . When you say to God, "O God, take me, for the highest thing that I can do with myself is to give myself to Thee,". . . you sweep into the current of the best, the holiest, and the most richly human of our humanity, which in every age has dedicated itself to God. The worshippers of all the world—the Jew, the Greek, the Hindu, the Christian in all his various cultures, take you for their brother. . . . You are never in such company as when you are before God's throne offering Him your brightest and most precious.   VI. 44, 45.

Be of good cheer, brave spirit; steadfastly
Serve that low whisper thou hast served; for
      know
God hath a select family of sons
Now scattered wide through earth, . . .
Who are thy spiritual kindred.
And Time, who keeps God's word, brings on
      the day
To seal the marriage of these minds with
      thine.
. . . Ye shall be
The salt of all the elements, world of the
      world.
                                EMERSON.

[W]HEN] ground is trodden hard, it is the very substance of the ground that lies impenetrable and catches the seed, and will not let it in and claim the soil and do its fruitful work. . . . This is the notion of the Crust. It is not a foreign material; but the thing itself, grown hard and rigid, shuts the soft and tender and receptive portions of the thing away. . . . Thus out of the very substance of a man's life, out of the very stuff of what he is and does, comes the hindrance which binds itself about his being, and will not let the better influences out. . . . That self-made barrier must be broken up, must be restored to its first condition and become again part of the substance out of which it was evolved, before the life can be fed with the dew of first principles and the rain of the immediate descent of God.

What is the crust upon your life that keeps out holy influences?

VI. 155, 156.

This crust of selfishness and sin
That shuts my better self within,—
If Thou canst make it soft and fine,
So bloom and fruitage there may shine
In answer to Thy dew and sun,
I can but say: Thy will be done!
For where the deepest cuts Thy plough,
And all is bare and broken now,
Faith sees the tender grain-rows spring,
The teeming valleys laugh and sing!

J. L. M. W.

IF, as we profess to believe, all right is forever antagonistic to all wrong, then what
a lesson there is to us in the steadfast law and
faithfulness of all the universe around us.
How each day coming to its task of crowding
labors, each night bringing in its blessed peace
of sleep in obedience to the old command of
Genesis, brings with it a remonstrance against
our faint-heartedness and constant wavering
of loyalty and truth.   The stars in their courses
fight against us as they fought against Sisera.
The duty that they are doing cries shame on
the duty that we are leaving undone every
day. . . .   While this morning's sunrise is rosy
with the memory of last night's sunset, while
noon looks longingly down the eastern sky
that it has travelled, and fondly onward to the
night toward which it hurries, while month
links in with month, and season works with
season, and year joins hand with year in the
long labor of the world's hard life, there is a
lesson for us all to learn of the unity and the
harmony of our existence.   Let us take the
lesson, and with it in our hearts go out to be
more tolerant, more kindly, and more true in
our dealings with our fellow-men. . . . It is
sympathy, it is love, it is healthy interest in
one another, that all these great teachers make
their lesson.

X. 243.

So links more subtle and more fine
Bind every other soul to thine
In one great Brotherhood divine.

ADELAIDE A. PROCTER.

The Father sent the Son to be the Saviour of the world.—1 JOHN iv. 14.

AND when an earnest soul accepts this everlasting Christ, is there not a new glory in his salvation when he thinks that it has been from everlasting?   He looks back, and lo, the Saviour was his Saviour before the worlds were made!   The covenant to which he clings had its sublime conditions written in the very constitution of the Godhead.   It was not spoken first on Calvary; nay, it did not begin when it was told to David, or to Moses, or to poor Adam crushed into the dust with his new sinfulness outside the garden-gate.   Before them all, in the very nature of the Deity, was written the prophecy that if ever in the unfolding of the ages one poor human soul like mine should need salvation, the eternal Christ, bringing His credential of Eternal Human Brotherhood, should come to save it.   The ages rolled along; my soul was born, and sinned; it cried out to be saved, and lo, Christ came! What is there left for me to do but cling to Him with a love strong as His precious promises and a faith firm as His Everlasting Saviourship ?

VI. 319.

Except the Cross, and Him who died
Upon it, now in earth or heaven
What own I, claim I ?   Now below
I seek no farther; here is woe
Assuaged forever: now above
I look no longer; here is love!

DORA GREENWELL.

He that soweth to the Spirit shall of the Spirit reap everlasting life.—GAL. vi. 8.

CHRIST had His word of encouragement and strength to say to every soldier in His army and to every worker at His work. . . . Not merely scholars in their studies, not merely missionaries in their martyrdoms, not merely saints in their closed closets, but every working man and woman everywhere,—they are all His. The spirit which proceeds from Him may pour through the whole mass and find out every particle, and give to each an impetus towards its own next higher stage of life, and so bear the whole along together towards the completion of each man and the completion of the whole social and business life, and politics and education, and then, as the crown of them all, Religion. "That is not first which is Spiritual, but that which is Natural; and afterward that which is Spiritual!" But they are all God's; and to make each instinct with what measure of His life it is capable of containing—that is to build them all into a flight of shining stairs, sweeping upward into even clearer and intenser light, until he who mounts to the full summit stands by the altar of God's unclouded presence and realizes the blessedness of perfect Communion with Him.

VI. 258.

For we are laborers together with God.
1 COR. iii. 9.

Life is too short to waste
    In critic peep or cynic bark,
Quarrel or reprimand,—
    'Twill soon be dark:
Up! mind thine own aim, and
    God speed the mark!   EMERSON.

MEN complain that God does not do this and that and the other thing for them, which He never undertook to do. They say, "He does not make me rich. He does not fill my life with friendships." So they flutter about with their complainings as a bird will sweep this way and that, doubtful and wandering and tempted on every side. But as at last the bird catches sight of the home where it belongs, though very far away, and all its flutterings cease, and setting itself straight towards that, it steadies itself and seeks it without a single turn aside; so by and by one of these wanderers among many hopes discovers far away the hope, the one only hope, for which God made him, and forgetting everything else thenceforth gives himself to that, to serve God and by serving Him to grow into His goodness.   I. 312.

        I go to prove my soul!
I see my way as birds their trackless way; I
    shall arrive! What time, what circuit,
I ask not; but . . .
In some good time—His good time—I shall
    arrive:
He guides me and the bird. In His good
    time!   BROWNING.

A central peace subsisting at the heart
Of endless agitation.   WORDSWORTH.

BUT motion without fatigue, or waste, or
need of refreshment or repair, that is
the finished idea of Peace.   We talk about the
" Peace of God."   Is not this really the conception which, carried to its highest, reaches
that sublime idea?   " My father worketh hitherto and I work," said Jesus.   It is no Orien-
tal apathy.   The Christian thought of God is
full of interest, zeal, emotion, action, only it
is always perfectly balanced with its surroundings, since its surroundings are the utterance
and creation of itself.   God and the universe
in their unbroken harmony.   The universe
never asking anything of God which God cannot do.   God having no power or affection
which the universe cannot utter.   That is the
Perfect Peace.   To match that consummate
Peace in our lower little sphere, to be to our
world as God is to His, to work as perpetually
and yet as calmly and so effectively as He
works; that is the real thing that we pray for
when we ask for one another the Peace of
God.   VI. 189.

Roll round, strange years; swift seasons, come
        and go;
    Ye leave upon us but an outward sign;
    Ye cannot touch the inward and divine,
    Which God alone does know;
There, sealed till summers, winters, all shall
        cease,
In His deep peace.   DINAH MULOCH CRAIK.

He was not that Light, but was sent to bear witness of that Light.—JOHN i. 8.

TO look different from other people, to wear other clothes, to be somehow eccentric, . . . this is the most superficial form of the desire for originality. . . . To start some new idea, to send forth something that shall show our fellows that this machinery within us does not work just the same with all the mental machinery in all the world—this is the higher ambition of a higher man. Different from both of them is that religious consciousness which the devout man has that God made him for a special purpose, for a special exhibition of himself; and so the desire to *be himself* completely, in order that no purpose which God had in his creation may fail through his being distorted or obscured. This is a desire for the divine originality of *character* which God intended. . . . Many men try to be John the Baptists by wearing the skins and eating the locusts and wild honey. Others would be John the Baptists by preaching strange doctrines. Very few seek to live the life that he lived by recognizing that they are sent into the world, not to shine themselves, but merely by some way of their own to bear witness of the Light of God. VII. 41.

O Lord Jesus Christ, Who didst make Thy forerunner, Saint John Baptist, to be as a bright light in Thy temple ; Grant that we may ever shine in Thy Church, with the ardor of faith, in works of charity, and in true humility ; through Thy mercy, O Christ our God, Who, with the Father and the Holy Ghost, livest and reignest, ever one God, world without end. Amen.—ANCIENT COLLECTS.

THERE are two persons to whom life is pretty clear, the man who does not think or feel at all, and the man who thinks and feels very deeply. . . . The sluggish creature who just runs his little fragment of the universe and asks no questions further is troubled by no doubts. The finished soul who sees with God's eyes the great moral laws which govern all God's worlds, he, too, may rest in peace. Between the two the great mass of men, seeing the difficulties, but not seeing their solutions, live in disquietude and questionings. And when one has once outgrown the first repose of ignorance and thoughtlessness, he never can go back to it—there is no hope for him except to go on to the higher repose of faith and knowledge and sympathy with God.

VI. 112.

Therefore to whom turn I but to Thee, the
    ineffable Name?
    Builder and maker, Thou, of houses not
      made with hands!
What, have fear of Thee who art ever the
    same?
    Doubt that Thy power can fill the heart that
      Thy power expands?
There shall never be one lost good! What
    was, shall live as before,
    The evil is null, is nought, is silence imply-
      ing sound:
What was good shall be good, with, for evil,
    so much good more;
On the earth, the broken arcs; in the heaven,
    the perfect round.

BROWNING.

A man should rejoice in his own works, for that is his portion.—ECCLES. iii. 22.

IT is the mere smatterer in any profession who thinks it is slight and is contemptuous about it. It is a universal rule that he is a poor workman who does not honor and respect his work. A man has no right to be doing any work which, as he grows greater within it, does not offer him new views of itself to call out an ever-increasing reverence and honor. And in all the good occupations of life (one would like to impress it upon every young merchant, young mechanic, and young student whom he can speak to) a man's best proof of growing greatness in himself is a growing perception of the greatness and beauty of his work.

VI. 40.

And everywhere, here and always,
    If we would but open our eyes,
We should find, through these beaten foot-
        paths,
    Our way into Paradise.

        .   .   .   .   .

Dull earth would be dull no longer,
    The clod would sparkle a gem;
And our hands, at their commonest labor,
    Would be building Jerusalem.

LUCY LARCOM.

Hereby we know that He abideth in us, by the Spirit which He hath given us.—1 JOHN iii. 24.

The branch cannot bear fruit of itself except it abide in the Vine.—JOHN xv. 4.

IN this truth of the believer's abiding in Christ, there are two notions involved—of Permanence and of Repose. . . . There is a new tranquillity which is not stagnation, but assurance, when a life thus enters into Christ. It is like the hushing of a million babbling, chattering mountain streams as they approach the sea and fill themselves with its deep purposes. It is like the steadying of a lost bird's quivering wings when it at last sees the nest and quiets itself with the certainty of reaching it, and settles smoothly down on level pinions to sweep unswervingly towards it. It is like these to see the calm of a restless soul that discovers Christ and rests its tired wings upon the atmosphere of His truth, and so abides in Him as it goes on towards Him.

VI. 299, 300.

O my soul, how noble thou art,
What a wonderful power lies hid in thee!
For thou canst not rest until thou attain the
    highest good,
And find out the ultimate end;
Which being recognized and found,
Thy restlessness shall cease.

THOMAS À KEMPIS.

We know that we have passed from death unto life because we love the brethren. — 1 JOHN iii. 14.

THAT man ought to distrust his Christianity very deeply who finds that when he has become a Christian he takes no more large and hopeful and charitable view of his fellow-men and their lives than he did before. The glory of a revealed immortality is that it exalts into struggle for a purpose that which seemed to be only the restless tossing and heaving of mere discontent . . . poor fitful efforts after goodness, broken and distracted; a mere unrest and moral turmoil everywhere. What can interpret it except the great opening of an eternity, and the sight of the power of that eternity working even here? With that in view, we come to a large and tolerant suspense of judgment that is good for us. Who can say how much of this which seems purposeless restlessness is really purposeful struggle? The wild, confused waves are going somewhere. We grow to a sure conviction that very much of what seems bad is only good unformed and struggling under the power of the resurrection to its full development and exhibition.

VII. 281, 282.

Only add
Deeds to thy knowledge answerable; add faith,
Add virtue, patience, temperance; add love,
By name to come called charity, the soul
Of all the rest: then wilt thou . . . possess
A Paradise within thee.

MILTON.

SIMON called Peter left his net and followed Jesus. He went out of the old life into the untried new life, following this Master. He went out to a friendship and a work that were to fill his days with delight and inspiration. He went to new thoughts, new hopes, new duties. But did he go to nothing else? As he turns and follows Jesus does he not go burdened with new *dangers* which he did not have before? . . . If from that moment of his choice it is possible for him to acknowledge Christ, is it not possible also to deny Him?

Does not such a truth as this, when it is understood and deeply felt, make men reject the privileges which bring such dangers with them? Happily it is not so . . . commonly the scale of men's construction is loftier than that. Commonly the man who is man enough to see this truth is man enough to meet it. It fills him with a soberness which is energy and not despair. And besides, men see that it is a danger which they *cannot* shirk. To avoid privilege in order to escape the chance of sin which it brings with it is essentially to commit the very sin of which we are afraid. For Peter to refuse to follow Jesus because he sees the denial looming in the distance is really only to anticipate his sin and to deny his Master *now*.

VII. 114, 115.

Fear ballasts hope, hope buoys up fear,
And both befit us here.

CHRISTINA G. ROSSETTI.

Yea, Lord, Thou knowest that I love Thee.
JOHN xxi. 15.

THE true sign of forgiveness is not some mysterious signal waved from the sky; not some obscure emotion hunted out in your heart; not some stray text culled out of your Bible; certainly not some word of mortal priest telling you that your satisfaction is complete. The soul full of responsive love to Christ, and ready, longing, hungry to serve Him, is its own sign of forgiveness. . . . I think that with all we know of the divine heart of Jesus He would far rather see a soul trust Him too much, if that is possible, than trust Him too little, which we know is possible enough. When a man who has sinned, and who, like Simon Peter, has not a shadow or a ghost of an excuse to offer for his sin, has so known Christ that he never thinks of Him as one to be propitiated, never doubts for an instant that if he is forgivable he is forgiven, and so lets his hatred of his old sin break out in an utterance of his love for the Holy One, and lets his sorrow for his treason only show itself in his desire for loyal work, then that poor sinner's sin is dead and gone.

VII. 127.

Turn all to love, poor soul;
  Be love thy watch and ward;
Be love thy starting-point, thy goal,
  And thy reward.
CHRISTINA G. ROSSETTI.

Behold, this stone shall be a witness unto us ; for it hath heard all the words of the Lord.

JOSH. xxiv. 27.

THERE are always people who are to the world they live in what that stone in Shechem was to the nation in the midst of which it stood. Not voluble people, not people with their glib and ready judgment upon everything which goes on about them, perhaps people who have seemed to the world at large mere stones; but people who some time in their lives had had the primary truth of God, the Divinity of Righteousness, spoken so into their ears that it has filled their being. Thenceforward they spoke that word in all its simplicity to everybody. All earnest struggle after righteousness feels their approval and sympathy, and counts it really God's. All shuffling, cowardly and wanton sin hides or hurries away from their rebuking presence. They declare no subtleties and no refinements. They simply, broadly utter right and wrong. Such people have a noble place and function in the world. Men who would not own God's judgments directly, own God's judgments as they come through them. They purify and bless the circle, the community in which they live, as that stone under the oak at Shechem must have seemed to purify and bless the whole land of Israel.

VI. 263.

Through such souls . . .

God, stooping, shows sufficient of His light
For us i' the dark to rise by.

BROWNING.

Unto one he gave five talents, to another two, and to another one ; to every man according to his several ability.—MATT. XXV. 15.

IN the life which that parable describes, the different talents of different servants are fully taken into the account. Duty is measured by chance, and yet the essential idea of duty is never weakened. I am bound to do less than you, but I am just as severely bound to do my little as you are to do your much. Where else could those ideas be kept in perfect harmony and peace, neither of them hurting the other, but within the larger idea of fatherhood ? In what group could the child take his little task, fitted to his little hands, and do it, with the entire conviction that he must do it, and, nevertheless, not vexed nor bewildered by the sight of tasks a thousand times greater than his own being done close by his side; and at the same time, the great man, the hero, dedicate himself to his vast work with no sense of oppression nor injustice, nor with any feeling of superiority or pride,—in what group could these two faithful souls work on, in such difference and yet in such identity, but in a family, where every child has his own special duty, great or small, clothed with the absoluteness of the Fatherhood which is over all ?

VIII. 63.

For what is infinite must be a home,
    A shelter for the meanest life,
Where it is free to reach its greatest growth,
    Far from the touch of strife.

FABER.

THE more we read the Psalms, and indeed all the Bible, we are impressed with the remarkable value which belongs to the Holy Land as representing not merely the localities of certain historical events, but also by a higher association the geography of the spiritual life of man. . . .　Though the historic land which lies between the Mediterranean sea and the Asiatic deserts should be blotted from the surface of the earth to-morrow, there would be eternally a Holy Land.　Still all over the world, the Jordan would roll down its rocky bed to the Dead sea; still the hills would stand about Jerusalem; still the desert would open between Judea and Galilee; still Egypt must mean captivity, and the Red sea deliverance, and the Gilgal providence, and Bethany domestic piety, and Calvary redeeming love,—although the visible places to which those names belong should cease to be forever.　We little know how much we owe to this eternal picture drawn in the hearts of men, this mapped-out Palestine of the inner life.

VI. 18.

For all of good the past hath had
Remains to make our own time glad—
Our common daily life divine,
And every land a Palestine.

WHITTIER.

Flag of Freedom and Union, wave!
Peace and order and beauty draw
Round thy symbol of Light and Law!

WHITTIER.

JESUS was a patriot. That sentiment which makes so much of the poetry of the earth—the love of men for their native land—was very strong in His bosom. . . . But why is it that His patriotism is a part of His life to which we least often turn? It is not only that He lived a larger life and did a larger work, which has far outreached the Jewish people and touched us with its influence. It is the constant predominance of the sonship to God over the sonship to David in His consciousness, making Him always eager for the land of David because of the interests of God which it enshrined. This is a distinct and definite quality when it appears in a man's patriotism. It makes his patriotism fine and lofty above the measure of the common patriotic feeling of mankind.

VIII. 131, 132.

Our country hath a gospel of her own
To preach and practise before all the world,—
The freedom and divinity of man,
The glorious claims of human brother-
    hood, . . .
And the soul's fealty to none but God.

JAMES RUSSELL LOWELL.

And be clothed with humility.—1 PET. v. 5.

IT is striking that almost without exception the word humility, used before the time of Christ, is used contemptuously and rebukingly. It always meant meanness of spirit. To be humble was to be a coward. It described a cringing soul. It was a word of slaves. Such is its almost constant classic use.

Where could we find a more striking instance of the change that the Christian religion brought into the world, than in the way in which it took this disgraceful word and made it honorable? To be humble is to have a low estimation of one's self. That was considered shameful in the olden time. Nobody claimed it for himself. Nobody enjoined it upon another. You insulted a man if you called him humble. It seemed to be inconsistent with that self-respect which is necessary to any good activity. Christ came and made the despised quality the crowning grace of the culture that He inaugurated. Lo! the disgraceful word became the key-word of His fullest gospel. He redeemed the quality, and straightway the name became honorable. It became the ambition of all men to wear it. To call a man humble was to praise him now. Men affected it if they did not have it. Pride began to ape humility when humility was made the crowning grace of human life.

I. 325.

Christ was pleased Himself to be
Our Pattern of humility:

To show no path of duty lies
Too low for highest dignities.   J. L. M. W.

JESUS was never guarding himself, but always invading the lives of others with His holiness. . . . His life was like an open stream that keeps the sea from flowing up into it by the eager force with which it flows down into the sea. He was so anxious that the world should be saved, that therein was His salvation from the world. He labored so to make the world pure that He never even had to try to be pure Himself. Health issued from Him so to the sick who touched His garments that He was in no danger of their infection coming in to Him. This was the positiveness of His sinlessness. He did not spend His life in trying not to do wrong. He was too full of the earnest love and longing to do right,—to do His Father's will.

So we are sure at once, and we learn it certainly from Christ, that the true spotlessness from the world must come, not negatively, by the garments being drawn back from every worldly contact, but positively, by the garments being so essentially, divinely pure that they fling pollution off, as sunshine, hurrying on its mission to the world, flings back the darkness that tries to stop its way.

I. 182, 184.

Have Jesus in thy heart,
And thou wilt be preserved from all defilement.
THOMAS À KEMPIS.

Be ye glad and rejoice forever in that which I create.—Is. lxv. 18.

IT means something that, in the disorder of thought and feeling, so many men are fleeing to the study of orderly nature.   And it is rest and comfort.   Whatever men are feeling, the seasons come and go.   Whatever men are doubting, the rock is firm under their feet, and the steadfast stars pass in their certain courses overhead.   Men who dare count on nothing else may still count on the tree's blossoming and the grape coloring.   It is good for a man perplexed and lost among many thoughts to come into closer intercourse with Nature, and to learn her ways and to catch her spirit.   It is no fancy to believe that if the children of this generation are taught a great deal more than we used to be taught of nature, and the ways of God in nature, they will be provided with the material for far healthier, happier, and less perplexed and anxious lives than most of us are living.

I. 171.

Nature . . . can so inform
The mind that is within us, so impress
With quietness and beauty, and so feed
With lofty thoughts, that neither evil tongues,
Rash judgments, nor the sneers of selfish men,
Nor greetings where no kindness is, nor all
The dreary intercourse of daily life,
Shall e'er prevail against us or disturb
Our cheerful faith that all which we behold
Is full of blessings.

WORDSWORTH.

I SEEM to hear a certain sort of apologetic tone among men of faith, which is not good. . . . The man who trusts God sometimes seems almost to say to his unbelieving brother, " Forgive me. I am not as strong as you are. I cannot do without this help. You are more strong and do not need it. But let me keep it still." No open foe of faith can do faith so much harm as that kind of believer. . . . It is a sick man apologizing to death because he is not quite ready yet to die. It is the meagreness of health in him that prompts his poor apology. Let him grow healthier and he begins to look not down to death with apologies, but up to life with hopes and aspirations. So let the weak disciple grow more strong in faith, and he will have no longer feeble words of shame and self-excuse to say about his trust in Christ; only his whole life will grow one earnest prayer for an increase of faith, as the child's life is one continued hope and prayer for manhood.

VI. 100.

Belief's fire, once in us,
Makes of all else mere stuff to show itself:
We penetrate our life with such a glow
As fire lends to wood and iron.

BROWNING.

*If any man thinketh he is wise, . . . let him
become a fool, that he may be wise.*

                              1 Cor. iii. 18.

BEHOLD, wisdom is the end of all! No
less in the Bible and in the Church than
in the schools. . . . If the Gospel discredits
any of man's achievements, declaring them to
be incompetent to satisfy the soul and educate
the nature, it is always only that it may insist
upon a higher knowledge. Christ was a
teacher. Christ is a teacher forever. If He
declares that no scholastic culture, and no skill
in the arts of life, and no acquaintance with
the ways of men can save a soul, it is only
that He may insist that man must know his
own soul, and the deep difference of right and
wrong, and the infinite holiness of God. These
are true knowledges. "That they might know
Thee, the only true God, and Jesus Christ
whom Thou hast sent." It is of all importance that we should know that the Christian
life is a life of knowledge, not of ignorance.
It is a separate, a higher region of knowledge
than that to which we generally give the
name; but it is knowledge still. It is the
apprehension of truths, of those vast truths
which the senses cannot discover, nor the
intellect evolve, but which through the open
avenues of the spirit enter in and occupy the
life.   VI. 167.

Have I knowledge? confounded it shrinks at
        wisdom laid bare!
Have I forethought? how purblind, how blank
        to the Infinite Care!   BROWNING.

IT is the law of God, that wherever there is duty there is also possible joy. Just as the man who sees foliage knows that somewhere there must be water, although his eyes or ears cannot discern it, and the trees seem to grow out of the sand; so the man who is sure that in any spot there is duty for him to do knows that there is a happiness for him somewhere in the doing of that duty, even though for the present it seems to be a dreadful drudgery. In the expectation of that joy he works. The expectation of joy *is* joy; and so the man who in his voluntariness surrenders some delight or privilege, finds that there is a subtler mastery of happiness which is to be gained only by giving it up and seeking something higher, though for the time it seems to separate us from the happiness we love. Many and many an experience there is in this world which gives us the right to believe that happiness is something very coy and wilful, which, when we chase it, runs away from us; but, when we turn away from it and seek for something better, and forget to seek it, changes its mind and chases us.

III. 238.

He was not all unhappy. His resolve
Upbore him, and firm faith, and evermore
Prayer from a living source within the will,
And beating up through all the bitter world,
Like fountains of sweet water in the sea,
Kept him a living soul.

TENNYSON.

_With what measure ye mete, it shall be measured
to you again._—MATT. vii. 2.

IT is a law of vast extent and wonderful
  exactness.   The world is far more orderly
than we believe; a deeper and a truer justice
runs through it than we imagine.   We all go
about calling ourselves victims, discoursing on
the cruel world, and wondering that it should
treat us so, when really we are only meeting
the rebound of our own lives.   What we have
been to things about us has made it necessary
that they should be this to us.   As we have
given ourselves to them, so they have given
themselves to us. . . .   Only, keep your minds
clear of any materialism which would think
that in mere earth itself resides this power of
just and discriminating reply.   It is as we and
all things exist together in the great embrac-
ing and pervading element of God that all
things give themselves to us as we give ourselves to them.   So all the phenomena of life
are at the same time divine judgments if we
are only wise enough to read them.

III. 268.

Vainly the lonely tarn its cup
  Holds to the feeding skies;
Unless the source be lifted up,
  The streamlet cannot rise:
By law inexorably blent,
Each is the other's measurement.

SUSAN COOLIDGE.

IN some strange shrine of Romish or Pagan religion, all glorious with art, all blazing with the light of precious stones, there bend around the altar the true devotees who believe with all their souls; while at the door. . . . lingers a group of travellers full of joy at the wondrous beauty of the place; and as when the music ceases and the lights go out they go away, each carrying what it was in him to receive,—the devotee his spiritual peace, the artistic tourist his æsthetic joy: so men bestow themselves on Christ, and by the. selves that they bestow on Him the giving of Himself to them must of necessity be measured. . . . Not merely with outstretched hands but with open hearts we must stand before Him. . . . Then to each of us even here upon the earth shall begin that which is to be the everlasting wonder and delight of heaven, the perfect giving of the Lord to souls that are perfectly given to Him, the everlasting action and reaction, the unhindered beating back and forth of need and grace between the Saviour on His throne and His servants at their tireless work for Him.

III. 286.

What Thou hast given, do Thou receive the
    same;
And whence the rivers rise, thither let them
    return.

THOMAS À KEMPIS.

Lord, is it I?—MATT. xxvi. 22.

NO sin is sudden.   The warning may be only half recognized, but when the sin of our life comes, who of us has not felt, strangely mingled with its strangeness, a certain dreadful familiarity, such as one might feel when a man whom he had never seen, but of whom he dreamed last night, and whose face he remembered from the dream, stepped in the living flesh across his threshold? . . .   The man in business, spurning the very thought of cheating, as ready as he ever was to strike down any man who dared approach him with temptation, finds himself some day questioning duty and trying to make it say that it is not duty, or seeing how close he can run under the lee of a doubtful transaction and yet sail out safe. He has not sinned, but if he is a sensitive and thoughtful man he sees, as he opens his eyes to what he is doing, how he *might* sin.   He shudders as a man might who, walking in his sleep, woke up and found that what he thought was music is the roaring in his ears of the chasm on whose brink he stands.   His coming sin has given him its warning.

VII. 119, 120.

Out of my soul's depths to Thee my cries have
    sounded;
Lord, shouldst Thou weigh our faults, who's
    not confounded?

CAMPION.

OUR best moments are the utterance of our highest, truest possibility. . . . They are the type of what we always might and ought to be. For the exceptionalness of an event is not properly measured by its rarity. The exception is the departure from the law of life, whether it comes rarely or comes often. If the law of a man's life, the standard, the ideal of it, is that he shall be true, and ninety-nine times to-day he lies and only once he tells the truth, those ninety-nine times are really ninety-nine exceptions. Once, only once, he has been his true self, conformed to his law.

If all the world could know that, what a great change would come! If we could all be sure that our best is our most natural—that it is the evil which is most unnatural; if I knew man simply in his intrinsic nature, nothing at all of this long dark history of his, I think that nothing he could do would be so good as to surprise me. It would be his wickedness that would seem strange. To keep that feeling about him, in spite of this long history of his—that is the triumph of the truest faith.

VII. 348, 349.

All is well, I know, without;
I alone the beauty mar,
I alone the music jar.
Yet, with hands by evil stained,
And an ear by discord pained,
I am groping for the keys
Of the heavenly harmonies;
Still within my heart I bear
Love for all things good and fair.

WHITTIER.

HAVE you been in the habit of thinking of Christ as of one so far away, so different from us, that what He is and does seems to throw no light on what we may be and do? But such a thought as that denies the very power of the Incarnation. Here stand our human lives, all dark and lustreless. Here stands one human life in which has been lighted the fire of an evident divinity. Shall we look on and see the fine lines and the fair colors of human nature brought out by the fire which burns within, and not make any glowing inference with regard to our own humanity, with regard to its unfulfilled possibilities and the attainments for which it may confidently hope? Surely not so! . . .

Let us believe indeed that in the experience of Christ there is such revelation of the possibility, such confirmation of the hopes of our humanity! So only does this life become that beacon on the mountain-top, that bugle-cry at the army's head, which He evidently counted it to be, which it has so often been through all the Christian centuries!

IV. 282, 283.

Jesus, Saviour, Friend most dear!
Dwell Thou with us daily here;
By Thine own life teach us this—
How divine the human is!

One with God, as heart with heart,
Saviour, lift us where Thou art;
Join us to His life, through Thine,
Human still, though all divine!

LUCY LARCOM.

And He answered to him never a word; insomuch that the governor marvelled greatly.
MATT. xxvii. 14.

SO the prisoner revealed Himself to His amazed and frightened judge. By silence often of necessity and not by speech He must make Himself known, because the revelation is too great for words to contain; because the hearer cannot hold the truth and yet, by his strange human capacity, can hold Him who speaks the truth, Him who is the truth; because words sometimes hide instead of revealing what they try to tell,—for all these reasons the Lord often when we pray to Him answers us not a word.

Oh, my friends, if our answered prayers are precious to us, I sometimes think our unanswered prayers are more precious still. Those give us God's blessings; these, if we will, may lead us to God. Do not let any moment of your life fail of God's light. Be sure that whether He speaks or is silent, He is always loving you, and always trying to make your life more rich and good and happy.
V. 139.

All as God wills, who wisely heeds
  To give or to withhold,
And knoweth more of all my needs
  Than all my prayers have told.

WHITTIER.

And a vision appeared to Paul in the night: There stood a man of Macedonia, and prayed him . . . Come over, and help us.—ACTS xvi. 9.

SO far as we know there was no one man in Macedonia who wanted Paul. . . . But what, then, means the man from Macedonia? . . . He is the utterance not of a conscious want, but of the unconscious need of those poor people. It is the unsatisfied soul, the deep need, all the more needy because the outside life, perfectly satisfied with itself, does not know that it is needy all the time,—it is this that God hears pleading. This soul is the true Macedonia. And so this, as the representative Macedonian, the man of Macedonia, brings the appeal. How noble and touching is the picture which this gives us of God. The unconscious needs of the world are all appeals and cries to Him. He does not wait to hear the voice of conscious want. The mere vacancy is a begging after fulness; the mere poverty is a supplication for wealth; the mere darkness cries for light. . . . The "man of Macedonia" was the very heart and essence of Macedonia, the profoundest capacities of truth and goodness and faith and salvation which Macedonia itself knew nothing of, but which were its real self. These were what took form and pleaded for satisfaction.   II. 94, 95.

> O Lord God, hear the silence of each soul,
>   Its cry unutterable of ruth and shame,
>   Its voicelessness of self-contempt and blame :
> Nor suffer harp and palm and aureole
> Of multitudes who praise Thee at the goal,
>   To set aside Thy poor and blind and lame !
>
>   CHRISTINA G. ROSSETTI.

Knowing that ye are thereto called, that ye should inherit a blessing.—1 PET. iii. 9.

THERE are always great unifying truths waiting to close around and bind into a surprising unity the fragmentary lives we live. For we certainly do live very much in fragments. Our special blessings stand isolated, and are not grasped and gathered into one great pervading consciousness of a blessed life,—of a life brooded over and cared for and trained by God the Blesser. . . . If you could believe in one great utterance of God, one incarnate word, the manifested pity of God and the illustrated possibility of man at once,—then, with such a central point, there could be no more fragmentariness anywhere. . . . Blessings of every sort are reflections of that great blessing. . . . The manifestation of the Son of God, of Christ, gives all other blessings a place and meaning, just as the sun in heaven accounts for and rescues from fragmentariness every little light of the innumerable host which, in every hue and brilliancy, sparkle and flash and glow from every point of our sun-lit world. V. 199, 202.

My being, Lord, will nevermore be whole
    Until Thou come behind my ears and eyes,
Enter and fill the temple of my soul
    With perfect contact—such a sweet surprise—
Such presence as, before it met the view,
    The prophet-fancy could not once foresee,
Though every corner of the temple knew
    By very emptiness its need of Thee.
                              GEORGE MACDONALD.

---

*The eyes of the Lord are over the righteous, . . .
and if ye suffer for righteousness' sake, happy are
ye.*—1 PET. xii. 14.

IT is so hard to do right, you say. Yes, of
course it is; and the soul that tries to do
right does wrong so constantly! But then it
is so glorious—glorious to do right through
struggle; glorious to mount from the lower to
the higher life, and seeing how God has
bound our perfection to His own, have but one
confident prayer for both: not, " Father, save
me from this hour "—from any hour, however
hard it be—but " Father, glorify Thy name."

And as to Christ when He prayed, so often
to us, sharers not only of His struggle, but of
His triumph, there shall come a voice from
heaven, saying, " I have both glorified it, and
will glorify it now again in thee." Who cannot
dare all things and bear all things in the
celestial courage of that promise ?

VII. 237.

God's trumpet wakes the slumbering world;
   Now, each man to his post!
The red-cross banner is unfurled;
   Who joins the glorious host ?

He who, with calm, undaunted will,
   Ne'er counts the battle lost,
But, though defeated, battles still,—
   He joins the faithful host!

He who is ready for the cross,
   The cause despised loves most,
And shuns not pain or shame or loss,—
   He joins the martyr host!

SAMUEL LONGFELLOW.

And I saw as it were a sea of glass mingled with fire ; and them that had gotten the victory . . . having the harps of God.—REV. xv. 2.

DISAPPOINTMENTS of every sort, sorrows, sufferings, trials, struggles, restlessness and dissatisfaction, false friends, poor health, low tastes and standards all about us—who shall catalogue the troubles of human life? Who shall tell the difference between two men who live in different aspects of all these things? Are they intrusions, accidents, thwartings and disappointments of the will of God? Or are they (this is what our doctrine says they are) Messiahs, things sent, having, like the ships that sail to our ports from far-off lands of barbarian richness, rare spices and fragrant oils and choice foods that we cannot find at home, whose foreign luxuriance forces its odorous way through the coarse and uncouth coverings in which their wealth was packed away in the savage lands from which they came? Are they prolific sources of spiritual culture, contributing what our best happiness could not have except from them, the energy and vitality which there is no way of stirring up in human nature but by some sense of danger, the fire to mingle with the glass?

IV. 117.

Happy is he whose heart
Hath found the art
To turn his double pains to double praise!

GEORGE HERBERT.

WHEN we open our eyes morning after morning and find the old struggle, on which we closed our eyes last night, awaiting us; . . . when all our habits and thoughts have become entwined and colored with some tyrannical necessity, which, however it may change the form of its tyranny, will never let us go,—it grows so hard as almost to appear impossible for us to anticipate that that dominion ever is to disappear, and that we shall ever shake free our wings, and leave behind the earth to which we have been chained so long.

But the day comes, nevertheless. Some morning we go out to meet the old struggle, and it is not there. . . . Things do get done, and when anything is really finished, then come thoughtful moments in which we ask ourselves whether we have let that which we shall know no longer do for us all that it had in its power to do, whether we are carrying out of the finished experience that which it has all along been trying to give to our characters and souls.   VI. 56, 57.

I search, but cannot see
What purpose serves the soul that strives, . . .
. . . unless the fruit of victories
Stay, one and all, stored up and guaranteed
    its own
Forever, by some mode whereby shall be made
    known
The gain of every life.   BROWNING.

Afterward it yieldeth the peaceable fruit of righteousness.—HEB. xii. 11.

He led them forth by the right way, that they might go to a city of habitation.—Ps. cvii. 7.

A TRAVELLER is going to a great city which is his final goal. At the very beginning of the journey the road leads over a high hill. Upon the summit the traveller can clearly see the spires of the far-away city flashing in the sunlight. He feasts his eyes on it. And then he follows the road down into the valley. It plunges into forests. It sounds the depths in which flow the dark waters which the sun never touches. But yet it never forgets the city which it saw from the hilltop. It feels that distant unforgotten glory drawing it toward it in a tight straight line. And when at last the traveller enters in that city, it is not strange to him, because of the prophecy of it which has been in his heart ever since he saw it from the hill.

If we read rightly, thus, the method by which God brings His children to their best attainment, it is certainly a method full of wisdom and beauty. First He lets shine upon them for a moment the thing He wants them to become, the greatness or the goodness which He wishes them to reach. And then, with that shining vision fastened in their hearts, He sets them forth on the long road to reach it. The vision does not make it theirs. The journey is still to be made, the task is still to be done. But all the time, that sight which the man saw from the mountain-top is still before the eyes, and no darkness can be perfectly discouraging to him who keeps that memory and prophecy of light. VII. 340.

Ye are My witnesses, saith the Lord, that I am God.—Is. xliii. 12.

NO man is a separate, rounded character, independent of any other, carrying his own qualities included within himself; every man is a medium through which God expresses Himself with more or less of clearness and effectiveness, according to the dimness or the transparency of the character on which His light falls. We are like windows through which a higher light is always falling; but the window is blurred and mottled because at some places it is stained deep and will not let the light through; and where it does receive it, it is always conscious of *receiving*. The radiance with which it shines comes to it from without—not *it* shines, but the light shines through it.

We learn to count men, thus, not by the witness that they bear of themselves, but by the witness that they bear of God. . . . Many of the most subtle and perplexing phenomena of human life become clearer to us when we have once reached this conception of the unity of the universe, of the way in which man exists and manifests himself only in relation toward God. "Christ is *all*, and *in all*;" or, in Paul's phrase, "None of us liveth to himself, and no man dieth to himself. Whether we live, therefore, or die, we are the Lord's."

VII. 38, 39.

No reflection so imperfect
  But it something clear doth speak
Of a fuller revelation
  Waiting for the eyes that seek;
Love is made in heavenly likeness
  Though the image be but weak.

J. L. M. W.

AS the sun shines upon a bank of snow no two of all the myriad particles catch his light alike or give the same interpretation of his glory. Have you ever imagined such a purpose for your commonplace existence? If you have you must have asked yourself what the quality is in a man's life which can make it *reflective* of God—capable of bearing witness of Him. There is some quality in the polished brass or in the calm lake that makes it able to send forth again the sunlight that descends upon it. What is it in a soul that makes it able to do the same to the God who sheds Himself upon its life? The Bible has its one great name for such a great transforming quality, and that is "*love.*" Love in the Bible is not so much an action of the soul as it is a quality in the soul permitting God to do His divine actions through it. The love of God is a new nature, a new fiber, a new fineness and responsiveness in the soul itself, by which God is able to express Himself upon and through it as He cannot when He finds only the medium of the coarse material of an un-loving heart.   VII. 46.

If any man love God, the same is known of Him.
1 COR. viii. 3.

Here is the patience and faith of the saints.
REV. xiii. 10.

BETTER that the whole calendar were swept away and every saint forgotten, than that one of them should take anything from that perfect prerogative of saviourship which is the Saviour's own.   But this need not be. . . .   Christ is more utterly my sole resource in strong temptation, the only Being I can flee to, when I see strong men of the saintly histories turned into weakness before the power of evil, and fleeing in desperation to that same Christ, to be restrengthened with a higher power than the old.   There is a use of the saints that can make Christ nearer, clearer, dearer to our souls.   They may be like a mere atmosphere between our souls and Him, whose every particle, filled with Him, has passed on His life to the next particle, and so at last sent Him down to us pure, as He is, uncolored with its own blueness, the "light that lighteth every man," lighting us all the more brightly because it has lighted them.

I. 128, 129.

What is the flame of their fire, if so I may
    catch the flame;
  What the strength of their strength, if also
    I may wax strong?
The flaming fire of their strength is the love
    of Jesu's Name,
  In whom their death is life, their silence
    utters a song.

CHRISTINA G. ROSSETTI.

*I am He that liveth, and was dead ; and, behold,
I am alive forevermore ; . . . and have the keys
of . . . death.*—REV. i. 18.

IT is because He died that He holds the keys
of death. . . . They who have under-
gone and overcome stand with their keys to
open the portals of life's great emergencies to
their brethren. The wondrous power of experience! And see how beautiful and enno-
bling this makes our sorrows and temptations.
Every stroke of sorrow that issues into light
and joy is God putting into your hand the key
of that sorrow to unlock it for all the poor
souls whom you may see approaching it,
through all your future life. It is a noble thing
to take that key and use it. There are no nobler
lives on earth than those of men and women
who have passed through many experiences of
many sorts, and who now go about with calm
and happy and sober faces, holding the keys,
some golden and some iron, and finding their
joy in opening the gates of these experiences
to younger souls, and sending them into them
full of intelligence and hope and trust. Such
lives, I think, we may all pray to grow into as
we grow older, and pass through more and
more of the experiences of life.

I. 217, 219.

*Blessed be God, . . . Who comforteth us in all
our tribulation, that we may be able to comfort
them which are in any trouble, by the comfort
wherewith we are comforted of God.*

2 COR. i. 3, 4.

*And at midnight Paul and Silas prayed, and
sang praises unto God.*—ACTS xiv. 25.

WHEN it enters like a flood of light into
the soul of some wretched invalid or
some victim of relentless misfortune, that by
a faithful patience under his suffering he can
glorify God and show forth the power of
Christ, then what a change comes to him!
How all is transfigured! How full of beauty
the hated sick-room grows! There is something behind the suffering for the suffering to
rest and steady itself upon. The light has
been kindled behind the dark window, and all
its fair lines and bright colors shine out. · In
the purpose of the suffering the escape from
the suffering is found; as when Paul and Silas,
in the book of Acts, sang praises to God by
night in prison, when they turned their im-
prisonment into a tribute to their Master, then
"the foundations of the prison were shaken,
and . . . the doors were opened, and every
one's bands were loosed."

VI. 51.

> We take with solemn thankfulness
> Our burden up, nor ask it less,
> And count it joy that even we
> May suffer, serve, or wait for Thee,
> Whose will is done.

WHITTIER.

Mark how the fire in flints doth quiet lie,
  Content and warm t' itself alone;
But when it would appear to others' eye,
  Without a knock it never shone.

GEORGE HERBERT.

SUPPOSE that years ago there came some crisis in your life which taught you the necessity and the glory of being brave. It was some mighty day of God with you. . . . You dared to fight because you dared not feebly run away. It was a revelation of you to yourself. What then? The crisis past, the lightnings faded and the thunders hushed, you came down from the mountain. Ever since that you have walked on in quiet, level ways. But many a time, in simple tasks which had not power of themselves to bring you such self-revelations, you have found yourself able to be brave with a bravery whose possibility you learned in that tremendous hour. . . . Men are meeting the petty enemies of the household and the street to-day with a fortitude and a fearlessness which they learned thirty years ago on the battle-fields of the Rebellion. Men are bearing little disappointments with a patience which was born in them while they stood by the death-bed of their best beloved. . . . It is good that the power which is first born under exacting and peculiar circumstances should then be set free from those circumstances. altogether and become the general possession of the life, available for all its needs. The cloud forms about the mountain-peak; but once formed there, it floats away and drops its blessing upon many fields. VII. 343.

And the day was dark over them.

MIC. iii. 6.

O MY dear friends, it is a terrible thing when one's religion is too small for the world, and is always leaving great parts of the world's life unaccounted for, unilluminated, and is always dreading to have the world made any larger, lest this religion shall seem even more meagre and insufficient.   But it is a great thing when the world is too small for one's religion, and the soul's sense of the glory and dearness of God is always craving larger and larger regions in which to range.   Then welcome all discoveries, all illuminations, all visions of the greatness of the world of God.

VII. 177.

Then the ever-lifted cry:
Give us light, or we shall die!
Cometh to the Father's ears,
And He hearkens, and He hears. . . .
They, hardly trusting happy eyes,
Discern a dawning in the skies:
'Tis Truth awaking in the soul;
Thy Righteousness to make them whole.
—What shall men, this Truth adoring,
Gladness-giving, youth-restoring,
Call it but eternal Light?
'Tis the morning, 'twas the night.

GEORGE MACDONALD.

EVERYWHERE the lower furnishes opportunities for the higher, and is a failure unless the higher blooms out of the ground which the lower has made ready. It is Paul's groaning and travailing creation. It is the unity of the universe in which, from end to end, there is no hardest, commonest, and cheapest thing which, living in simple healthiness and self-respect, may not become the gathering point and manifestation point of the most infinite celestial light,—no stone that may not make an altar. Reverence the simple, the prosaic, the natural, the real; but demand of every common thing of life, whether it be your body or your money or your daily experience, that it shall bloom to fine results in your own soul and in your influence upon the world.

VI. 254.

One small life in God's great plan,
    How futile it seems as the ages roll,
Do what it may, or strive how it can,
    To alter the sweep of the infinite whole! . . .
But the pattern is rent where the stitch is lost,
Or marred where the tangled threads have
        crossed;
And each life that fails of its true intent
Mars the perfect plan that its Master meant.

SUSAN COOLIDGE.

Love mocks thee, whose mounting desire
Doth not to the Perfect aspire.

TWO men who have known each other for
years become together the servants of
Christ. His spirit comes to them. They
begin the new life of which He is the centre
and the soul. How their old friendship
changes! How it is all the same, and yet how
different it is! It opens depths and heights
they never dreamed of. Where they used to
do so little for each other, now they can do so
much. Where they used to touch only on the
outside, now their whole natures blend. They
have taken friendship and planted it where it
belongs, in the soil and air of the divine love;
and it opens its essential richness as the trop-
ical flower which has been living a half-life in
the northern soil tells its whole sweet and
gorgeous story of itself when it is carried to
the bright skies and warm ground for which
God made it.

VII. 312.

A friend! Deep is calling to deep!
A friend! The heart wakes from its sleep,
To behold the world lit by one face,
With one heavenward step to keep pace.

.   .   .   .

O Heart wherein all hearts are known,
Whose infinite throb stirs our own,
O Friend beyond friends, what are we,
Who ask so much less, yet have Thee!

LUCY LARCOM.

Jesus saith unto them, How many loaves have ye?—MATT. xv. 34.

WHEN you stand face to face with a hungry-eyed creature whom you want to feed with better life, be sure that you imitate your Lord. Be sure that you begin by asking him " How many loaves have you, my poor friend ? What can you give me to begin with ? What has God done for you already ? Show me your best, and we will pray to God together that as you put it into His hands He will bless it and multiply it, till your whole life is fed with the grace which is all His but which He has made yours by bidding it work upon the substance of what He had given you already."

" How many loaves have you ?" It is the Lord's first question; and the hands of those who really want His help, search their robes to see what they have hidden there. One brings his joy; another brings his pain; another brings his helpless desire; another brings his poor resolution; another has nothing to bring except just his sorrow that he has nothing. It is a poor collection; only seven loaves, and a few little fishes; but it is enough. His blessing falls upon them, and they come back to the souls which gave them up to Him, multiplied into the means of healthy, holy, happy life.

May God help us all, every day of our lives, to come to Christ just as we are, that He may make us more and more just what we ought to be.

II. 142, 146.

THE home, school, and shop must be here on the fairest hillsides and plains of the world for something. If we will not claim them for their best use, and by our use of them exalt them to their best explanations, we need not wonder at the low and godless explanations which men give of them. When we are willing to see in them the ministrations of God; when men, asking for the means of grace, are pointed, first of all, to the duties and relations of their lives as the places where they will meet God, where they will find the deepest experiences,—conviction of sin, utter humility, the need of Christ, and the ideal of holiness,—then how the dead earth and all that is upon it will glow with a fire that no materialism will quench. Till then, so long as we fail to use the world for spiritual culture, no wonder if it be dead; and who cares whether the dead thing sprang from the hand of a creator or took shape of chaos by a force as dead as itself ?

X. 31.

Not he who spins with subtle art
  The webs of fine philosophy,
Not he who dwells alone, apart,
  In scorn of poor humanity,
Nor he who cries, Lo, here! Lo, there!
  The hidden Christ is sure to be!
But he who treads the narrow path
  Of homely duty day by day,
And lends whatever strength he hath
  To help his brother on the way,
Will surest hear at set of sun,
The Master's loving word, " Well done! "

J. L. M. W.

THE best and noblest natures are marked by hardly anything so much as this,—the simultaneousness and reasonableness of the lives they live. . . . The spontaneousness does not obscure the reason, and the reason does not hamper and clog the spontaneousness. So it always seems to me that it is with Jesus. He presses His brother's hands with brotherly affection. His brother's sneer wounds as no stranger's can. His mother's sorrow enters into its own secret chamber of sympathy in Him where no other sorrow can intrude. And yet all the while, with all the instinctive value which He gave to them for their own sake, these home affections all are ties to bind Him to humanity, windows through which He looks into the depths of human life, interpretations to His soul of the wider brotherhood in the vaster family.

Surely here is a noble indication of what the family affections may be to all men.

VIII. 184.

To Thee our full humanity—
  Its joys and pains belong;
The wrong of man on man to Thee
  Inflicts a deeper wrong.

Who hates, hates Thee; who loves becomes
  Therein to Thee allied;
All sweet accords of hearts and homes
  In Thee are multiplied.

WHITTIER.

IF human sin needs a humanity to judge it, do not these weak and struggling efforts of our life after goodness crave some sympathy to which they can appeal as they go up to judgment?   What! shall I send these poor pretences of holiness up to heaven, this ineffective virtue which is not a being good, but only a trying to be so,—shall I send them up to lay themselves against the fiery purity of God and be burnt off like spots of blemish from the white light of His perfectness?   Oh, no, give me a man!   Though He be perfect, He will know what human imperfection is. . . .   He will comprehend what my poor struggles mean. . . .   If we look deep enough, we ought to feel, every time when we see a little child at night trustfully laying his day's life, made up of faint desires, feeble effort and continual failures, into the hands of God, what a blessed thing it is that there is in that everlasting God an everlasting Christ, an undying humanity, which will take that day's life into a brother's hands and count it precious with all the intelligence of sympathy.   VI. 322.

> Thou, O Elder Brother, who
> In Thy flesh our trial knew,
> Thou who hast been touched by these,
> Our most sad infirmities,
> Thou alone the gulf can span
> In the dual heart of man,
> And between the soul and sense
> Reconcile all difference,
> Change the dream of me and mine
> For the truth of Thee and Thine.
>   WHITTIER.

IN this mixture of good and evil which we call Man, this motley and medley which we call human character, it is the good and not the evil which is the foundation color of the whole. Man is a son of God on whom the Devil has laid his hand, not a child of the Devil whom God is trying to steal. . . . The great truth of Redemption, the great idea of Salvation, is that the realm belongs to Truth, that the Lie is everywhere and always an intruder and a foe. He came in, therefore he may be driven out. When he is driven out, and man is purely man, then man is saved. It is the glory and the preciousness of the first mysterious, poetic chapters of Genesis that they are radiant all through their sadness with that truth.

V. 9, 10.

'T were glorious, no doubt, to be
One of the strong-winged hierarchy,

  .   .   .   .

Yet I, perhaps, poor earthly clod,
Could I forget myself in God,
Could I but find my nature's clue
Simply as birds and blossoms do,
And but for one rapt moment know
'Tis Heaven must come, not we must go,
Should win my place as near the throne
As the pearl-angel of its zone.

JAMES RUSSELL LOWELL.

And He went up into a mountain to pray. And as He prayed, the fashion of His countenance was altered, and His raiment was white and glistering.
LUKE ix. 28, 29.

IN Jesus our humanity went up into the mountain and was transfigured. It shone with light there on the cross. Thenceforth, into whatever depths of selfishness it might descend, it carried the power of that transfiguration with it. In its certainty that He who suffered there was one with it and really bore its nature, it knew that not to be selfish, but to be unselfish, was its true life. That is the reason why so wonderfully, through all the years of miserable self-seeking which have come since, souls everywhere have come out under the power of that cross and let themselves be crucified for fellow-men, and why the dream of a world glorious with mutual devotion has never been lost out of men's hearts.

Those lives of self-devotion, however humble and obscure they seem, have always themselves the same power which belongs to the sacrifice of Jesus. They too throw light on darker lives. They are lesser hill-tops grouped around the great mountain. Such lives may we live in any little world where God has set us!
VII. 345.

But we would be of those who do Thy will,
And unto whom Thou dost in love disclose
The brightness of Thy face, to overfill
Their heart with sweetness, we would be of
those. CHRISTINA G. ROSSETTI.

And Peter answered and said unto Jesus, Master, it is good for us to be here.

MATT. ix. 5.

TO many, if not to all, men's lives come such splendid moments as came to Peter on the mountain of the Transfiguration. . . . Once on a certain morning you felt the glory of living, and the misery of life has never since that been able quite to take possession of your soul. Once you knew for a few days what was the delight of a perfect friendship. Once you saw for an inspired instant the idea of your profession blaze out of the midst of its dull drudgery. Once, just for a glorious moment, you saw the very truth and believed in it without the shadow of a cloud. . . . And often the question must have come, "What do they mean? What value may I give to these transfiguration times?"

The first instinct is to feel that they are not complete and final; that they point to something which is yet to come; that they are the premonitions, the anticipations, of a fuller condition, in which that which they manifested fitfully and transiently shall become the constant and habitual possession of the life.

VII. 338, 339.

Nothing resting in its own completeness
  Can have worth or beauty, but alone
As it leads and tends to further sweetness,
  Fuller, higher, deeper than its own.

Life is only bright when it proceedeth
  Toward a truer, deeper life above;
Human love is sweetest when it leadeth
  To a more divine and perfect Love.

ADELAIDE A. PROCTER.

Ye shall know them by their fruits.
MATT. vii. 16.

CONDUCT is the mouth-piece of character. What a man is declares itself through what he does. . . . Character without conduct is like the lips without the trumpet, whose whispers die upon themselves and do not stir the world. Conduct without character is like the trumpet hung up in the wind which whistles through it, and means nothing. The world has a right to demand that all which claims to be character should utter itself through conduct which can be seen and heard. The world has a right to disallow all claims of character which do not utter themselves in conduct. "It may be real,—it may be good," the world has a right to say, "but I cannot know it or test it; and I am sure that however good and real it is, it is deprived of the condition of the best life and growth, which is activity."

V. 308, 309.

Therefore love and believe; for the works will
    follow spontaneous,
Even as day does the sun: the Right from the
    Good is an offspring,
Love in a bodily shape; and Christian works
    are no more than
Animate Love and Faith, as flowers are the
    animate spring-tide.

LONGFELLOW.

*We are debtors, not to the flesh, to live after the
flesh.*—ROM. viii. 12.

SELF-MORTIFICATION, self-sacrifice, is
not the first or final law of life. You are
right when you think that these appetites and
passions were not put into you merely to be
killed, and that the virtue which only comes by
their restraint is a poor, colorless, and feeble
thing. You are right in thinking that not to
restrain yourself and to refrain from doing, but
to utter yourself, to act, to do, is the purpose
of your being in the world. Only, this is not
the self you are to utter, these are not the acts
you are to do. There is a part in you made to
think deeply, made to feel nobly, made to be
charitable and chivalric, made to worship, to
pity, and to love. You are not uttering yourself while you keep that better self in chains
and only let these lower passions free. Let me
renew those nobler powers, and then believe
with all your heart and might that to send out
those powers into the intensest exercise is the
one worthy purpose of your life. You will
not so much have crushed the carnal as em-
braced the spiritual. Christ will have made
you free. You will be walking in the Spirit,
and so will not fulfil the lusts of the flesh.

I. 364, 365.

> To this life things of sense
>   Make their pretence:
> In the other angels have their right by birth:
>   Man ties them both alone,
>   And makes them one,
> With the one hand touching heaven, with the
>   other earth.   GEORGE HERBERT.

Are the consolations of God small with thee?
JOHN xv. 11.

THEY do not take your sorrow off; and oh, . . . whatever be your suffering, I beg you to learn first of all that not that, not to take your sorrow off, is what God means, but to put strength into you that you may carry it as the tired man, who has drunk the strength-giving river, lifts up his burden by the river-bank and goes singing on his way. Be sure your sorrow is not giving you its best . . . unless it opens to you ideas that have before been unfamiliar; mostly these three ideas, education, spirituality, immortality. Those ideas are the keys of all the mysteries of life, and so the gateways to consolation. And it is wonderful to see how, just as soon as a man is really crushed and sorrowful, God seems by every avenue to be offering those great ideas for that man's acceptance. He seems to write them on the sky, to whisper them from every movement of the commonest machinery of life, to fill books with them that never seemed to know anything of them before, to make the vacant house and the full grave declare them. You are a child of God whom He is training. You have a soul which is your true value. You are to live forever. Know these truths. By them triumph over the sorrow that He cannot take away, and be consoled.

I. III.

> Trusting that sorrow is but love's disguise,
> And all withholding but another way
> Of making richer by what love denies—
> So grows the soul a little, day by day.
> MARY C. SEWARD.

Blessed be God, . . . the Father of mercies, and the God of all comfort ; who comforteth us in all our tribulation, that we may be able to comfort them which are in any trouble, by the comfort wherewith we are comforted of God.

2 COR. i. 3, 4.

THE power of Paul or of any man to grasp and realize this high idea of the purpose of the help which God sends, shows a very clear understanding that it is really God who sends the help. Indeed, I think no man can really mount up to the idea that God truly and personally cares for him enough to reach down and turn the bitterness of his cup to sweetness, without being, as it were, compelled to look beyond himself. All strong emotions, all really great ideas, outgo our individual life, and make us feel our human nature. If you are not sure that any mercy comes to you from God; if, whatever pious words you use about it, the recovery of your health, or the saving of your fortune, seems to you a piece of luck, some good thing which has dropped down upon you from the clouds, then you may be meanly and miserably selfish about it. You shut it up within the jealous walls of your own life. It is a light which you have struck out for yourself, and may burn in your own lantern. But if the light came down from God, if He gave you this blessing, it is too big for you to keep for yourself. He must have meant it for a wider circle than your little life can cover, and it breaks through your selfishness to find for itself the mission that it claims. I. 3.

Lord, show us the Father.—JOHN xiv. 8.

NOW we are very apt to take it for granted, that however we may differ in our definitions and our belief of the deity of the Son and of the Holy Spirit, we are all at one, there can be and there is no hesitation, about the deity of the Father. God is divine. God is God. And no doubt we do all assent in words to such a belief; but when we think what we mean by that word God; when we remember what we mean by " Father," namely, the first source and the final satisfaction of a dependent nature . . . think how many of us look for neither of them any farther back or any farther on than this routine in which we live. We devote ourselves to it; we deck it with all the graces we can bestow upon it, because there is no higher fatherhood present to our thoughts, because we know no loftier God. Now to such a man what is the first revelation that you want to make? Is it not the divinity of the Father?

I. 234, 235.

With gentle swiftness lead me on,
　Dear God, to see Thy face;
And meanwhile in my narrow heart
　Oh, make Thyself more space!

FABER.

*Through Him we both have access by one Spirit
unto the Father.*—EPHES. ii. 18.

EVERY act is made up of a purpose, a
method, and a power. And so the purpose and the method and the power are here.
What is the purpose or the end? "To the
Father we all have access." What is the
method? "Through Christ Jesus." What is
the power? "By the Spirit." . . . In this
one total act, the end, the method, and the
power are distinguishable, . . . and what is
more, each is distinctly personal. . . . This
salvation, which is all the work of God, first,
last, and midmost, has its divine personalities
distinct for its end and its method and its
power. It is salvation to the Father, through
the Son, and by the Spirit. The salvation is
all one; yet in it method, end, and power are
recognizable. It is a three in one.

The end of the human salvation is "access
to the Father." That is the first truth of our
religion—that the source of all is meant to be
the end of all, that as we all came forth from
a divine Creator, so it is into divinity that we
are to return and find our final rest and satisfaction, not in ourselves, nor in one another,
but in the omnipotence, the omniscience, the
perfectness, and the love of God.

I. 231, 234.

Enough for me to feel and know
That He in whom the cause and end,
The past and future, meet and blend, . . .
Guards not archangel feet alone,
But deigns to guard and keep my own.

WHITTIER.

"MAN shall not live by bread alone, but by every word that proceedeth out of the mouth of God,"—by every word, from the gentlest to the severest, that the eternal lips know how to speak. . . . And remember this is not a doctrine for the world's heroes and martyrs only; it is for every living soul when it is called on to give up the lower that it may attain the higher life. It is for the man who has to give up his dollar that he may keep his honesty, to give up a doubt that he may win a truth. It is for the young man who has to give up a fascinating acquaintance that he may keep his purity, to let go a tempting chance of business because there is something about its associations that is going to degrade his life . . . for the woman who abandons worldliness to serve her God, who turns her back on fashion and its wretched littleness that she may go up into eternal life. . . . Wherever truth and interest conflict, wherever the desire to be popular, to be rich, to be wise, to be anything else, has to be cut away and cast behind a man that he may go on unhindered to be good and true and holy, there the law of the martyrs and the heroes, there the law of the Christ, whose meat was to finish His Father's work, and who for the eating that eternal meat fasteth from the bread that perisheth, comes down and proves itself the law of all true life.

VII. 162.

With love for all around
　　Our days and hours to fill:
Thus be it ever found
　　Our meat to do Thy will!

LUCY LARCOM.

God is faithful, who will not suffer you to be tempted above that ye are able : but will with the temptation also make a way to escape, that ye may be able to bear it.—1 COR. X. 13.

ONLY those temptations which we encounter on the way of duty, in the path of consecration, only those has our Lord promised us that we shall conquer. He sends us out to live and work for Him. The chances of sin which we meet while that divine design of life, the life and work for Him, is clear before us, shall not hurt us. When we forget that design, our arm withers, our immunity is gone. This is what we really mean, what we often put blindly enough, when we ask whether such a man is a religious man or not. We mean, or we ought to mean, whether religion or the service of God is present with him as a continual purpose; not whether he is ever tempted; not whether he ever sins; we know the answers to those questions well enough; but whether behind all the temptation, under all the sin, his soul is still set toward God with genuine and strong devotion. If it is, we know that he must come out safe.

IV. 340.

The lightning and thunder,
　They go and they come;
But the stars and the stillness
　Are always at home.

GEORGE MACDONALD.

IN all artificial religiousness, all that is not bound to life, educated through life, and uttering itself in life, there are gaps and breaks. It is the sadness of every Christian experience,—the loveless time between the moments of ecstatic apprehension; the total secularness between the points of religious performance. . . . The Spirit of God, expected only at certain seasons and by certain doors, finds sometimes those doors closed, and no welcome waiting Him at any other. It is only when we know that any door capable of admitting any influence may admit the blessed influence of God, only then can we be hopeful of keeping the breadth and variety of life, and at the same time of always receiving the culture and the grace of God. Let only the western shutters be open, and we shall see only the western sun. Let all the windows be open and expectant, and from sunrise round to sunset there shall be no interval in the unbroken light. The sun, in the course of the day, will look into them all.

X. 27.

Light of the world! undimming and unsetting,
　Oh, shine each mist away!
Banish the fear, the falsehood, and the fretting,
　Be our unchanging day!
HORATIUS BONAR.

All of you are the children of the Most High.
                              Ps. lxxxii. 6.

IT seems to me absolutely certain that if there is in man a real essential belonging with God, if in a true and indestructible sense he is God's child, then the reaching out of the child's soul after the Father's soul, of the human soul after the divine soul, must be a perpetual fact, it can never be stopped. . . . Agnosticism, Nescience, Pessimism, Secularism must be all temporary phenomena; none of them can be the settled and permanent condition of the human soul if man is the child of God. If he is not, then one is ready to accept whatever comes; for who cares whether a beast that is but a beast dreams that he is an angel, or with a bitter wisdom knows his beasthood?
                              III. 122.

If thou hast wanderings in the wilderness,
And find'st not Sinai, 'tis thy soul is poor:
There towers the mountain of the Voice no
        less,
Which whoso seeks shall find; but he who
        bends
Intent on manna still and mortal ends,
Sees it not, neither hears its thundered lore.
                    JAMES RUSSELL LOWELL.

WHEN we see the man in great trouble or great joy grown suddenly religious—the glad "Thank God!" or the agonized "God help me!" bursting out of unaccustomed lips, it does not mean desperation, and it does not mean hypocrisy. It means that for once in that man's life the true soil of his nature has been laid bare, and it has claimed the divine relations for which it was made; just as you strip the layer of rock off from a bed of earth that lay below it, and in a day the newly exposed earth is sprouting all over with grass that you never planted. It has caught the grass seeds out of the air. The wandering birds have brought them to it. It has found them treasured in itself. It puts forth upon them its own simple nature, and grows green from side to side. The man's hard surface may close over when the great agony or the great joy is past, and all may seem just as before, but he who once has known the movements of this new capacity never can think of himself as he was used to think. . . . He may go on living a most earthly life, but he knows forever that there is a spiritual heaven and a spiritual hell. He never can say of himself again, "I have no spiritual capacity." . . . He has looked upon God, and his soul can never forget how it answered when it met the gaze of the love and power which made it, and for which it was made.   I. 152.

For God, who commanded the light to shine out of darkness, hath shined in our hearts, to give the light of the knowledge of the glory of God.
    2 COR. iv. 6.

Go into the city, and it shall be told thee what thou must do.—ACTS ix. 6.

'Tis here, O pitying Christ, where Thee I seek,
Here where the strife is fiercest, where the sun
Beats down upon the highway thronged with
    men,
And in the raging mart. Oh, deeper lead
My soul into the living world of souls
Where Thou dost move!
RICHARD WATSON GILDER.

THE final spiritual state of man is pictured as a heavenly city, a place of a thousand relationships springing out of his human nature. The training-place of his spiritual life must be a city, a place of many relationships as well. . . . Continuity, variety, influence, reality—these are the things after which our spiritual life is hungering and thirsting. To grow spasmodic, monotonous, uninfluential, unreal, is not this the familiar death of the spiritual life that saddens many a closet and many a church ?

I have not said superficially that to labor is to pray. Prayer lies behind all; but I am sure that by the finite act of labor the infinite act of prayer is helped to its completeness, as the soul grows by the body's ministries to its perfect life. Labor which is conscious of ministering to prayer—that is, of giving the soul deeper perceptions of God and of itself—grows proud of and rich in its mission. It catches much of the loftiness of prayer itself. It goes enthusiastically and buoyantly upon its way, sowing the spiritual life. X. 32.

HAVE you grown weary of looking for any signs of promise in this dull mass of fellow-men and withdrawn yourself into some luxury of self-culture, feeling as if what you had and were was too good to be wasted upon such creatures as these sick and poor and ignorant ? You must be rescued from this proud conceit, not simply by counting yourself lower, but by valuing more highly the spiritual natures of these fellow-men. You must value them as He valued them, who gave His life for them, before you can be as humble in their presence as He was; and that can come only by making yourself their servant. Only he who puts on the garment of humility finds how worthily it clothes his life. Only he who dedicates himself to the spiritual service of his brethren, simply because his Master tells him they are worth it, comes to know how rich those natures of his brethren are, how richly they are worth the total giving of himself to them.

I. 348.

And know that pride

Howe'er disguised in its own majesty,
Is littleness; that he who feels contempt
For any thing, hath faculties
Which he hath never used; that thought with him
Is in its infancy. The man whose eye
Is ever on himself doth look on one,
The least of Nature's works, one who might
    move
The wise man to that scorn which wisdom holds
Unlawful, ever. Oh, be wiser, thou!
Instructed that true knowledge leads to love.

WORDSWORTH.

ALL life tends to encrust itself, to imprison itself within itself, and its crust needs to be constantly broken and returned into the general mass out of which it was formed, in order that the best influences may be received. Ever there must be a return to a primitive simplicity, to a condition of first principles, in which the power to receive may be freshened and renewed. Do you not recognize that? It is part of the old craving to begin the game of life again. It is not that life has been miserable, or has wholly failed, but it has lost simplicity. . . . Is not that craving for a return to simplicity just what St. Paul has in his mind when he says of the man whom he wants to see made wise, " Let him become a fool " ? Is it not just this getting rid of the crust of life, in order that life itself may be open to the sunshine? This is what he means by his strange word " fool," I think. It may have some reference to what the world will think of him who accepts the Gospel in its simpleness; but more than that, I think it also must refer to that condition of simplicity to which the nature must return before Christ with all His great enlightenment can take possession of it.

VI. 160, 161.

Wisdom ofttimes is nearer when we stoop
Than when we soar.

WORDSWORTH.

And when He was come near He beheld the city, and wept over it.—LUKE xix. 41.

WE may picture the approach of Jesus to our souls under the figure of His entrance into Jerusalem. He comes to one of us as He came to that city of His and of His Father's. Think how sacred it was to Him. Think how He loved it. Think what vast precious possibilities he could see sleeping behind its brilliant walls. There was His Father's temple. There was the whole machinery for making the complete manhood. And yet there was defiance, selfishness, unspirituality, and cruelty—the house of prayer turned into the den of thieves. O my dear friends, if Christ, as He comes to any one of us to offer us His salvation, never forgets for a moment what we might be in the sight of what we are, and never forgets for a moment what we are in the vision of what we might be; if He always sees our sins in the light of our chances, and our chances against the shadow of our sins, then what Jerusalems we must be to Him! He loves us as He loved that city, with a love full of reproach and accusation. He stops as He comes in sight of us, and "beholds the city, and weeps over it." I can think of no picture which so lets me into the very depths of the soul of Christ, as He approaches a soul of man which He longs to save, as that which depicts Him stopping on the Mount of Olives, where Jerusalem first comes into sight, and beholding the city, and weeping over it.

VII. 212.

"YE must be born again," said Jesus. Ponder these divine words of His, and ever more and more they seem immeasurably deep. To think of them is like gazing into endless space. But one great truth which they assuredly contain is this: that life for any man is not complete until a deeper and a higher life is put beneath and over the mere life of action, into which the soul can perpetually retreat, and on whose breast the life of action can be buoyantly upborne. There are men who the world thinks are always failing who are themselves conscious of a success which is a truer truth to them than all their failures. They are the men who have been born again, and who carry the new life underneath the old life all the while. The Master of that new life is Christ. The soul worried and torn with disappointments, haunted by the taunts of fellow-souls which tell it it has failed, suspicious of itself, yet keeping still its faithfulness and consecration, goes to Him, to Christ, and lo! it finds a new fact there. Below its failures He has for it success. Through all its deaths He brings out for it, as He brought out for Himself, life! "I too," He says, "seemed to fail, but in my Father I succeeded." "You shall share with me. Ye are they which have continued with Me in My temptations. And I appoint unto you a kingdom, as My Father hath appointed unto Me."

Whatever failures He may have for us to pass through first, may He bring us all at last to that success in Him.

VII. 207.

Beloved of God, called to be saints.—1 Cor. i. 2.

IT is out of the very heart of the discipleship that the apostleship proceeds. . . . Jesus calls all His disciples together, and out of them He chooses twelve. It is no inattentive idlers hanging on the outskirts of the group who listen to Him, that he thinks good enough to go and carry His message. It is they who have listened to Him longest, and most intelligently, and most lovingly. It is Simon and Andrew his brother, James and John, Philip and Bartholomew, Matthew and Thomas; it is men like these, the very heart and soul of the discipleship, whom he selects and calls apostles. And so it always is. Always it is the best of the inward life of anything, that which lies the closest to its heart and is the fullest of its spirit, which flowers into the outward impulse which comes to complete its life. The heart of any good thing is catholic and expansive. It claims for itself the world. It longs to give itself away, and believes in the capacity of all men to receive it. This noble and beautiful truth, whose illustrations are everywhere, was it not declared by Jesus when out of the choicest heart of the group of His disciples, He chose His apostles?

IV. 154, 155, 156.

The footprints of the Life divine
Which marked their path remain in thine;
And the great Life transfused in theirs
Awaits thy faith, thy love, thy prayers.

WHITTIER.

WHEN I see the noble life of a man whose faith I believe is all wrong, or is wofully imperfect, let me not dare to say that his is not true nobleness.   That confuses my moral standards and throws me into the worst hopelessness.   Let the sight of him give me a new faith in the power of human nature to be generous and good, which can break through the most oppressive circumstances, and open into flower out of the most barren soils.   Let it make me ashamed of the small show of generosity and goodness which I with my better faith am able to display; but let it not delude me into saying that what I know is my better and fuller faith is a thing of no consequence; let it not hide from me the fact that my infidel friend, with all his excellence, would be a finer and nobler man than his own present self if he believed in the truth and lived in the power of that which I know to be the faith of God; let it not lead me to forget that the real power of a faith is to be estimated not by the influence of its presence or its absence in individuals who may be exceptional, but by its effect upon broad stretches of human history over wide areas of time and space.

III. 215.

Noble, gentle, self-forgetting,
    In earth's best affections rife,
There is yet one thing thou lackest—
    'Tis the Spirit's breath of life.

CAROLINE M. NOEL.

Judge righteous judgment.—JOHN vii. 24.

THE - great question after all is this: Shall we judge man by God or God by man? Does light and understanding flow upward or downward? If we judge man by God, at once we have true and discriminating thoughts of human life. We have absolute standards. We have a test of the worth of all we do or see. But if we judge God by man, we only have over again what the world has been so full of,—the persuasions of self-interest, the disbelief in absolute righteousness, the changing standards of the changing times. Men have gone into the sanctuary of their own selfishness, the sanctuary of themselves, and straightway they have seemed to see an end of God. All sense of a supreme and awful Fatherhood on which all men depended, to which all action must go back for judgment, has been lost. No higher power than the human has seemed to be moving under and giving meaning to the events of ordinary life.

VI. 124.

If He could doubt on His triumphant cross,
How much more I, in the defeat and loss
Of seeing all my selfish dreams fulfilled,
Of having lived the very life I willed,
Of being all that I desired to be?
My God, my God! why hast Thou forsaken
   me!

W. D. HOWELLS.

Blessed is the man that endureth temptation.
JAMES i. 12.

ANY temptation through which a man may go without yielding is a glory and a strength. But shall men go on courting temptations, finding them out, and running into them, so that they may come out glorious and strong? Look at Christ's temptation. There is one phrase which lights up the whole story. Christ was " led up *of the Spirit* to be tempted of the devil." He had a certain work to do. That work was not His own, but was His Father's. His Father's Spirit guided Him, and told Him how to do it. . . . We too have a work, a duty. . . . In doing our duty the Spirit of our Father may lead us into temptation, but if He really leads us there He will protect us there. If He does not lead us, if we go of our own self will, we have no pledge of His protection. . . . If your duty lies right by the gates of hell, walk there boldly, and the gates of hell shall not prevail against you. If your-duty does not carry you there, you cannot be too fastidiously careful for your purity, to keep it out of the way of every lightest zephyr of temptation. Such is the manifest difference of the temptations into which God leads us and those into which we run ourselves. VII. 135, 136.

Evil knowledge acquired in one wilful moment of curiosity may harass and haunt us to the end of our time.
And how after the end of our time?
CHRISTINA G. ROSSETTI

In all points tempted like as we are, yet without sin.—HEB. iv. 15.

THERE will come a world where there will be no temptation—a garden with no serpent, a city with no sin. The harvest day will come and the wheat be gathered safe into the Master's barn. It will be very sweet and glorious. Our tired hearts rest on the promises with peaceful delight. But that time is not yet. Here are our tempted lives, and here, right in the midst of us, stands our tempted Saviour. If we are men we shall meet temptation as He met it, in the strength of the God who is the Father of whom all men are children. Every temptation that attacks us attacked Him and was conquered. We are fighting with a defeated enemy. We are struggling for a victory which is already won. That may be our strength and assurance as we recall, whenever our struggle becomes hottest and most trying, the wonderful and blessed day when Jesus was "led up of the Spirit into the wilderness to be tempted of the devil."

VII. 148.

> "Tempted and tried!"
> Yet the Lord shall abide
> Thy faithful Redeemer, thy Keeper and Guide,
> Thy Shield and thy Sword,
> Thy exceeding Reward.
> Then enough for the servant to be as his Lord!

FRANCES R. HAVERGAL.

I was glad when they said unto me, Let us go up to the house of the Lord.—Ps. cxxii. 1.

SOMETHING very beautiful and grand, almost awful . . . is the yearly gathering from every corner of the land to the sacred festival meeting at Jerusalem. The land swarms and hums with movement. The men of the seashore and the hills, they are all stirring. Every pass is full, every hillside is alive. . . . Every man brought his own burden, his own sorrow, his own sin. The problems of the year, the things that had perplexed them as they worked in the fields alone, or debated with their brethren, or met the troubles of the household—all these they brought to offer to the Lord, to seek solution for them in the higher, calmer atmosphere of the temple. There was the place where their darkened and frightened understandings would find light and peace.

It is an old-time picture. We do not go to church so now. . . . But woe to us if our more rational belief, instead of lifting all the earth up to heaven, only crowds down the hill-tops and leaves no heaven, and makes our whole earth earthly.

VI. 110, III.

The Lord answer thee in the day of trouble ;
The name of the God of Jacob defend thee ;
Send thee help from the sanctuary,
And strengthen thee out of Zion ; . . .
Grant thee thy heart's desire,
And fulfil all thy mind.

Ps. xx. 1, 2, 4.

*It was too painful for me, until I went into the
Sanctuary of God ; then understood I the end of
these men.*—Ps. lxxiii. 15, 17.

HOW old the bewilderments of the world
are! . . .   Here, almost three thousand
years ago, is a poor man who . . . has been
puzzled because the ungodly were rich, as if
riches were the appropriate premium of goodness; but when he comes to stand with God all
that is altered.   He comes in sight of larger
circles of bliss.   He sees that God has other
rewards to give His chosen besides these little
trinkets. . . .   So long as he knows no higher
happiness than prosperity, it puzzles him that
the bad should have it.   So soon as he comes
to know the infinitely higher joy of company
with God, and sees that that can be given only
to the good,—" without holiness no man can
see the Lord,"—it no more troubles him that
bad men should have the poor counterfeit of
happiness, than it troubles the solid merchant,
sitting in his houseful of plain and solid comfort, to see a miserable fop strut by in cheap
and gaudy finery making believe and perhaps
thinking that he is rich.

VI. 109.

Happier he whose inward sight,
Stayed on his subtile thought,
Shuts his sense on toys of time,
To vacant bosoms brought.

EMERSON.

And Israel saw the Egyptians dead upon the seashore.—Ex. xiv. 30.

DO we believe in the death of our Egyptian ? What is your Egyptian ? Some passion of the flesh or of the mind ?

It was on the farther shore of the Red Sea that the Egyptian pursuers of the Israelites lay dead. It was when the people of God had genuinely undertaken the journey to the land that God had given them, that the grasp of their enemy gave way and the dead hands let them go. You must go forth into a new land, into the ambition of a higher life,—then, when he tries to follow you there, he perishes. . . . Not merely by trying not to be selfish, but by entering into the new joy of unselfish consecration, so only shall you kill your selfishness. When you are vigorously trying to serve your fellow-men, the last chance that you will be unjust or cruel to them will disappear. When you are full of enthusiasm for truth, the cold hands of falsehood will let you go. . . . Seek not the same low things by higher means; seek higher things, and the low means will know that they cannot hold you their slave.

VI. 65, 66, 67.

Nor can I count him happiest who has never
Been forced with his own hand his chains to
    sever,
And for himself find out the way divine.
JAMES RUSSELL LOWELL.

OVER a broad open plain there blows a strong steady wind. It never stops, it never changes. All over the plain there are men and women on their journeys. Hear them cry out. "This wind, this dreadful wind!" cries one, all out of breath and gasping. "How bitter it is, how cruel, how it hates me!" "This wind, this blessed wind!" cries another, within hail of him. "How kind it is, how helpful, how it loves me!" Are there two winds, or has the one fickle wind its favorites? No, the one constant wind is blowing steadily and is no respecter of persons; but one man has set his face against it and the other man is walking with it.

Through this great open world moves God like a strong wind or spirit, finding out all the public and the secret places of the life of man. . . . But while your brother at your side is full of the sense of God's love, to you God seems the hindrance of your life; His righteousness defeats your plans, His purity rebukes your lust, His nature and being smite you in the face like a blast that blows bitter and cold from a far-off judgment day. Does God hate you and love your brother? No, He loves you both: but you with your disobedience are setting yourself against His love. You must turn round.   IV. 312, 313.

The blast that smites thee, face and breast,
  Is God's clear voice to thee:
" This way is neither joy nor rest,—
  Turn, turn, and go with me!"
                          JULIA WOOD.

Lead me in Thy truth and teach me ; for Thou art the God of my salvation.—Ps. xxv. 5.

NO familiarity of religion, no presentation of it as a regulative force, no offer by Christ of Himself as the friend of daily life, must seem to us to depreciate the power of our salvation or make it appear to us other than the touch of God. There will come to you hours of great exaltation; you will go up to mountain-tops of vision. The Divine Voice will speak to you out of the sun and out of the cloud. Those will come in their time as it is best. But let no experience and no expectation of them make you careless or distrustful when out of commonest things, out of daily tasks, and daily difficulties, and daily joys, and the simplest needs of your nature, and the most domestic familiarities of life, God speaks to you and offers you His Son. Know His voice so truly that you cannot mistake it from whatever unexpected quarter it may speak. Watch for the Divine Light so anxiously that you may never say that it is not divine from whatever humblest quarter it may shine.

VI. 294.

All common things, each day's events,
  That with the hour begin and end,
Our pleasures and our discontents,
  Are rounds by which we may ascend.

LONGFELLOW.

If ye abide in Me, and My words abide in you, ye shall ask what ye will, and it shall be done unto you.—JOHN xv. 7.

CAN he in whom the words of Christ abide pray an unanswered prayer? . . . Can he in whom this word of Christ's abides—"Seek ye first the Kingdom of God and His righteousness"—go on clamoring with miserable mercenary prayers for food and drink, houses and lands, as if they were the first things to seek? Or he in whom this everlasting word of Christ abides—"In this world ye shall have tribulations,"—can you conceive of him as vexing God with querulous supplications to be released from suffering, and not delighting God with holy petitions that he may be brave and patient under it, that he may be purified and made perfect by it? . . . How many times we have complained that our prayer brought no answer, when it was a prayer that we never could have prayed unless we first drove out every word of Christ from its abiding-place within us! Is there a Christian here who can declare before God that he ever prayed to God in perfect submission to Christ's will, in perfect conformity to Christ's words, and got no answer? Not here; not in all the world; not in all the ages!   VI. 305.

> No voice of prayer to Thee can rise,
> But swift as light Thy love replies;
> Not always what we ask, indeed,
> But, O Most Kind! what most we need. . . .
> For bread may nourish less than stone
> If eaten thankless or alone;
> And many a pure, desirèd thing
> Might prove a snare or hide a sting.
>
> HARRIET McEWEN KIMBALL.

Thy will be done.—LUKE xi. 2.

WHAT is it that you ask for when you kneel and pray? Directly, no doubt, it is some special mercy. It is the coming in of your ship; it is the recovery of your friend; it is the opportunity of usefulness which you desire for yourself. But do you want any of those things if God does not see that it is best that you should have them? . . . Is it not His will which is your real, your fundamental, your essential prayer? You must keep that essential prayer very clear, or the special prayer becomes wilful and trivial. You must pray with the great prayer in sight. You must feel the mountains above you while you work upon your little garden. Little by little your special wishes and the eternal will of God will grow in harmony with one another, —all conflict will die away, and the great spiritual landscape from horizon to horizon be but one. That is the prayer of eternity, the prayer of heaven, to which we may come—no one can say how near—on earth:—

V. 121.

> Which brings to God's all-perfect will
>   That trust of His undoubting child,
> Whereby all seeming good and ill
>   Are reconciled.
>
> WHITTIER.

For if the ministration of condemnation be glory, much more doth the ministration of righteousness exceed in glory.—2 COR. iii. 9.

THINK of the minister's necessary relation to God. God is the granary from which he must be immediately fed, the armory from which his weapons must be immediately drawn. . . . . He must sanctify himself that the people may be sanctified through him. . . . Then think of the minister's relation to mankind. Whatever tells upon his people's characters he shares with them. Their temptations and their victories are his. He goes with them up into the heavens and down into the depths. His personal life is multiplied by theirs. What is it to live? To crawl on in the dust, leaving a trail which the next shower hastens to wash away? Is it to breathe the breath of heaven as the tortoise does, and to bask in the sunshine like the lizard? Or is it to touch the eternal forces which are behind everything with one hand, and to lay the other on the quivering needles and the beating hammers of this common life? Is it to deal with God and deal with man? Is it to use their powers to the utmost, and to find ever new power coming into them constantly with their use? If this is life, then there is no man who lives more than the minister; and the generous youth whose cry is, "Let me live while I live," must some day feel the vitality of great service of God and man, and press in through the sacred doors, saying, "Let me, too, be a minister!"

VI. 339.

The spirit of man is the candle of the Lord.
PROV. xx. 27.

[THERE is a] perpetual revelation of God by human life. . . . See how at the very bottom of His existence, as you conceive of it, lie these two thoughts—purpose and righteousness; how absolutely impossible it is to give God any personality except as the fulfilment of the intelligence that plans in love, and the righteousness that lives in duty. Then ask yourself how any knowledge of these qualities—of what they are, of what kind of being they will make in their perfect combination—could exist upon the earth if there were not a human nature here in which they could be uttered, from which they could shine. Only a person can truly utter a person. Only from a character can a character be echoed. You might write it all over the skies that God was just, but it would not burn there. It would be, at best, only a bit of knowledge; never a Gospel; never something which it would gladden the hearts of men to know. That comes only when a human life, capable of a justice like God's, made just by God, glows with His justice in the eyes of men, a candle of the Lord.

II. 6.

As the planets to the sun,
    We would moor our souls to Thee;
Kindle us, All-Heavenly One,
    · Torches of Thy truth to be!

LUCY LARCOM.

Methinks we do as fretful children do,
Leaning their faces on the window-pane
To sigh the glass dim with their own breath's
        stain,
And shut the sky and landscape from their view;
And thus, alas!—since God the Maker drew
A mystic separation 'twixt those twain,
The life beyond us and our souls in pain—
We miss the prospect which we're called unto.
. . . . Be still and strong,
O man, my brother, hold thy sobbing breath,
And keep thy soul's large window pure from
        wrong,
That so, as life's appointment issueth,
Thy vision may be clear to watch, along
The sunset, consummation-lights of death.
ELIZABETH BARRETT BROWNING.

PAUL tells of Christians who "through fear of death are all their lifetime subject to bondage." There are some men and women who haunt their lives and make them cheerless, for fear they will not be able to meet the king of terrors when he comes. Dear friends, learn from your Saviour that no duty reveals itself till we approach it. The duty of death, when you approach it, will light itself up, you may be sure, and seem very easy to your soul. Till then do not trouble yourself about it. To live, and not to die, is your work now. When your time comes the Christ who conquered death will prove Himself its Lord, and pave the narrow river to a sea of glass for you to cross. The work of life is living, and not, as we are so often told, preparing to die, except by living well.   VII. 235.

Whatsoever ye do, do it heartily, as to the Lord.
Col. iii. 23.

AN act of yours is not simply the thing you do: it is the reason why you do it. Why are you selling your goods? If without falsehood you can say, " Because it is my duty, in order that I may maintain my family and serve my generation and honor God by usefulness," then certainly the act opens itself and becomes a church. It is the house of God. It is the gate of heaven. . . . In every act consciously and devoutly done for God's sake, God gives Himself to the soul and feeds it, in the act; not after it and in reward of it, but *in* it.

Seek your life's nourishment in your life's work. Do not think that after you have bought or sold or studied or taught, you will go into your closet and open your Bible, and repair the damage and the loss that your day's life has left you. Do those things certainly, but also insist that your buying or selling or studying or teaching shall itself make you brave, patient, pure and holy! Do not let your occupation pass you by, and leave you only the basest and poorest of its benefits—the money with which it fills your purse. Compel it to give up to you the charity and faith and character and godliness which it has as its heart, which it hides charily, but which it must give to you if you insist upon it and are able to receive it.

IV. 238, 242.

I will lift mine eyes unto the hills, from whence cometh my help.—Ps. cxxi. 1.

I TURN to Jesus, and in all His human life there seems to me nothing more divine than the instinctive and unerring way in which He always reached up to the highest, and refused to be satisfied with any lower help. In the desert the Devil offered Him bread, good wholesome bread. Apparently He could have had it if He would; but he replied, " Man shall not live by bread alone, but by the word of God." . . . On the cross they held up to Him the sponge full of vinegar; but the thirst that was in Him demanded a deeper satisfaction, and He gave His soul to His Father and finished His obedient work. So it was everywhere with him. The souls beside Him found their helps and satisfactions in the superficial things of earth. . . . He could not rest anywhere till He had found God His Father, and laid the burden which was crushing Him into the bosom of the eternal strength and the exhaustless love.

It is your privilege and mine, as children of God, to be satisfied with no help but the help of the highest. When we are content to seek strength or comfort or truth or salvation from any hand short of God's, we are disowning our childhood and dishonoring our Father.

II. 285.

Oh! there is never sorrow of heart
That shall lack a timely end,
If but to God we turn, and ask
Of Him to be our friend.

WORDSWORTH.

What is the chaff to the wheat? saith the Lord.
JER. xxiii. 24.

NEVER be afraid to bring the transcendent mysteries of our faith, Christ's life and death and resurrection, to the help of the humblest and commonest of human wants. There is a sort of preaching which keeps them for the great emergencies, and soothes the common sorrows and rebukes the common sins with lower considerations of economy. Such preaching fails. It neither appeals to the lower nor to the higher perceptions of mankind. It is useful neither as law nor gospel. It is like a river that is frozen too hard to be navigable but not hard enough to bear. Never fear to bring the sublimest motives to the smallest duty, and the most infinite comfort to the smallest trouble. They will prove that they belong there if only the duty and the trouble are real.

IX. 27.

For He who bore all sorrow weighed,
  Nailed to His own, each lesser cross;
He knows the burden on us laid,
  The secret pain, the hidden loss.

Touched with our woes, He lifteth up
  The humblest follower in His train;
He maketh sweet the bitter cup,
  And death itself is blessèd gain.

HARRIET McEWEN KIMBALL.

HOW many of us have said, "I will love God; I ought to, and I will," and so have wrestled and struggled to do what they could not do,—what in their hearts they knew no real reason for doing,—and have miserably failed, and now are satisfying themselves with loveless obedience, or else have left God altogether and tell their hearts that they must forego all such beautiful, hopeless ambitions. Ah, my friend, what you need is to get away round upon the other side of the whole matter. It is not whether you love God but whether God loves you. If He does, and if you can know that He does, then give yourself up totally and unquestioningly to the assurance of that love. Rejoice in it by day and night. Go singing for the joy of it about your work and your play. And as you go singing for joy that God loves you, behold the response is born before you know it, and you are loving God as countless souls have always loved Him, "because He first loved us."

V. 51.

If I Him but have,
  If He be but mine,
If my heart, hence to the grave,
  Ne'er forgets His love divine—
Know I naught of sadness,
Feel I naught but worship, love, and gladness.

GEORGE MACDONALD.

Jesus said unto him, Thou shalt love the Lord thy God . . . with all thy mind.
MATT. xvii. 37.

EVERYWHERE, to think that divine truth lies beyond or away from the intelligence of man, is at once to make divine truth unreal and unpractical, and to condemn the human intelligence to dealing not with the highest, but only with the lowest themes. . . . Love God with all your mind, because your mind, like all the rest of you, belongs to Him, and it is not right that you should give Him only a part to whom belongs the whole. When the procession of your powers goes up joyfully singing to worship in the temple, do not leave the noblest of them all behind to cook the dinner and to tend the house. Give your intelligence to God. Know all that you can know about Him. In spite of all disappointment and weakness, insist on seeing all that you can see now through the glass darkly, so that hereafter you may be ready when the time for seeing face to face shall come!
III. 41, 42.

No religion that does not think is strong. . . . Mysticism, disowning doctrine and depreciating law, asserts that religion belongs to feeling, and that there is no truth but love. . . . The hard theology is bad.   The soft theology is worse. . . . Value no feeling which is not the child of truth and the father of duty.
IX. 243, 244.

OH, how we separate our knowing and our obeying powers, our mental and our moral natures, as if either of them could live without the other! No, the promise that we shall know includes the promise that we shall obey. So it attains its fullest richness.

When we say that, eternity springs into life and lives. No longer a bare doctrine, no longer a great, arid fact, that we shall live forever, but a great, actual reality! Hark, through the atmosphere of that belief can you not hear the music of the activity which fills the streets of the New Jerusalem? I hear the feet hurrying over the glassy pavements, the voices calling to each other in the joy of service, the ringing of the hammers on the anvils where in the fire of the love of God, the perfect obedience of His redeemed is forging His perfect will into the instruments of perfect deeds. . . . You need not live alone, for you may, if you will, know and obey God. You and God, you and God, one system of power knit together in mutual knowledge, and in common standards. That is what Christ claimed you for. . . . Come by Him to the Father, and then live! O Christ, draw us, thy Father's children, to our Father now!

IV. 295.

I need drawing, yea, much drawing.
For unless Thou drawest,
No one comes, no one follows,
Because every one turneth to himself.

THOMAS À KEMPIS.

*Now I know in part ; but then I shall know
even as I am known.*—1 Cor. xiii. 12.

THE more one thinks and studies, the more
he becomes aware how infinite is truth.
. . . Upon the subject which we know best we
are still out at sea. Every time a fellow-man's
finger touches our faith, it makes it rock, and
compels us to feel that, however well anchored
it is, so that it will not drift, it is very far
from being bolted and mortised into the solid
ground. . . . We know this is not good;
yet we very often do not see how it is to be
escaped. The real escape, I think, lies here.
The Christian faith is not primarily a belief in
Christian truth, but a belief in Christ. All
truth which we believe, we believe in and because of Him. We know that though we have
truly taken Him for our Master, He is very
far yet from having told us all that He has to
tell. That knowledge binds us to Him not
merely by what He has already taught us, but
by the far greater truth which He is keeping
for us, which He will give us in His good time.

III. 304, 305.

For veils of hope before Thee drawn,
    For mists that hint the immortal coast
Hid in Thy farthest, faintest dawn,—
    My God, for these I thank Thee most.

Joy, joy! to see, from every shore
    Whereon my step makes pressure fond,
Thy sunrise reddening still before!—
    More light, more love, more life beyond!

Lucy Larcom.

Now we see through a glass darkly, but then face to face.—2 COR. xiii. 12.

It doth not yet appear what we shall be, but we know that when He shall appear, we shall be like Him.—1 JOHN iii. 2.

ALL these words reach forward. They all own a present incompleteness. The soul which uses them is discontented, and lives upon its hope. And when their great fulfilment comes, he who has entered into the joy they promise will look back as from a mountain top, and see all experience till then only as the climbing, shining stairway, so built that along it this complete destiny, this entire life, might be attained.   XII. 21.

Enough that blessings undeserved
  Have marked my erring track;
That wheresoe'er my feet have swerved
  His chastenings turned me back,—

That more and more a Providence
  Of love is understood,
Making the springs of time and sense
  Sweet with eternal good,—

That care and trial seem at last,
  Through memory's sunset air,
Like mountain ranges overpast
  In purple distance fair,—

That all the jarring notes of life
  Seem blending in a psalm,
And all the angles of its strife
  Slow rounding into calm.   WHITTIER.

The Beautiful Gate of the temple.—ACTS iii. 10.

EVERY human life starts in the beautiful mystery of childhood. Through that Beautiful Gate every man comes into the temple. . . . And that sets us to asking whether to the beautiful temple of a mature religious life there is also a beautiful gate. . . . Here are children all among us, and yet we often talk to one another as if nobody under twenty had anything to do with the great things which are of such unspeakable importance after we have come of age. . . . The current idea of the churches, which has only just begun to be dislodged, that adult conversion is the type and intended rule of Christianity, comes largely from the fact that the first preachers had of necessity to be occupied with men who had known nothing of Christianity in their youth. Peter and Paul had to go to grown-up men, and ask them to begin the Christian life. But surely that was not to be the perpetual picture of Christian culture. Christ was too human for that. . . . Christ had been too evidently a child; the Incarnation had too evidently taken all of life into its benediction for the children ever to be wholly counted out.

IV. 128, 129, 130.

The innocence that is so wise,
The trust that dreams of no disguise,
The simple faith in mysteries,—
These still shall in the world survive
So long as God doth children give,
To keep the child in us alive.
SAMUEL LONGFELLOW.

W E hear much in these days of the precocity of childhood. . . . Josephus tells us that once in the siege of Jerusalem this golden gate which we have made the image of childhood, "was seen to be opened of its own accord about the sixth hour of the night." Some thought it was a good omen, "as if God did open to them the gate of happiness." Others thought it was very bad, "as if the gate were open to the advantage of their enemies." So in this critical time of ours, not the least critical sign is this: that the golden gate stands open wide, that childhood is exposed and sensitive to new impressions and ideas. Is it for good or evil? . . . The wider open the gate the better, if only the truth can be poured in. The more receptive the children's life the better, if only they who train the children can thoroughly believe that there is a manly and beautiful religion of which the child is capable, and work with God to bring their children to it. When that conviction takes possession of the Church, then the Church shall indeed have her children in her arms. Then Isaiah's vision of the complete New Jerusalem shall be fulfilled: "Thou shalt call thy walls salvation, and thy gates praise."

IV. 150.

" Beautiful gates are for beautiful things,—
Beautiful thought on beautiful wings,
Beautiful love that heavenward springs."

IN almost every Christian's experience come
times of despondency and gloom, when
there seems to be a depletion of the spiritual
life, when the fountains that used to burst and
sing with water are grown dry, when love is
loveless, and hope hopeless, and enthusiasm so
utterly dead and buried that it is hard to believe that it ever lived.   At such times there is
nothing for us to do but hold with eager hands
to the bare, rocky truths of our religion, as
a shipwrecked man hangs to a strong, rugged
cliff when the great retiring wave and all the
little eddies all together are trying to sweep
him back into the deep. . . . Then, when the
tide turns, and we can hold ourselves lightly
where we once had to hang heavily, when faith
grows easy, and God and Christ and responsibility and eternity are once more the glory and
delight of happy days and peaceful nights,
then certainly there is something new in them,
—a new color, a new warmth. The soul has
caught a new idea of God's love when it has
not only been fed but rescued by Him.

IV. 120.

I know not what the future hath
    Of marvel or surprise,
Assured alone that life and death
    His mercy underlies.

.   .   .   .   .

I know not where His islands lift
    Their fronded palms in air;
I only know I cannot drift
    Beyond His love and care.

WHITTIER.

*And one of them, when he saw that he was
healed, turned back, and fell down on his face at
His feet, giving Him thanks.*

LUKE xvii. 15, 16.

THERE is such a difference between coming
out of sorrow thankful for relief, and
coming out of sorrow full of sympathy with
and trust in Him who has released us. Nine
lepers hurry off to show themselves with their
white skins to the priest. One leper only
waits to cast himself at the feet of Jesus and
worship Him. Tell me, will not those nine
be different from that one if ever a new disease should fall upon them all ?

Let that one leper be the type of the soul
to whom the whole blessedness of a blessing
from Christ has come. Not only the health
but the Healer he delights in. Not only the
salvation but the Saviour is his glory and his
joy. Such souls there are; souls to which all
the deliverances and the educations that have
filled their past lives are precious, not merely
for the safety and the instruction which they
have brought, but far more for the personal
knowledge of the Deliverer and the Teacher
which has been won in them, and in whose
strength the soul looks on and faces all that
the future has to bring without a fear.

II. 333.

Faith sees the future in the past:
Its Saviour is its First and Last.

WE cannot believe in our Christ for ourselves, unless we believe in Him for all the world. The more deeply we believe in Him for ourselves, the more certain we shall be that he is the Saviour of the world. A deeper personal faith, a more complete discipleship, that is what you want. Have that, and the apostleship must come. If there is any part of your life not wholly consecrated to Him, if there is any of His love which you have not appropriated, if there is any undone duty which, as you do it, will open a new door into His heart, if there is any word by speaking which you may the more utterly commit yourself to Him; just as surely as in any of these ways you deepen your own spiritual life and make Jesus more your Saviour, just so surely you will believe in Foreign Missions, and long to tell all men that He is their Saviour too.

IV. 172.

Oh, if our brother's blood cry out at us,
   How shall we meet Thee who hast loved us
      all,—
Thee whom we never loved, not loving him?
The unloving cannot chant with seraphim,
Bear harp of gold or palm victorious,
   Or face the vision beatifical.

                CHRISTINA G. ROSSETTI.

Then came the disciples to Jesus apart, and said, Why could not we cast him out?

MATT. xvii. 9.

IN our story Christ, when He came and found the Disciples helpless before their task, put forth His hand and healed the sick boy with no help of theirs.   But that was an exceptional event. . . .   The great method of His operation when it was thoroughly established was to work through obedient men.   It was Matthew's obedience in the hand of Christ's commandment that saved Matthew. . . .   If any of you are struggling with your sins, I beg you to learn the truth and see it wholly. You cannot cast them out, but if you will give yourself to Him, He can cast them out with you.   Hate your sins for His sake; let His love fill you with love, and then the conquering of your sins by His help shall be in its course one long enthusiasm, and at the end a glorious success.   III. 198, 199.

I could not do without Thee,
   O Saviour of the lost!
Whose precious blood redeemed me,
   At such tremendous cost.
I could not do without Thee;
   I cannot stand alone;
I have no strength or goodness,
   No wisdom of my own.
But Thou, belovèd Saviour,
   Art all in all to me;
And weakness will be power,
   If leaning hard on Thee.

FRANCES R. HAVERGAL.

The good will of Him that dwelt in the bush.
DEUT. xxxiii. 16.

THE identity of God's eternal being stretches under, and gives consistence to, our fragmentary lives.   God's eternity makes our time coherent.   And so it was God in the old bush that made it still visible to Moses across the eventful interval.   He saw that bush when all the other bushes of Egypt had faded out of sight, because that bush was on fire with God. And as Christianity is the most vivid of all religions, with its personally manifested God, there is a more perfect unity in a Christian life than in any other.   It keeps all its parts, and from its consummations looks back with gratitude and love to its beginnings.   The crown that it casts before the throne at last is the same that it felt trembling on its brow in the first ecstatic sense of Christ's forgiveness, and that has been steadily glowing into greater clearness as perfecting love has more and more completely cast out fear.   The feet that go up to God into the mountain, at the end, are the same that first put off their shoes beside the burning bush.   This is why the Christian, more than other men, not merely dares but loves to look back and remember.

II. 40.

Help me to look behind, before,
   To make my past and future form
A bow of promise, meeting o'er
   The darkness of my day of storm.

PHEBE CARY.

"THE good will of Him that dwelt in the bush." . . . In some church-pew, in some closet's privacy, in some stillness or some crowd, years ago the fire came; the common life about you burned with the sudden presence of Divinity; God called you, and you gave yourself to God. I bid you look back and see the mercy that has led you ever since, and strengthen your hope and courage and charity and faith as you remember the long, long good-will of Him that dwelt in the bush. And some of you are standing just by the bush-side still, the shoes off your feet, the voice of God in your ears, lifted up with the desire for the new life of Christ. You are determined to be His, for He has called you. Well, till the end, life here and hereafter will be only the unfolding of this personal love which seems to you so dear and so mysterious now. . . . The mercy which takes you into its bosom at last in heaven, will be still the old familiar good-will of Him that dwelt in the bush.

II. 58.

My soul is melted by that love,
  So tender and so true;
I can but cry: My God and Lord,
  What wilt Thou have me do?

My blessings all come back to me,
  And round about me stand;
Help me to climb their dizzy stairs,
  Until I touch Thy hand!

ALICE CARY.

There is some soul of goodness in things evil,
Would men observingly distil it out.

SHAKESPEARE.

THE sins Christ has forgiven are dead, but they are not gone. If none of the dead go from us, if when death comes a new and finer life begins, and he whom we call dead is with us in sweetest, subtlest portion of his life, with everything of harshness, every disagreement, every power of harm taken out, why may it not be so with our dead sins? It is so, surely! There is a soul in them which lives on still while their body of wickedness has perished—a soul of patience, of watchfulness, of gratitude, and of never-dying love. O my dear friends, we have not done with a sin of ours, we have not finished its history, until, long, long after it has died in the kind forgiveness of the Saviour, we have traced the eternal career of the spirit which its death has liberated into life, giving steadfastness to duty, and charity to friendship, and unutterable tenderness to the love of the Saviour till eternity shall end.

That is what our sins shall be to us forever. They die as sins in forgiveness that they may live forever as the impulses of holiness and the exhaustless fountains of love.

VII. 128.

From rank decay the fairest flowers grow;
From buried springs the sweetest waters flow.

JULIA WOOD.

JUST as a delightful study, into which some dear friend first initiated you, has always over and above its own delightfulness a beauty that comes from your love to him; so the soul that Jesus has made holy lives always in the beauty of holiness, made more exquisite and dear by the loveliness of Christ. Of every earthly grace as well as of the heavenly glory it is true that " the Lamb is the light thereof." Every new attainment which the Christian makes is but an entrance into another mansion which his Saviour has made ready for him. He grows brave, but Christ was brave before him. He enters into self-sacrifice, but Christ leads him with His cross. He finds the home of his soul at last in perfect union with God; but the Godhood is familiar and doubly dear to him because of the Christhood through which he enters it. All virtue, holiness, and truth, throughout the universe, loses the chill of abstractness and glows with the warmth of personal love.

VI. 184.

Love greatens and glorifies
Till God's a glow to the loving eyes
In what was mere earth before.

BROWNING.

Do not I fill heaven and earth? saith the Lord.
JER. xxiii. 28.

From henceforth let no man trouble me, for I bear in my body the marks of the Lord Jesus.
                              GAL. vi. 17.

IN its clumsy, halting way the outer is the record of the inner life. The body is the story of the soul. We bear in our flesh the marks of our masters. . . . "Who is your master?" is the question that includes all questions. If a man tries to push that question aside, he declares that he is his own master. And then he bears in his body the marks of himself; the faded colors and the scars mean only wilfulness and selfishness. But now suppose that life has meant for that man, from the beginning, the claiming of his soul by a higher soul; . . . that the life is Christ's life, uttering His wishes, seeking His purposes, filled and inspired by His love, reckoning its vitality by the degree of conscious and realized sympathy with Him,—and then it will be true that every outward sign in which those inward experiences are recorded will become a mark of the Lord Jesus, a sign of the occupation of the nature by His nature which is what it has meant for this man to live.

II. 357, 358, 359.

Yea, let the fragrant scars abide,
    Love-tokens in Thy stead,
Faint shadows of the spear-pierced side
    And thorn-encompassed head.
                    JOHN HENRY NEWMAN.

No man can serve two masters.—MATT. vi. 24.

SHALL you be God's or the world's? Be both! Not in any low miserable compromise. Not by the effort to serve God and mammon. But by a brave and filial questioning of God that He may tell you just how He wants a child of His to live in this peculiar time and under these peculiar circumstances of yours. There is a type of universal human life in harmony with the best life of all the ages, in tune with the sublimest and finest spiritual music of the universe, in harmony also with the profoundest dictates of your own personal conscience, which you can live in your parlor and your shop; and that life you can reach if you are consecrated to God in your own place and time. If you live that life, the world of the present owns you and claims you and rejoices in you. The most distant life of man looks in on you and recognizes you as a part of itself, and says, "Well done!" Up from your own conscience speaks your self-approval. And God your Father bends His love around you, and out of His blessing feeds you with His strength.   VI. 240.

> Take my life, and let it be
> Consecrated, Lord, to Thee.
>
> Take my will, and make it Thine;
> It shall be no longer mine.
>
> Take myself, and I will be
> Ever, only, all for Thee.
>
> FRANCES R. HAVERGAL.

TO be religious, to be a Christian, means
something accurate and specific. It is
not to be a little stronger than the strongest, a
little wiser than the wisest, a little truer than
the truest. It is something more. It is something different from all. It is to have taken
up a new quality of being, which God only
gives through Jesus Christ, . . . to have become the subject of forces deeper, dealing with
profounder regions of the nature, than were
ever stirred before. . . .

Let a plant try to be a bird forever and it
will forever fail. It may grow to be a very
superior plant, unfold a lordly beauty to the
wondering sun, but between it and the song
and the flight and the nest lies forever the gulf
that separates flower-life from bird-life and
never can be crossed. Let a man try to be a
Christian forever. The struggle may make
him, I believe it will make him, a better man;
but between him and the strength and the
peace and the love yawns forever the gulf that
separates man-life from God-life, and which no
man ever yet crossed save as he stretched out
both his helpless hands to God and felt a hand
too powerful not to trust clasp them and lift
him, whither he knew not, till lo! the gulf was
crossed, and he had entered on the new life
that they live who live in God.

VII. 160.

In Thy presence is fulness of joy.—Ps. xvi. 11.

NOTICE the mysterious personalness with which sin presents itself as a tempter to the hearts of men,—what we usually hear stated as the doctrine of "besetting sins." . . . Why is it that he who is most liable to pride, has such continual incitements to over-weening vanity? Why is it that the poor inebriate, trying to give up his drink, finds the whole world full of beckoning fingers and tempting voices that keep calling back again his dying passions into life? To the light and over-frivolous character all nature shapes itself into a chorus and sings siren songs to scare incipient thoughtfulness away. . . . Does it not seem that we are living in the midst of mysterious forces leagued against our souls,— that our enemy is mysterious, is superhuman? Mysterious and superhuman, then, must be our safety and defence. . . . "We wrestle not against flesh and blood, but against . . . powers, against the rulers of the darkness of this world."

VI. 9, 10, 27.

Michael, the leader of the hosts of God,
Who warred with Satan for the body of him
Whom, living, God had loved! If cherubim
With cherubim contended for one clod
Of human dust, for forty years that trod
The gloomy desert of man's chastisement,
Are there not ministering angels sent
To battle with the devils that roam abroad,
Clutching at living souls? The living, still,
The living, they shall praise Thee!

DINAH MULOCH CRAIK.

When Jacob slept in Bethel, and there dreamed
  Of angels ever climbing and descending
A ladder, whose last height of splendor seemed
  With glory of the Ineffable Presence blend-
    ing, . . .
Foretold they His descent, the Son of God,
  Who humbly clothed Himself in vestments
    mortal,
And so, encumbered with our weakness, trod
  With us the stairway to His Father's portal—
To life whose inner secret none can win
Save by surmounting earthliness and sin ?

Lucy Larcom.

BE sure that you mount up to Christ by gaining His view of yourself, and that you do not drag Him down to yourself by your selfishness, and then you may freely claim Him in your commonest life, and bid Him do, and honor Him for doing, the work which He craves and delights in when He says: "I am among you as He that serveth." . . . I will be studiously on my guard not to mistake the cravings of my nature for the voice of the coming Christ, but I will not silence those cravings of my nature when they welcome the coming Christ,—I will bid them speak, I will listen for God's answer to them, and when Christ does come it shall make the witness of His coming perfectly conclusive and complete that it is not merely in the clouds of heaven, but through the worn and torn avenues of my conscious human necessities, that He comes.

VI. 293.

If I lay waste and wither up with doubt
The blessed fields of heaven where once my
    faith
Possessed itself serenely safe from death;
If I deny the things past finding out;
Or if I orphan my own soul of One
That seemed a Father, and make void the place
Within me where He dwelt in power and grace,
What do I gain by that I have undone?

W. D. HOWELLS.

THERE is a great deal of danger of our forgetting that to believe much, and not to believe little, is the privilege and glory of a full-grown man. There will come times—and upon such a time our lot has fallen—when men are led to sing the praise and glorify the influence of doubt. Assuredly it has its blessings, but while we magnify them we ought never to forget that they are always of the nature of compensation. . . . There do come times when you must cut a tree down to its very roots in order that it may grow up the richer by-and-by; but a whole field of stumps is not the ideal landscape. The forest, with its wealth of glorious foliage, is the true coronation of the earth. . . . Seek faith—as full and rich a faith as you can find. Try to know all you can about God and your own soul. Count every new conviction which is really won a treasure and enrichment of your life.

VII. 319.

Help Thou mine unbelief.—MATT. ix. 24.

YOU say: "Why is it so easy for others to believe, so hard for me?" There is a willing and an unwilling unbelief. Man must not complain that the sun does not shine on him, because he shuts his eyes. If it is unwilling unbelief; if you really want the truth; if you are not afraid to submit to it as soon as you shall see it; . . . then you are not to be pitied. To climb the mountain on its hardest side, where its granite ribs press out most ruggedly, where you must skirt round chasms and clamber down and up ravines,—all this has its compensations. You know the mountain better when you reach its top. It is a realler, a nobler, and so a dearer thing. . . . If you can only keep on bravely, perseveringly, seeking the truth, saying, "I must have it or die;" saying that till you do die; dying at last, if needs be, in the search; then I declare not only that somewhere—here or in a better world—the truth shall come to you, but that, when it comes, the peace and the serenity of it shall be made vital with the energy of your long search. . . . For perfect truthfulness must find the truth at last, or where is God?

IV. 122.

If thou seek for truth, and *do it*,
Not in vain shalt thou pursue it.

If thou seek for truth, and *live it*,
He who is the Truth will give it.

L. M.

That ye may be filled with all the fulness of God.—Ephes. iii. 19.

THE Incarnation, the beginning of the earthly life of Christ, was the fulfilment, the filling full, of a human nature by Divinity. It made the man in whom the miracle occurred absolutely perfect man. It did not make Him something else than man. . . . Whenever He says to men "Follow Me," He is declaring that He is man as they are men, that the peculiar Divinity which filled Him, while it carried humanity to its complete development, had not changed that humanity into something which was no longer human. Can we picture that to ourselves? Is it not just as when the sunlight fills a jewel? The jewel throbs and glows with radiance. All its mysterious nature palpitates and burns with clearness. It opens depths of color which we did not see before. But still it is the jewel's self that we are seeing. The sunlight has made us see what it is, not turned it into something different from what it was. . . . One thing evidently appears; which is that the developing power, which brings the being into which it enters to its best, has essential and natural relations to the being which it develops. The jewel belongs to the light. And this must always be the truth which must underlie all understanding of the Incarnation. Man belongs to God. The human nature belongs to the Divine.

II. 255, 256, 257.

I am come that they might have life, and that they might have it more abundantly.—John x. 10.

That ye, being rooted and grounded in love, may be able . . . to know the love of Christ, which passeth knowledge.—EPHES. iii. 17, 19.

HEAVEN is not only real because His humanity is there, not merely glorious because His greatness is there. It is dear because His love is there—the love which filled His earthly life, the love of the miracle and of the wayside teaching and of the cross. The nearness and the glory might be there and yet Heaven not lay hold of our hearts. We might be well content to stand far off and gaze. We might not want to go there. We might not listen for messages, nor send our feeble voices forth in prayer. But now our Christ is there, our Saviour, what wonder if the earth a thousand times seems dull and wearisome, and always gets its best brightness from that other world in which He is, of which this is the vestibule! . . . What wonder if the hope that He will some day take us to Himself abides calm and constant behind all the transitory hopes of life, which are lighted and go out again and again, while that hope remains always as the deep sky remains behind the coming and the going of the stars!

VII. 301.

Some are resigned to go,—might we such grace
    attain
That we should need our resignation to re-
    main.

RICHARD G. TRENCH.

Lo, I come.—HEB. x. 7.

THE great Christian doctrine of the Atonement tells us that when man fell from holiness to sin, there appeared in the whole universe only one nature which had in itself a fitness to undertake the work of reconciliation and restoral. . . . Then comes the question, When did that fitness of the Christ begin? . . . What if He had borne forever the human element in His Divinity, anointed Christ from all eternity? What if there had been forever a Saviourhood in the Deity, an everlasting readiness which made it always certain that, if ever such a catastrophe as Eden came, such a remedy as Calvary must follow? Does not this deepen all our thought of salvation? Does it not teach us what is meant by " the Lamb slain from the foundation of the world "?

And see how such a truth tallies with all God's ways. This natural body of ours has in itself the fitness for two sets of processes, —the processes of growth and the processes of repair. You keep your arm unbroken, and nature feeds it with continual health; you break that same arm and the same nature beautifully testifies her completeness, which includes the power of the Healer as well as the Supplier. So it is to me a noble thought, that in an everlasting Christhood in the Deity we have from all eternity a provision for the exigency which came at last,—a provision, not temporary and spasmodic, but existing forever, and only called out into operation by the occurrence of the need.

VI. 316, 317.

I am not come to destroy, but to fulfil.
MATT. v. 17.

IT is redemption and fulfilment that Christ comes to bring to man. There is a true humanity which is to be restored, and all whose unattained possibilities are to be filled out. . . . Man is a child of God, for whom his Father's house is waiting. The whole creation is groaning and travailing until man shall be complete.

As soon as we understand all this, then what a great, clear thing salvation becomes. Its one idea is health. Not rescue from suffering, not plucking out of fire, not deportation to some strange, beautiful region where the winds blow with other influences and the skies drop with other dews, not the enchaining of the spirit with some unreal celestial spell, but health,—the cool, calm vigor of the normal human life; the making of the man to be himself; the calling up out of the depths of his being and the filling with vitality of that self which is truly he,—this is salvation!

V. 7, 9.

In Christ I touch the hand of God,
  From His pure height reached down,
By blessed ways before untrod
  To lift us to our crown;
Victory that only perfect is
Through loving sacrifice, like His.

LUCY LARCOM.

He answered and said, Who is He, Lord, that I might believe on Him? And Jesus saith unto him, Thou hast both seen Him, and it is He that talketh with thee.—JOHN ix. 36, 37.

HOW touching in this special story is the allusion to the light which the Lord had given only that day!

Jesus reminds him of the lower mercy that He may assure him of the higher. . . . It is as the Saviour of the past life that He offers Himself for the future.

There have been great creative moments in the history of the world, as all history and science seem to show,—moments when after long, silent preparations, suddenly the old order broke and a new, as if by magic, came into its place. So it has been in physical and social and political history. But in neither was there any magic. The same force which was in the last changing conviction had been in all the preparation. The flower is but the ripening of the same juices that built the stem. So it is with conversion to the very last. The Christ who in eternity opens the last concealment, and lays His comfort and life close to the deepest needs of the poor, needy, human heart, is the same Christ that first laid hands upon the blind eyes, and made them see the sky and flowers.

V. 213, 214.

No stranger, but the Friend unseen,
Who from the first thy Friend hath been.

WHAT will heaven be ? . . . I find manifold fitness in the answer that tells us it shall be " a sea of glass mingled with fire." Heaven will not be pure stagnation, not idleness, not any mere luxurious dreaming over the spiritual repose that has been safely and forever won; but active, tireless, earnest work; fresh, live enthusiasm for the high labors which eternity will offer. These vivid inspirations will play through our deep repose and make it more mighty in the service of God than any feverish and unsatisfied toil of earth l.s ever been. The sea of glass will be mingled with fire.

Here too we have the type and standard of that heavenliness of character which ought to be ripening in all of us now, as we are getting ready for that spiritual life. . . . Surely, there is a very high and happy life conceivable, which very few of us attain, yet which our religion evidently intends for all of us. Calm and active; peaceful and yet thoroughly alive; resting always upon truth, but never sleeping on it for a moment; working always intensely, but serene and certain of results, never driven crazy by our work; grounded and settled, yet always moving forward in still but sure progress; always secure, yet always alert, —glass mingled with fire.   IV. 125, 126.

I dare not pray to Thee to give
  The heaven which shall appear;
My cry is: Help me Thou to live
  Within the heaven that's here!

ALICE CARY.

"NO man hath seen God at any time," said Jesus, but [beyond death] the power of the new life is to be that "we shall see Him as He is." It is our privilege to dwell upon the untold, unguessed glory of the world that is to come. It is a poor economy of spiritual motive which tries to make heaven real by taking out of it all thought of inexpressible and new delight, and bringing it down to the tame repetition of the scenes and ways of earth. But no one listens to the talk or reads the books which are written about heaven, without feeling that the glory and delight which they speak of are far too completely separated in kind from any which this world's experience has taught us how to value. It ought not to be so. The highest, truest thought of heaven which man can have is of the full completion of those processes whose beginning he has witnessed here,—their completion into degrees of perfectness as yet inconceivable, but still one in kind with what he is aware of now.

V. 303.

Our Past had held our Future, like a rose
That may not yet its perfect self disclose,
　　Lest angry winds should scatter and molest;
So, shut within this narrow bud, its woes
　　Were but the crumpled leaves too closely
　　　　pressed,
And all its loveliness did but enclose
　　The germ of after beauty—now a Guest,
But soon to be a Dweller.

DORA GREENWELL.

Whosoever exalteth himself shall be abased; and he that humbleth himself shall be exalted.
                    LUKE xiv. 11.

SET a man to work, and if he were great enough to be humble at all, his work would bring him to humility. He would be brought face to face with facts. He would measure himself against the eternal pillars of the universe. He would learn the blessed lesson of his own littleness in the way in which it is always learnt most blessedly, by learning the largeness of larger things. And all this, which the ordinary occupations of life do for our ordinary powers, Christianity, with the work that it furnishes for our affections and our hopes, does for the higher parts of us.

It seems to come to this, that Christianity is the religion of the broadest truthfulness. It does not set men at any work of mere resolution, saying, "Come, now, let us be humble." That would but multiply the endless specimens of useless self-mortification. But true Christianity puts men face to face with the humbling facts, the great realities, and then humility comes upon the soul, as darkness comes on the face of the earth, not because the earth has made up its mind to be dark, but because it has rolled into the great shadow.   I. 350, 351.

> " His state
> Is kingly.   Thousands at his bidding speed
> And post o'er land and ocean without rest."

TO live in such a universe of obedient activity, to feel its movement, to be sensible of its gloriousness, and yet to make no active part of it would be dreadful.   Milton felt this, and in his last great line was compelled to pierce down to the deepest truth about the matter, and assert that he, too, even in his blindness, had share in the obedience of the untiring worlds:

> " They also serve who only stand and wait."

Here is the deepest reason, here is the reasonable glory of that which is perpetually exalted and belauded in cheap and superficial ways—the excellence of work, the glory of activity.   Many of our familiar human instincts live and act by deeper powers than they know.   That which is really the noble, the divine element in the perpetual activity of man is the sympathy of the obedient universe. The circling stars, the flowing rivers, the growing trees, the whirling atoms, the rushing winds,—all things are in obedient action, doing the will of God.   It is the healthy impulse of any true man who finds himself in this active world to share in its activity.   It is the healthy shame of any true man to find himself left out, having no part in that obedience which keeps all life alive.

V. 265.

A MERICA was discovered in the fulness of time. First there had to come the long education of the world which made possible the energy and patience and skill that achieved the task. And then we can see how it had to be kept until the pressure of the crowded life of the old world called for another continent to work out to greater issues the problem of human history. Then the great curtain was withdrawn—then, in the fulness of time.

So let men work away with their statistics and their averages and prove how beautifully under all our life there run the great necessities of God. . . . The curse or blessing *causeless* cannot come. And into the clear light of all such speculations we may look to get a clearer and more loving understanding of our God. I see Him now as He stands holding back the inventions and discoveries and institutions that are to make the next generation glorious—more glorious than ours,—holding them back until their time is full. The home of the future, the republic of the future, the Church of the future—they must be built upon the present, and they must wait until their foundations shall be laid.

VII. 57, 60.

God's gracious purpose comes to fulfilment
  Never too soon and never too late;
Bright o'er the clouded arch of His future
  Shineth the legend: *Trust thou and wait.*

J. L. M. W.

WHO are the men who have succeeded in the best way,—who have done good work while they lived, and have left their lives like monuments for the inspiration of mankind? They are the men who have . . . questioned the circumstances in which they found themselves, and asked what was the best thing which any man in just those circumstances might set himself to do? These are the men before whom there rises by-and-by a dream, which later gathers itself into a hope, and at last solidifies into an achievement. Columbus discovers America because he is Columbus, and because the study of geography and the enterprise of men have reached just this point. Luther kindles the Reformation because he is Luther, and because the dry wood of the papacy has come to just the right inflammability. You and I, who are not Luthers nor Columbuses, but simply, by the grace of God, earnest, true-hearted men, conceive some purpose for our lives and keep it clear before us, praying that we may not die before we do it; and at last doing it before we die, because we are we, and because the world in which we live is just the world it is.

IV. 322.

Such faith, O God, our souls sustain,
Free, true, and calm, in joy and pain,
That even by our fidelity
Thy Kingdom may the nearer be!

SAMUEL LONGFELLOW.

'Tis sorrow builds the shining ladder up,
Whose golden rounds are our calamities,
Whereon our firm feet planting, nearer God
The spirit climbs, and hath its eyes unsealed.

JAMES RUSSELL LOWELL.

THE final purpose of all consolation and help is revelation. The reason why we are led into trouble and out again is not merely that we may value happiness the more from having lost it once and found it again, but that we may know something which we could not know except by that teaching, that we may bear upon our nature some impress which could not have been stamped except on natures just so softened to receive it.   II. 272.

Great truths are greatly won.   Not found by
        chance,
    Nor wafted on the breath of summer dream,
But grasped in the great struggle of the soul,
    Hard buffeting with adverse wind and
        stream;

And in the day of conflict, fear and grief,
    When the strong hand of God, put forth in
        might,
Ploughs up the subsoil of the stagnant heart,
    And brings the imprisoned truth-seed to the
        light.

Wrung from the troubled spirit, in hard hours
    Of weakness, solitude, perchance of pain,
Truth springs, like harvest from the well-
        ploughed field,
And the soul feels it has not wept in vain.

HORATIUS BONAR.

*Because thou hast kept the word of My patience,
I also will keep thee from the hour of temptation.*

REV. iii. 10.

TAKE the man whose life has known be-reavement, who has passed sometime through those days and nights which I may not try to describe to you, but which come up to so many of you as I say the old word, death. Days and nights when he watched the slow untwisting of some silver cord on which his very life was hung, or suddenly felt the golden bowl dashed down and broken of which his very life had drank. The first shock became dulled. The first agony grew calm. The lips subsided into serenity. But was there not something in him that made him greater and purer and richer than of old; something that let any one see who watched the change, that it was " better to have loved and lost than never to have loved at all " ? A whole new quality, that rich quality which the Bible calls by its large word " patience," the power of his trial, was in his new serenity, until he died.

IV. 114.

Grant us, O Lord, that patience and that faith:
　Faith's patience imperturbable in Thee,
　Hope's patience till the long-drawn shad-
　　ows flee,
Love's patience unresentful of all scathe.

CHRISTINA G. ROSSETTI.

THE soul which God is training in solitude thinks its life wasted because it is cut off from society, and the soul that God keeps in the very midst of its fellows sighs for the joy and culture of being alone.

If we could only know that in its time only is any Christian mood or condition beautiful, and that God only knows its time! When the day is over the stars will come, and then it is good to see them; but to see them before that, in the sunlight, you must go, men say, down to the bottom of a well, where you do not belong, which is unnatural and unhealthy. When we have done with earth the heaven will come; and, till that, only such heaven— and it is not a little—as is possible upon the dear old earth.

IV. 257.

What Thou wilt, O Father, give!
All is gain that I receive. . . .
Let the lowliest task be mine,
Grateful, so the work be Thine;
Let me find the humblest place
In the shadow of Thy grace. . . .
Clothe with life the weak intent,
Let me be the thing I meant;
Let me find in Thy employ
Peace that dearer is than joy;
Out of self to love be led
And to heaven acclimated,
Until all things sweet and good
Seem my natural habitude.

WHITTIER.

In everything ye are enriched by Him.
                                    1 COR. i. 4.

From Thee is all that soothes the life of man,
His high endeavors and his glad success,
His strength to suffer and his will to serve.
But O Thou sovereign Giver of all good,
Thou art, of all Thy gifts, Thyself the
        crown;—
Give what Thou canst, without Thee we are
        poor,
And with Thee rich, take what Thou wilt
        away.   COWPER.

THE knowledge of God lies behind everything, behind all knowledge, all skill, all
life.   That is the sum of the whole matter.
And then comes the great truth . . . that it is
only by the experiences of the soul, only by
penitence for sin, only by patient struggle
after holiness, only by trust, by hope, by love,
does God make Himself known to man. . . .
As the man becomes more pure, more peni-
tent, more sensitive to the least touch of sin,
more passionately eager to be good, so does
he grow for ever more and more sure of God.
And to him, thus growing ever surer of God,
the world he lives in becomes clothed with an
ever diviner light. . . .

Of heaven it is written that " the Lord God
Almighty and the Lamb are the light thereof."
This part of heaven at least may be begun below.   Not merely the earth we live in, but our
own especial life—our work, our study, our
daily toil—may live already in the light of
God.   III. 110.

Luke, the beloved physician.—COL. iv. 14.

OF Luke alone it would appear as if he continued to do as a Christian the same thing which he had done before.   In him alone we see what since his time has been the natural and normal type of Christian life,—the inspiration of a definite old occupation by a new spiritual power, so that it continued to be exercised, and showed its genuine capacity, and fulfilled its true ideal.

Luke must have gone among his patients saying, "I do this by the faith of the Son of God."   Tell me, when he could say that, was there no holier sacredness in the finger which he laid on the sick man's pulse?   Was there no truer sense of sympathy with the men whom he saw on every side of him engaged in other works than his?

Not by deserting your profession but by deepening it, by seeking a new life under it, by praying for and never resting satisfied until you find regeneration,—the new life lived by the faith of the Son of God; so only can your life of trade or art or profession be redeemed; so only can it become both for you and for the world a blessed thing.   The necessary labors which the nature of man and his relations to this earth demand, all done by men full of the love of God, and each using to its best the special faculty that is in him,—the world needs no other millennium than that.

V. 219, 224, 227.

*And Balak said unto him, Come, I pray thee,
unto another place. . . . Thou shalt see but the
utmost part of them, and shalt not see them all:
and curse me them from thence.*

NUMB. xxiii. 13.

THERE are parts of it [life] and aspects of it
which, if they were all, would make existence an accursed thing. "Come," says the
pessimist, "you shall not see the whole. I will
set you where you shall only see a part, and
curse me it from thence." There is where
pessimism is made. The man who sees the
whole of life must be an optimist. I know
dark points of view, grim gloomy crags of
moral vision, hideous observatories on which
if a man stands he can see nothing but the
dreadful side of life, its wretchedness, its disappointment, its distress, its reckless, wanton,
defiant sin. I can see gathered on those hor-
rible observation points the despisers, the re-
vilers, the cursers of our human life. I know
that if I went up there and stood by their side,
my tongue would curse like theirs. But there
I will not go. If there be any point whence
I can see it all, however dimly, through whatever clouds, there I will go. So will I keep
my faith that life is good, and work with what
strength I can against its evils, knowing that
I work in hope. VI. 212.

"With patient step thy path of duty run:
  God nothing does or suffers to be done,
  But thou thyself would'st do it, didst thou see
  The end of all events as well as He."

Pray without ceasing.—2 THESS. v. 17.

PRAYER involves far more than we ordinarily think,—a certain necessary relation between the soul and God. The condition of prayer is personal; it looks to character. How this rebukes our ordinary slipshod notions of what it is to pray! God's mercy-seat is no mere stall set by the vulgar roadside, where every careless passer-by may put an easy hand out to snatch any glittering blessing that catches his eye. It stands in the holiest of holies. We can come to it only through veils and by altars of purification. To enter into it, we must enter into God.

VI. 308.

O Infinite of joy and light,
  Wherewith we are surrounded,
We lift our spirits to Thy height
  Unfathomed and unbounded:
Thy greatness drowns our petty cares,
Thy heaven is in us, unawares.

O Infinite of Righteousness,
  Breath of our inmost being!
Thy purity will cleanse and bless
  The soul from evil fleeing:
We hide our sin-stained hearts in Thee,
And pray, " As Thou art, let us be! "

LUCY LARCOM.

YOU cry, "O Lord, solve me this problem!" and the solution does not come. "What! must I walk in darkness?" your poor soul cries out; and then He comes and takes your hand and says, "He that followeth Me shall not walk in darkness, but shall have the Light of Life." In place of the answer to your prayer comes He to whom you prayed. You have not got the solution of your problem; it still floats in doubt. You have not got the sure prophecy of the future; it is hid behind the wavering and trembling veil. You have not got the brother's dear presence for whose life you cried and wrestled; he is walking beside the river of Life in the new Light of Heaven. You have not got what you prayed for, but you have got God! You have the source, the fountain, the sun! You have taken hold of the essential meaning and essence of all these things for which you prayed, in taking hold of Him to whom you prayed. In His silence you have pressed back to Him. . . . Not in the word He speaks but in the word He is, you have found your reply.

V. 132.

Reach downward to the sunless days,
　Wherein our guides are blind as we,
And faith is small and hope delays,—
Take Thou the hands of prayer we raise,
　And let us feel the light of Thee!

WHITTIER.

WHAT man goes bravely and faithfully through doubt and does not bring out a soul to which truth seems to be infinitely precious, and the human soul the most mysterious, sacred thing in the world? Out of the union of these two persuasions has come the prophetship of this life which now you cannot look at without seeing the infinite behind it made clear by it.

Surely, if we believe this, then the way in which God lets His children encounter great, and sometimes terrible, experiences is not entirely inexplicable. Surely if these souls which are now deep in sorrow, or are being cast up and down and back and forth in doubt, are being thus annealed and purified that they may come to be revealers, mediators between God and their fellow-men, then into our wonder at the existence of doubt and sorrow in God's world there comes a little ray of light. Who would not bear anything that could refine his life into fitness for such a privilege as that?

IV. 15.

> Happy they who learn from crosses,
>   Changeful clouds and fears,
> Life may richer be for losses,
>   Joyfuller for tears,
> Faith by doubts be clearer made—
> Stronger doubting souls to aid.
>
> JULIA WOOD.

Though our outward man perish, yet the inward man is renewed day by day.—2 COR. iv. 16.

IT is hard for us to imagine how flat and shallow human life would be if there were taken out of it this constant element—the coming up of the spiritual life where the physical life has failed. A man who never knew an ache or a pain comes to a break in health, from which he can look out on nothing but years of sickness ; and then the soul within him . . . claims its independence and supremacy, and stands strong in the midst of weakness, calm in the very centre of the turmoil and panic of the aching body. The temper of the fickle people changes, and the favorite of yesterday becomes the victim of to-day; but in his martyrdom he sees for the first time the full value of the truth he dies for, and thanks the flames that have lighted up its preciousness. . . . By this revelation of the spiritual through the broken physical life other men may learn its value. This is what makes the sick-rooms and the martyr-fires reasonable. In them has been made manifest by suffering that the soul is really more than the body, that the soul can triumph when the body has nothing left but disease and misery.

I. 11.

Most gladly, therefore, will I rest in my infirmities, that the power of Christ may rest upon me.—2 COR. xii. 9.

Arise, take up thy bed, and go into thine house.
MATT. ix. 6.

And I saw as it were a sea of glass mingled with fire.—REV. xv. 2.

HOW does the fire get into the sea of glass ? . . . It is repose mingled with struggle . . . calmness still pervaded by the discipline through which it has been reached. . . . You may go through the crowded streets of heaven, asking each saint how he came there, and you will look in vain everywhere for a man morally and spiritually strong, whose strength did not come to him in struggle. . . . There is no exception anywhere. Every poor soul that the Lord heals goes up the street like the man at Capernaum, carrying its bed upon its back, the trophy of its conquered palsy. There are no glassy seas which will really bear the weight of strong men but those that have the fiery mingling. All others are counterfeits, and crack or break. IV. 112, 119, 120.

Dust as we are, the immortal spirit grows
Like harmony in music: there is a dark,
Inscrutable workmanship that reconciles
Discordant elements, makes them cling to-
    gether
In one society. How strange that all
The terrors, pains, and early miseries,
Regrets, vexations, lassitudes interfused
Within my mind, should e'er have borne a part,
And that a needful part, in making up
The calm existence that is mine when I
Am worthy of myself. Praise to the end!
Thanks to the means! WORDSWORTH.

THIS time of ours, these men of ours, are marked by a singular depth of personal experience. The personal emotions, the anxieties with regard to personal conditions, are very intense. It is a time of much morbidness, and so I think that the danger under which men always labor, of letting the universe take the color of the windows of their own life through which they look at it, was never so dangerous as to-day. More men to-day think the world is wretched because they are sad and bewildered, than would have transferred their own conditions to the outside universe in less introspective and self-conscious times. The simplest men in the simplest ages, when they were in sorrow, opened their windows inward to let the world's sunlight in. The elaborate and subtle men in the elaborate and subtle ages, in their sorrow, open their windows outward and darken the bright world with their darkness. And among such men, in such an age, we live.

II. 157, 158.

We make the light through which we see
　The light, and make the dark:
To hear the lark sing, we must be
　At heaven's gate with the lark.

ALICE CARY.

Our destiny, our being's heart and home,
Is with eternity, and only there.
WORDSWORTH.

THE history of man bears witness, that man, though himself finite, demands infinity to deal with and to rest upon; he claims to have relations with the infinite. That fact is borne testimony to by all the ages; that fact is the perpetual witness of the consciousness in man's heart that he is the child of God. The child may be reminded every moment of his limitations and his youth, and yet he always mounts up to claim the largeness of his father's life for himself. And so man, the more you make him feel his finiteness, so much the more obstinately will he insist on his right to a potential possession of the infinite. The power of adoring love of which he is distinctly conscious, brings him assurance that there is a being worthy of such love.

III. 120, 121.

Into the heaven of Thy heart, O God,
I lift up my life like a flower;
Thy light is deep, and Thy love is broad,
And I am not the child of an hour.
LUCY LARCOM.

Behold, as thou passest through things mortal,
And amidst creatures visible,
Seeking to be contented with them,
Thou losest better things.
Thou separatest thyself from the Sovereign
    Good when thou doest this,
And turnest away from the true and blessed
    life which is eternal.

THOMAS À KEMPIS.

HAVE you ever stood in the midst of the world of fashion and marvelled how it was possible that men and women should care, as those around you seemed to care, about the little conventionalities which made the scenery and the problems of its life ? . . . There is a noble economy of the deepest life. . . . The people of Nazareth wanted to stone Christ, and He quietly passed away and left them with their stones in their hands; but the cross demanded Him, and He went up to the terrible experience with a soul consecrated to endure it all, and spared Himself not one blow of the scourge upon the shoulders, and not one piercing of the nails into the hands and feet. He knew what was worth while; and He knew that because He was one with God, the Son of God could not count the great little nor the little great. That was the secret of His perfect life.

V. 247, 248, 251.

And when it was day, He called unto Him His disciples, and of them He chose twelve, whom He also named Apostles.—LUKE vi. 13.

THINK what they must have been before they knew their master. The open life of free and thoughtless young men they must have lived, easily making friends, easily entering into everybody's superficial interests because they had only superficial feelings of their own, liking to be liked, and full of ready sympathies. Then they met Jesus. They were drawn away to Him. By Him they were drawn in upon themselves. To know Him and their own deeper lives in Him, became their longing. . . . Their lives were folded in upon themselves, and upon Him who was at the centre of each. But by-and-by a new power began to work at the unfolded heart. He who had drawn them in upon Himself began to send them abroad. Another kind of love for their old friends, and all the world whom those friends represented, came to them. They began to be seen again upon the streets. Only now they are telling every one of the new life. They have been drawn in from the world upon Christ, that He might send them out, full of Himself, into the world.   IV. 159.

   And that Thou sayest " Go! "
Our hearts are glad, for he is still Thy friend
And best beloved of all, whom Thou dost send
   The farthest from Thee; this Thy servants
     know:
Oh, send by whom Thou wilt, for they are blest
Who go Thy errands.   DORA GREENWELL.

If they drink any deadly thing, it shall not hurt them ; they shall lay hands on the sick, and they shall recover.—MARK xvi. 19.

IS that a prize ? Is it wages which is offered for a certain meritorious act which is called faith ? Not so, surely! It is a consequence. It is a necessity. Safety and helpfulness. These come out of the full life of Christ in the soul of man as the inevitable fruits. Safety, so that what hurts other men shall not hurt him. Helpfulness, so that his brethren about him shall live by his life. . . . It is by life, by full, vigorous, emphatic existence that men are safe in this world, and that they save other men from death. I glory in such a statement as that. It makes my Bible shine. Men everywhere are trying to be safe by stifling life; by living just as low as possible. Men everywhere are trying not to do one another harm, trying to spare each other's souls by tender petting, by guarding them against any vigorous contact with life and thought. The Bible comes glowing with protest. " Not so," it says. " Only by the fulness of life does safety come. Only by the power of contact with life are sick and helpless souls made whole. None but the live man saves himself or quickens the dead to life; saves himself or saves his neighbor."

IV. 337.

Light is light which radiates,
Blood is blood which circulates,
Life is life which generates.

EMERSON.

Hold hard, hope hard, in the subtle thing
That's spirit; though cloistered fast, soar free.
BROWNING.

I THINK there never was a materialist so complete that he did not realize that the great mass of men were not materialists, but believed in spiritual forces and longed for spiritual companies. He might think the spiritual tendency the wildest of delusions, but he could not doubt its prevalence. How could he? Here is the whole earth full of it. Language is all shaped upon it. Thought is all saturated with it. In the most imposing and the most vulgar methods, by solemn oracles and rocking tables, men have been always trying to put themselves into communication with the spiritual world and to get counsel and help from within the veil. And if we hear the cry from one another, how much more God hears it, . . . and has prepared a way of aid. The power of the Holy Ghost!—an everlasting spiritual presence among men. What but that is the thing we want? That is what the old oracles were dreaming of, what the modern spiritualists are fumbling after. The power of the Holy Ghost . . . that is God's one great response to the unconscious need of spiritual guidance which He hears crying out of the deep heart of every man.   II. 105.

Heavenly things my soul hath seen,—
    Things the Holy Spirit shows,—
Things on which the heart can lean
    When the flesh has no repose.
ANNA L. WARING.

*In everything by prayer and supplication . . .
let your requests be made known unto God.*

PHIL. iv. 6.

TRUE, the most earnest Christian may err about the will of God. He may pray for sunshine when it is the will of God that it should rain. He may ask for comfort when it is God's will that he should suffer. But this can only come in superficial things. In the one central thing of all—his own spiritual life—he cannot err. He knows that "this is the will of God, even his sanctification." He may cry out for that with perfect certainty; and for all other things, if he prays as every Christian ought, submitting his prayer to God's revision, "Nevertheless, not my will, but Thine be done;" then, whether the special blessing that he asked is sent or not, the larger petition with which he covered in and included his lesser one is surely answered. The thing he really "willed" is "done unto him."

VI. 305.

"Not as I will": the sound grows sweet
Each time my lips the words repeat. . .
"Not as I will," because the One
Who loved us first and best has gone
Before us on the road, and still
For us must all His love fulfil
   "Not as we will."

HELEN HUNT JACKSON.

The riches of the glory of His inheritance in the saints.—EPHES. i. 18.

I AM sure that the world is a better place for you and me to live in to-day, not merely for the hundred great pattern lives which have passed into the heavens and which we call still by their names, but far more for the countless, nameless multitude of men and women who have wrought into the very substance of the earth, where at last they lay their bodies in unnoticed graves, the great, first, simplest words of God—that man was sacred, that duty was possible, that self-sacrifice was sweet, and that love for one's brother was the crown of life.   And you ought not to be satisfied until you find yourself able to feel that the hope of doing something by your living to make the world in a real, although an unappreciable, degree more full of these words for the men who are to follow us, is the noblest and most inspiring promise which can be set before your soul.

VI. 268.

For he who blesses most is blest,
  And God and man shall own his worth
Who toils to leave as his bequest
  An added beauty to the earth.

WHITTIER.

WE have all stood upon the margin which was the farthest which feet untransfigured by death might reach, and sent some beloved soul into the unknown world. Where have we sent it? To God, we say, bowing our heads with resignation. But is there no bleakness, no forlornness in our answer? God is so far off! However loving, kind, or wise, He is all God; the child we sent Him was all man in his fresh, genuine humanity. But what if there be a humanity in God to which they go? What if, since it went out from us, that human nature, made first in the image of Christ the human, has touched again that perfect nature out of which it sprang and finds itself at home? Yes, let me set this Christ eternally in the midst of the other world, and then the human soul that goes there goes to its own. It meets no strangeness on the other shore. . . . The child is gathered into the arms of a fatherhood and knows no strangeness or surprise. The brother clasps hands with a newer and more trusty brotherhood. . . . They go to Jesus and rest in Him, and wait for us till our humanity, made perfect too by death, shall find its place beside them.

VI. 325.

Praise God the Shepherd *is* so sweet!
Praise God the Country *is* so fair!
We could not hold them from His feet;
We can but haste to meet them there.

B. M.

Who, passing through the valley of Baca, make it a well.—Ps. lxxxiv. 6.

IN man, the user, rests the real nature of the things he uses. They have no invariable, fixed nature apart from him.

Now, let this great user, man, this one moral force, be called upon to go down into the vale of misery. He finds there all the circumstances of suffering—poverty, sickness, bereavement, sin itself; what then? these are things, and he is man. Let him rule them, not be ruled by them. Let him take down there a religious, trustful nature, a pious, cheerful heart, and there is more promised him than just that his cheerful piety shall support him through; he shall exercise his human right of ruling and using these, and shall come out with a more perfect joy and certain faith than he carried in. He shall not come out half-dead with thirst, just able to drag himself up to the fountain at the end, but it shall be as David so beautifully says: " He shall drink of the brook in the way, therefore shall he lift up his head."

VI. 28.

O Lord, of good the fountain free,
  Close by our hard day's journeying,
  Be Thou the all-sufficing spring,
And hourly let us drink of Thee!

Susan Coolidge.

When no low thoughts of self intrude,
  Angels adjust our rights;
But love that seeks its selfish good
  Dies in its own delights.

How much we take, how little give!
  Yet every life is meant
To help all lives; each man should live
  For all men's betterment.

ALICE CARY.

MEN think that they can be safe without being helpful, and thence come all the selfish notions of salvation.   Merely to crawl through life with face and mouth so bandaged up with caution that the foul air of life cannot affect us; merely to strike out from the wreck of a fallen world and swim ashore, shaking off all the drowning men who clutch at us in the wild water, and leaving the screaming wretches to their fate,—the man who seeks salvation so, finds at last to his disappointment and dismay that he is not saved.   It is not the hands that catch us and hold on to us, it is the hands of helpless men which we shake off in our selfishness that drag us down.   IV. 347.

Wherever upward—even the lowest round—
  Man by a hand's help lifts his feebler
      brother,
There is the house of God, and holy ground:
  The gate of heaven is Love; there is none
      other.
When generous act blooms from unselfish
      thought,
The Lord is with us, though we know it not.

LUCY LARCOM.

IT is not only the suffering in life that needs to be spoken to and helped. There is something else, I think, that is almost more exhausting than suffering in its constant wearing pressure upon the hearts of men. It is that feeling of the insignificance of life that often grows so hard to bear, . . . the wonder whether it means anything, the utter loss of any insight into what it means—this work of living. . . . Who can speak to and dispel this spectre? Who can tell us with authority that life has a meaning, and make us see it and rejoice to live for it? Who but the gospel of reconciliation? If *that* is true, if all these heavenly forces are at work upon our life, if all this watchful interest hovers over what we are doing, if we may really go on and be the children of God, where is there any insignificant detail? Who can help feeling *purpose* run like life-blood through the half-dried veins of his discouragement? How life lifts itself up with interest and dignity when it really becomes the culture of God's redeemed children for their Father's house!

VII. 107.

I hear from all-wards, allwise understand,
The great bird Purpose bears me 'twixt her
    wings,
And I am one of all the kinsmen things
That e'er my Father fathered. Oh, to me
All questions solve in this tranquillity!

SIDNEY LANIER.

GREAT is the power of a life which knows that its highest experiences are its truest experiences, that it is most itself when it is at its best. For it each high achievement, each splendid vision, is a sign and token of the whole nature's possibility. What a piece of the man was for that shining instant, it is the duty of the whole man to be always. . . . Strive for your best, that there you may find your most distinctive life. We cannot dream of what interest the world will have when every being in its human multitude shall shine with his own light and color, and be the child of God which it is possible for him to be,— which he has ever been in the true home-land of his Father's thought.

The hope of the world is in the ever richer naturalness of the highest life.

V. 21, 22, 23.

Upward the soul forever turns her eyes;
The next hour always shames the hour before;
One beauty, at its highest, prophesies
That by whose side it shall seem mean and
    poor.
No Godlike thing knows aught of less and less,
But widens to the boundless perfectness.

JAMES RUSSELL LOWELL.

For we wrestle not against flesh and blood, but against principalities, against powers, against the rulers of the darkness of this world.

EPHES. vi. 12.

LIFE is a battle. . . . The merchant is fighting with the competition of his brethren. The legislator is fighting with the barbarous tendencies which still haunt the most civilized societies. The philanthropists are fighting with abuses and ignorance and cruelty. And everywhere man, hopefully or hopelessly, is fighting with what he calls his fate,—the general aggregate of things about him which seems set to keep him down and to impede his way. The world is full of all these ideas of battle. And then right into the midst of them steps Paul, with his clear, ringing Christian word, " What are you fighting with ? Do you ask that ? " he says. " Lo, I can tell you. You are fighting with great evil principles and powers. . . . The rivalry of men, imperfect institutions, cruel habits,— all those are ugly enemies, but the real enemy is Badness itself. The real fight is with that."

VI. 71, 72, 73.

But shall I shun the sacred fight
  Which good maintains with ill ?
No: strong in my Redeemer's might,
  Be mine to wrestle still.
Here only, in this strife,
  Can I His soldier be;
Here only spend or lose a life
  For Him who died for me.

J. CONDER.

And to keep himself unspotted from the world.
JAMES i. 27.

WE set out for the battle in the morning strong and clean. By and by we catch a moment in the lull of the struggle to look down upon ourselves, and how tired and how covered with dust and blood we are. How long back our first purity seems—how long the day seems sometimes—how long since we began to live. You know what stains are on your lives. Each of us knows, every man and woman. They burn to our eyes, even if no neighbor sees them. They burn in the still air of the Sabbath even if we do not see them in the week. You would not think for the world that your children should grow up to the same stains that have fastened upon you. You dream for them of a " life unspotted from the world," and the very anxiety of that dream proves how you know that your own life is spotted and stained.

I. 176.

Whiteness most white. Ah, to be clean again
  In mine own sight and God's most holy
    sight!
To reach through any flood and fire of pain
  Whiteness most white;

To learn to hate the wrong and love the right,
  Even while I walk through shadows that are
    vain,
Descending through vain shadows into night.
CHRISTINA G. ROSSETTI.

IT is wonderful how mere power, or mere
   brightness, will win the confidence and
admiration of men from whom we might have
expected better things.   A bright book or a
bright play will draw the crowd, although its
meaning be detestable.   A clever man will
make a host of boys and men stand like
charmed birds while he draws their principles
quietly out of them, and leaves them moral
idiots.   A whole great majority of a community will rush like foolish sheep to the polls
and vote for a man whom they know is false
and brutal, because they have learned to say
that he is strong.   All this is true enough;
and yet while men do these wild and foolish
things, they know the difference between the
illumination of a human life that is kindled
from above and that which is kindled from
below.   They know the pure flames of one
and the lurid glare of the other; and however
they may praise and follow wit and power, as
if to be witty or powerful were an end sufficient in itself, they will always keep their
sacredest respect and confidence for that
power or wit which is inspired by God, and
works for righteousness.

II. 12.

Oh, we are sunk enough, God knows! but not
      quite so sunk that moments,
Sure, though seldom, are denied us, when the
      spirit's true endowments
Stand out plainly from its false ones.

BROWNING.

With twain he covered his face.—Is. vi. 2.

YOU can know nothing which you do not reverence. You can see nothing before which you do not veil your eyes!

All of the mystery which surrounds and pervades life is really one mystery. It is God. Called by His name, taken up into His being, it is filled with graciousness. It is no longer cold and hard; it is all warm and soft and palpitating. It is love. And of this personal mystery of love—of God—it is supremely true that only by reverence, only by the hiding of the eyes, can He be seen. He who thinks to look God full in the face and question Him about His existence, blinds himself thereby, and cannot see God. He sees something, but what he sees is not God, but himself. There is in Christ the continual awe of a nature from the perfect knowledge of which the conditions of His human life excluded Him. And if He could not know the Father perfectly while He lived here in the flesh, shall we complain that we cannot? Shall we not rather rejoice at it? Shall it not be a joy to us to feel, around and through the familiar things which we seem perfectly to understand, the wealth and depth of Divinity, outgoing all our comprehension?   V. 256, 257.

For greatness which is infinite makes room
    For all things in its lap to lie;
We should be crushed by a magnificence
    Short of infinity.

FABER.

And with twain did he fly.—Is. vi. 2.

THERE are two extremes of error. In the one, action is disparaged. The result is that character itself fades away out of the inactive life. In the other, action is made everything. The glory of mere work is sung in every sort of tune. . . . The result is that work loses its dignity, and the industrious man becomes a clattering machine. Is it not just here that the vision of the wings comes in? Activity in obedience to God. Work done for Him and His eternal purposes. Duty conscious of Him and forgetful of the doer's self, and so enthusiastic, spontaneous,—there is the field where character is grown, there is at once the cultivation of the worker's soul and the building of some corner of the Kingdom of God.

Oh, my young friends, listen to the great modern Gospel of Work which comes to you on every breeze, but do not let it be to you the shallow, superficial story that it is to many modern ears. Work is everything or work is nothing according to the lord we work for. Work for God. . . . Then you are standing with your flying wings which will assuredly bear you into fuller light as they carry some work of God towards its fulfilment.

V. 267.

As the servants of Christ, doing the will of God from the heart.—EPHES. vi. 6.

I ask not that for me the plan
Of good or ill be set aside,
But that the common lot of man
Be nobly borne and glorified.

PHEBE CARY.

IS it not true that any man makes his trade or occupation ready to be filled with the high motive of the love of God when he trains himself to look at it in its ideal, and, at the same time, is thoroughly conscientious in its duties ?   The shoemaker who, having opened his heart to God's love, comes soonest and fullest to find the work of his lapstone and his bench touched and inspired by that motive, will be the shoemaker who most conceives of his daily work as one connected with human comfort and strength, and who, at the same time, is most conscientiously faithful to its details.   These things a man can do: he can resolutely abandon the sins which cannot be spiritualized; he can open all the channels of his life to spirituality by the study of the ideal, and by faithful work in every part of his living.   One is the turning out of strangers; the other is the preparing of the chambers for the entering guest.   The one is negative, the other positive.   When both are done, then the man who has learned in one little spot— the conversion spot of his nature—that God loves him, and who has there begun to love God, may look to see that new motive run into all these newly opened chambers of his life, making the half-ready places completely ready by its touch.   X. 23.

WHAT is it that perpetuates the blighting influence of fashion? What are the channels through which are spread abroad the false standard of wealth, the base idea of manliness which poisons countless hearts? Are they not the same God-created channels through which the holiest influences were meant to flow?—"Simon, called Peter, and Andrew his brother; James the son of Zebedee, and John his brother"? Many and many a time their brotherhood is the power of a common curse, instead of a common blessing. . . . What shall we do then? . . . It is a very wide law and a very beautiful one, that the best way to make a thing fit for the use for which it was first made is to put it to that use. The best way to make the dusty trumpet clear is to blow music through it. The best way to make the sluggish mind capable of thinking is to think with it. And so the best way to make the natural relationships capable of carrying religious influence is to give them religious influences to carry, so strong and ardent that they shall force and burn their own way through whatever artificial obstructions may have stopped up the channel through which they were meant to go.

V. 86, 89.

Pour Thy Holy Spirit in!
Sweep away the bars of sin;
For the grace that comes from Thee
Make us channels pure and free
Unto those that nearest be!

JOHN WORDEN.

THE Holy Ghost is the constructive principle and power in human life. By Him
every society of good men is bound together.
By Him the Christian Church rises into the
sky of God's grace like a majestic tree full of
all precious fruit. By Him the family wins
new sacredness, and every friendship of men
who are trying to serve God is bound into in-
dissoluble union with an unseen but strong
compulsion. If you are afraid of yourself as
you find how you are drawing away from your
fellow-men and growing into a more and more
selfish life, you must come to God; you must
enter into the communion of the Holy Ghost.
If you have a quarrel which you hate and
know is miserable, but which holds you fast,
your only freedom from it is in the communion of the Holy Ghost. Come there and
your quarrel will break and scatter as the ice
melts when you bring it into the sun. . . . It
is the communion of a common forgiveness
and a common inspiration.

VII. 316.

If thou be dead, forgive and thou shalt live;
  If thou hast sinned, forgive and be for-
     given;
God waiteth to be gracious, and forgive,
  And open heaven.

Set not thy will to die and not to live;
Set not thy face as flint refusing heaven;
Thou fool, set not thy heart on hell: forgive
  And be forgiven.

CHRISTINA G. ROSSETTI.

The Lord make you to increase and abound in love, one toward another.—1 THESS. iii. 12.

WHAT is there that can keep the purity and loftiness of domestic life ? What is there that can preserve the color and glory of the family like the perpetual consciousness, running through all the open channels of its life, that they are being used to convey the truth and the power of God ?

IV. 83.

What does it mean when religion enters into a family, when over all the home life is stretched out the hand of God, and all a household is converted ?   I do not know how to tell the story of what happens then—of the deep, sweet, solemn change that comes over all the family experience—except by just this phrase: that the communion of natural affection has passed into the communion of the Holy Ghost.   All these loves which were there before move on still, but they are all surrounded by and taken up into one great comprehending love; and he who enters in at the door of that converted house hears them all in deepened, richened music, the same strains still, only full of the power of the new atmosphere in which they are played.

VII. 312.

Sweetest things in Thee are sweeter,
Holiest things in Thee completer;
Therefore, Lord, our home-life enter,
Be its light, its joy, its centre!

LOUISE MATHILDE.

I am not come to destroy but to fulfil.
                    MATT. v. 17.

INFLUENCES come from man to man as
the dew and sunshine come from the bounteous heavens to the ready ground. . . . Your
child, your scholar, your servant—you may
fulfil him or you may destroy him. You destroy him if you fasten on everything that is
bad and crude and ridiculous about him, and
pour out upon it rebuke and contempt. You
destroy him if you make him feel himself
weak and insignificant, and drive him to despair. You destroy him if you make his great
feeling about his own life to be shame. On
the other hand you fulfil him, you fill him out
to his full, to his fullest, if you catch everything that is good about him and water it with
judicious encouragement and praise. You
fulfil him if you recognize every feeblest and
clumsiest effort to do right, if you inspire him
with hope, if you make him seem to himself
worth cultivating and watching and developing.

Therefore, with all the strength which God
has given us, let us be fulfillers. Let us . . .
with sympathy and intelligence, patience and
hope, bring up the lagging side in all the vitality around us, and assert for man the worth,
the meaning and the possibility of this his
human life.   IV. 213.

O Sun of our souls first arisen,
    Give us light for the spirits that grope;
Make us loving and steadfast and loyal
    To bear up humanity's hope!
                    LUCY LARCOM.

AS the sun that lightens us makes all the objects round us the reflectors and distributers of his radiance, and so brings his light to us clothed with the clearness that belongs to them, so to the Christian the Spirit of his Saviour seems to have subsidized everything to make some new and more perfect revelation of Him. The home relations and the things in nature, our books, our friends, our thoughts, have all been made interpreters of Christ. Oh, there are times when, as one sits in meditation or moves quietly about in work for Jesus—when all this seems so rich and plain. A beautiful, serene simplicity seems to come forth out of this complicated snarl. We catch the music of one great pervading purpose in all this tumult and clatter. It is all *redemption* working out its plans. God made that hillside so perfect in order that He might show me His fatherly love. Christ gave me this task to do that I might understand His self-sacrifice for me. The Spirit brought me into my friend's friendship that it might so interpret to me the friendship of my God. At such times all seems plain. The world is for the sons of God.

VII. 105.

O Centre of all forms!   O concord's home!
O world alive in one condensèd world!
O Face of Him in whose heart lay concealed
The fountain-thought of all this kingdom of
　　heaven!

GEORGE MACDONALD.

WE can well believe while the rose is but a bud, shut in between hard, glossy green leaves, gathering only the first dream of color into its pale petals, that its own color should seem to it the purpose of its life, just to be the perfect rose for the pure beauty of its perfectness. But when the bud bursts and the rose is born—what then? A world is waiting for its fragrance and its loveliness. To serve that world, to send the colorless light interpreted through its soft hues, and the odorless atmosphere translated by its fragrance, to be all that it may be for the sake of all that it may do—this is the larger purpose of its being, and, learning this, it ripens to the perfect flower. So may the scholar dream of pure self-culture for its own sake. It is a noble dream. . . . But if he grows he must outgrow it. He must grow in the direction of humanity. All the vast needs of life lay hold on him. . . . All that he knows and loves must go out with him into all his life, and his scholarship must be part of the father who sits in the family, of the citizen who votes at the polls,—if need be, of the soldier who fights in the ranks. . . .

X. 272.

Yea, plant the tree that bears best apples,
    plant,
And water it with wine, nor watch askance
Whether thy sons or strangers eat the fruit:
Enough that mankind eat and are refreshed.

EMERSON.

I CANNOT conceive of God standing and deliberately withholding from His world, or from any least and humblest of His servants, till to-morrow any blessing which it is possible for Him to give to-day. But, on the other hand, I cannot conceive of God's giving to-day any blessing which to-day His world or His servant is unready to receive. Why is it that ages have lived on without the blessings of popular liberty and free government and well-guarded rights? Is it that God has said, "The world shall not have them until my favorite century and race appear"? Is it not rather that God has said, "The world cannot have them until it has won by hard experience the heart and hand to which these blessings can be given, in which they can be held"? Why is it that God did not give you long ago the peace, the moral strength, which He will certainly give you some day if you persevere? Has He been keeping them from you wantonly and wilfully? Has He not rather been, nay, *is* He not, standing over you, eager to give them at the first moment when the gift is possible?

XII. 28.

No more in heaven than earth will he find
   God,
  Who does not know His loving mercy swift
But waits the moment consummate and ripe,
  Each burden from each weary heart to lift.

HELEN HUNT JACKSON.

And shall I behold Thee face to face,
O God, and in Thy light retrace
How in all I loved here, still wast Thou?

BROWNING.

I LOVE to think of this, that where men to-day are most unconscious of His presence, Christ is laying foundations for His future work.   Here is a perfectly worldly man who cares nothing for Christ or Christianity, but yet Christ's touches are on him.   He is surrounded with blessings; he is pressed upon with sorrows; he is led through apparently meaningless experiences; and all that some day, when he is really moved to cry out for a Son of God, Christ may be able to come to him, not new and strange, but with the strong claim of years of care and thought and unthanked mercy.   It makes the world very solemn to think how much of this work Christ must be doing everywhere.   It makes our own lives very sacred to think how much of it He may be doing in us.

V. 213.

Our want and weakness, shame and sin,
   His pitying kindness prove,
And all our lives are folded in
   The mystery of His love.

His sun is shining pure and vast
   O'er all our nights of dread;
Our darkness by His light at last
   Shall be interpreted.

ALICE CARY.

And He took the seven fishes and the loaves, and gave thanks, and brake them, . . . and they did all eat and were filled.—MATT. xv. 36, 37.

ALL the history of the progress of men's thought bears witness that when God wants to give men knowledge which they have not had before, He always opens it to them out of something which they have already known. Paul stands upon Mars' Hill at Athens, and wants to show those people Christ. How does he begin? He takes what he finds there. He points to their altar to the unknown god, and says, "Him whom ye ignorantly worship I declare to you." He opens the books of their own writers and finds there his text, "As certain of your own poets have said." Out of their bit of truth he opens the rich completeness of the truth he has to tell. Is it not just exactly the miracle of Christ? . . . Continuity and economy; these are the laws of Him who is leading us, the Captain of our salvation. He always binds the future to the past, and He wastes nothing.

II. 134, 143.

Not by strange, sudden change and spell,
  Baffling and darkening Nature's face;
Thou takest the things we know so well,
And buildest on them Thy miracle,—
  The heavenly on the commonplace.

SUSAN COOLIDGE.

And Jesus said: Make the men sit down.
JOHN vi. 10.

QUIET has come in place of the noise; repose instead of action. It [the crowd] has become receptive. It is waiting to be fed. . . . Some day the headlong current of your life was stopped. The river ceased to flow. The waves stood still, and then the ocean which the flowing of the river had kept out poured up and in, and there were sacreder emotions in the old channels, and deeper hopes and fears were beating upon the well-worn banks. The day when your great bereavement came, . . . the day when joy, with that subtle possibility of deep pain which is always in her eyes, came to your door and knocked, . . . the day when, being weak and ill, you did not go to your business, . . . those were the days when God was feeding you. . . . No life is complete which does not sometimes sit trustfully waiting to be fed of God.

IV. 227, 232, 234.

For not by bread alone
  Can we, Thy children, live:
Some heavenly food unknown
  Thou unto us must give.

Thy life, O God! Thy Word,
  Outspoken through Thy Son
In Him our prayer is heard,
  Our heart's desire is won.

The hidden manna this,
  Whereof who eateth, he
Grows up in perfectness
  Of Christlike symmetry.   LUCY LARCOM.

THERE is danger for many men, if not for
all, in the perpetual outgo of energy
which so much of our life involves. . . . "All
is going out, nothing is coming in;" is not
that the dismay and the despair which settles
down upon many an experience as it attains to
middle life? Existence comes to feel to many
of us like a great river, which is always flowing with unbroken force downward to the sea.
It never stops. It is always pushing its life
outward. It gives the sea no chance to flow
up into it. So is the ever energetic life of one
whose sole idea is to exert influence, to make
himself felt in some result. How often the
river must long to pause. How often it must
become aware that its impetuous rush is losing
for it the richness of the great deep salt sea.
How often the busy life of man becomes aware
that somewhere round it there is richness
which it does not get because it opens outward
only, and not inward. . . . There is need of
rest and receptivity.   IV. 229, 230, 231.

Many are coming and going with busy and
    restless feet,
And the soul is hungering now, with " no lei-
    sure so much as to eat," . . .
Oh, for a Sabbath of life, a time for renewing
    of youth,
For a full-orbed leisure to shine on the foun-
    tains of holy truth,
And to fill my chalice anew with its waters
    fresh and sweet,
While resting in silent love at the Master's
    glorious feet.   FRANCES R. HAVERGAL.

LABOR and patience, activity and the growth which comes by passive suffering, ought always to make one single total life. . . . Make your most restful contemplation and your most receptive listening at the lips of God, not to be mere spiritual luxuries, but to be forms and modes of action. Make them acts. Let them call your powers into play. Let them be not listless, but full of vigor. Let them anticipate work for God and service of His children so earnestly and eagerly, that they themselves shall be work and service.

He who learns these lessons lives a life as deep as the ocean and as powerful. There is no tedium or fretfulness for him. His life catches the quality of the life of God. He works while it is called to-day, and yet he has already reached the rest which remaineth for God's people. Such lives may God help us to live.

IV. 241, 243.

Toil is sweet, for Thou hast toiled;
  Rest is sweet, for Thou didst rest;
Be our works from sin assoiled!
  Be our rest upon Thy breast!

Be our work for Thee our rest!
  Be our strife for Thee our peace!
Till our sun sink in the west,
  And we reap Thy joy's increase.

J. L. M. W.

*He said unto me: Son of man, stand upon thy
feet.*—EZEK. ii. 1.

*Giving thanks always for all things unto God
and the Father, in the name of our Lord Jesus
Christ.*—EPHES. v. 20.

SHALL we, can we, thank God for His mercies, standing upon our feet and rejoic-
ing that we are men, thoroughly grateful for
the real joy of life?   Back of all the special
causes for thanksgiving which our hearts recognize, is there a thankfulness for that on
which they all rest and in which they are sewn
like jewels in a cloth of gold; for the mere
fact of human life, for the mere privilege and
honor of being men and women? . . .
  If you have been dwelling solely on the evil
that is in man, or on the special evil which you
think is in your church, your nation, or your
age . . . stand up!   Stand up upon your feet!
Believe in man!   Soberly and with clear eyes
believe in your own time and place.   There is
not, there never has been, a better time or a
better place to live in.   Only with this belief
can you believe in hope.

II. 149, 161, 162.

How good is man's life, the mere living! how
    fit to employ
All the heart and the soul and the senses for-
    ever in joy!

BROWNING.

Thou hast kept the good wine until now.
JOHN ii. 10.

MAN says, "I choose to let the best come first; and then, if need be, things must degenerate. I would make sure of what good there is. I am so sure of nothing, that anything I can catch shall be caught instantly." But God says, "No! The world grows better and better. The best must be kept waiting till its time shall have arrived. The best cannot come until its time is ready. The best must not come first but last." It is a difference which one immediately feels when he comes into the region of the religion of Christ. The essence of Christianity is to believe that the world is growing better, that the life of man is growing better, under the discipline of Christ. It is calm and hopeful with great assurances. It sets the old man, at the end of his career, in the midst of fulfilled promises and finished educations, splendidly saying, as he looks back over his life: "It has all been good, but this is the best of all. Thou, O Christ, O Master, hast kept the best wine until now!"
XII. 7.

As Thou hast made the world without,
  Make Thou more fair the world within;
Shine through its lingering clouds of doubt;
  Rebuke its haunting shapes of sin;
Fill, brief or long, my granted span
Of life with love to Thee and man;
Strike when Thou wilt the hour of rest,
But let my last days be my best!
WHITTIER.

When I would do good, evil is present with me.
ROM. vii. 21.

PAUL'S story has been your story. You never sprang most bravely from the low order of your living, that a hand did not seem to catch you and draw you back. You never felt a new power start up within you that a new weakness did not start up by its side. . . . Awful has grown this certainty that no good impulse ever could go straight and uninterrupted to its victorious result, and yet is it not wonderful how you have kept the assurance that good and not evil is the master-power of your life? The resolution has been broken. It has limped and halted. It has stood for months, and made no progress, but it has never died.

VI. 13.

Lord, I have laid my heart upon Thy altar,
　But cannot get the wood to burn;
It hardly flares ere it begins to falter,
　And to the dark return.
Old sap, or night-fallen dew, has damped the
　　fuel;
　In vain my breath would flame provoke;
Yet see—at every poor attempt's renewal
　To Thee ascends the smoke!
'Tis all I have—smoke, failure, foiled en-
　　deavor,
　Coldness and doubt, and palsied lack:
Such as I have I send Thee; perfect Giver,
　Send Thou Thy lightning back!
GEORGE MACDONALD.

*When the fulness of time had come, God sent forth His Son.—*GAL. iv. 4.

IT was the emptiest age that the whole moral and spiritual history of man had seen; and just that emptiness it was which made it the fulness of time for Christ. . . . It was out of the deadness of millions and millions of souls that the cry for life came,—unconscious, unmeant, but no less recognized by Him who watches and answers not only the desires but the needs of men.

And so with all of us is it not the fulness of time indeed? Is there one of us who can say, "It is not my time yet?" Now while the morning is at hand, the night far spent; now while we have, it may be, but a little while left us to come to Christ or to come closer to Christ, to be a Christian or to be a better Christian; now while the Bridegroom's feet are close upon us, are sounding already in the distance, oh, let our loins be girded about, and our lights burning, and we ourselves like unto men that wait for their Lord.

VII. 67, 71.

Said Mark to Martin, "Wherefore spend
Such constant care thy vines to tend?
It may be months, it may be years,
Before the vineyard's lord appears."

Said Martin, "Though it may be long
Before I hear his harvest-song,
If of that hour can no man say,
It may be that he comes to-day."

JULIA WOOD.

ONLY when all was ready, only in the fulness of time, did Jesus come . . . and
the men of whom He was the representative
and the chief—have they their advents too?
It is easy to believe it about the greatest of
them. . . . But it is hard to think the same
of common people such as you and I.   [Yet]
hard as it is, great as is the strain which it
puts on all our low habits of thinking about
ourselves, the Bible is a strong and glorious
call to men to gird up the loins of their minds
and believe that God had a place for them and
put them in their own place. . . .   The beginning of a life goes back before the man is
here, a visible fact upon the earth.   It lays
hold of the thought of God, which runs back
to eternity.   God knew your nature.   He
had a plan and pattern of your being in His
mind.   As David says, His eyes did see your
substance, yet being imperfect, and in His
book were all your members written.   Knowing you, He made ready a place for you; He
shaped a cradle for you in the ages, and when
it was all done He laid your new life in it—the
advent before the nativity.   VII. 4, 5.

So take and use Thy work,
Amend what flaws may lurk,

What strains o' the stuff, what warpings past
  Thy aim!

My times be in Thy hand,
Perfect the cup as planned!

Let age approve of youth, and death complete the same!
BROWNING.

In my Father's house are many mansions.   I go to prepare a place for you.—JOHN xiv. 2.

AH! there is no friendship worthy of the sacred name where each of the two friends is not always thus making ready places for the other in higher and higher mansions of the Father's house, where each is not always opening to the other some higher life.   Do not dare to think that friendship is a mere pleasant amusement.   Do not dare to take out of it the moral responsibility that makes its depth and sacredness. . . .   Husband and wife live together in perfect domestic sympathy.   Not a thought of either that the other does not share.   But when one of them enters into Christ and knows His peace and joy, it seems as if for the first time they had separated.   But the soul that has found the Saviour comes back with its love, and tells the story of the Saviour it has found, and, Andrew-like, brings the other soul to the Christ in whose love it has found a place.   Everywhere this ministry of life to life is finding its illustrations.

VI. 175, 176.

Come home with me, belovèd,—
  Home to God's waiting heart!
In gladness met together
  From paths too long apart;
Strangers no more, but brethren,
  One life with Him to live;
Eternally receiving,
  Eternally to give!

LUCY LARCOM.

To every man according to his ability.

MATT. xxv. 15.

IT is a young man's right—almost his duty —to hope, almost to believe, that he has singular capacity, and is not merely another repetition of the constantly repeated average of men. Before he unfolds the bundle which his Lord has given him, he may well see in his imagination the ten bright talents shining through its folds. To see those dreams and visions gradually fade away; little by little to discover that one has no such exceptional capacity; to try one and another of the adventurous ways that lead to the high heights and the great prizes, and find the feet unequal to them; to come back at last to the great trodden highway, and plod on among the undistinguished millions—that is often very hard. . . . Yet the man of two talents has a great chance in the world. Alas for the world if he had not! For it is of him that the world is mainly composed. . . . And Christ must come with special welcome and appreciation and delight to any man who feels his insignificance, and is in danger of losing himself in the vague mass of his fellows.

IV. 198, 204.

Be sure no earnest work
Of any honest creature,—howbeit weak,
Imperfect, ill-adapted,—fails so much,
It is not gathered as a grain of sand
To enlarge the sum of human action used
For carrying out God's end.

ELIZABETH BARRETT BROWNING.

MEN get tired, one after another, of the fantastic and one-sided types of character which the world admires, and which seem to us very attractive at first. Expectant without impatience; patient without stagnation; waiting, but always ready to advance; loving to advance, but always ready to wait; full of confidence, but never proud; full of certainty, but never arrogant; serene, but enthusiastic; rich as a great land is rich in the peace that comes to it from the government of a great, wise, trusty governor,—this is the life whose whole power is summed up in one word—Faith. "Here is the patience and faith of the saints." This is the life to which men come who, through long years, "follow the 'Lamb whithersoever He goeth."

II. 58.

The bravely dumb that did their deed,
  And scorned to blot it with a name,—
Men of the plain heroic breed,
  That loved Heaven's silence more than fame:
Such lived not in the past alone,
  But thread to-day the unheeding street,
And stairs to Sin and Famine known
  Sing with the welcome of their feet.

LOWELL.

With good will doing service, as to the Lord, and not to men.—EPHES. vi. 17.

SUPPOSE—for it is at least supposable—that behind every other motive, shining through every other motive which made a man work, there had been this—the love of Christ. Whoever he worked for secondarily, he worked for Jesus first of all. Would that have made no difference? Like an electric atmosphere poured around the shrine in which a jewel rests, so that no hand can be thrust through to steal the jewel; so round the work, full of its joy, is poured the love of Christ, out of which no man can snatch it. Suppose that some strong opponent keeps him from doing what he wants to do,—there is still the assurance that his doing that is but a part of a vaster accomplishment,—the will of his great Master,—which he knows must come in its completeness whether this special act of his attain success or not.

III. 300.

I seem to halt, and yet I know
  The breath of God is in the sails:
  Whether by zephyrs or by gales,
The ships of God must onward go.
  E'en when to rest He singeth them,
  He to the haven bringeth them.

C. G. HAZARD.

As unknown, and yet well known.

2 COR. vi. 9.

ARE there not moments in your life when it seems to you as if you understood and knew yourself through and through? You have listened to this clank of your machinery so long, that you know every sound that it makes. . . . "Know myself!" you say; "indeed I do," grasping your own warm, hard flesh. "Am I not this, which lives thus? Why should I think myself mysterious?" And then instantly, "Know myself! God forbid! Who am I that I should enter into the bosom of His eternal purpose, and study there what has only there real and final being? Let me stand before my unknown self, and wonder." Poor and mangled is the life which has not thus seemed both to understand and be ignorant about itself. It must be either useless or visionless.

VI. 284.

But O my soul, as I thy good
   And evil ways explore,
I seem to see the Christ in thee
   His earthly life live o'er. . . .
Thou art that Temple where the Lord
   Out-teacheth scribes of law,
Whence afterward with cords He makes
   Coarse mammon priests withdraw;—
Thine inmost court, a holy place,
   The Lord's own glory-home,
Thine outer, sentencing Him oft
   To shame and martyrdom.

DENIS WORTMAN.

Whatsoever things were written aforetime, were written . . . that we, through patience, and comfort of the Scriptures, might have hope.

ROM. xv. 4.

Welcome, dear Book! soul's joy and food! the
    feast
Of spirits! heaven extracted lies in thee:
Thou art life's charter, the Dove's spotless
    nest,
Where souls are hatched unto eternity.

VAUGHAN.

WE circulate the Bible by the million. Some parts of it we read as a religious duty. But there are whole books of it teeming with interest which few of us ever touch. One sometimes feels that some day or other a great increase of the spiritual power of the Bible will come with what will be almost a rediscovery of its literary attractiveness. When people break through the strange feeling which has gathered around it that it is dull and unreal, and find that it is the most interesting book in all the world, then they will be open for its deeper power to lay hold upon their consciences and hearts. IV. 298.

Above all, get the great spirit of the Bible . . . the idea without which it would all drop to pieces,—that there is not one life which the great Life-Giver ever loses out of His sight; not one which ever sins so that He casts it away; not one which is not so near to Him that whatever touches it touches Him with sorrow or with joy. I. 110.

THE New Testament is a biography. Make it a mere book of dogmas, and its vitality is gone. . . . Make it the history of Jesus of Nazareth, and the world holds it in its heart forever. Not simply His coming or His going, not simply His birth or His death, but the living—the total life of Jesus in the world's salvation. And the Book in which His life shines orbed and distinct is the world's treasure. There, as in all best biographies, two values of a marked and well-depicted life appear. It is of value, first, because it is exceptional, and also because it is representative. Every life is at once like and unlike every other. Every good story of a life, therefore, sets before those who read it something which is imitable and something which is incapable of imitation; and thereby come two different sorts of stimulus and inspiration. It gives us help like that of the stars which guide the ship from without, and also like that of the fire which burns beneath the engines of the ship itself.

X. 428.

Why must He lay His infant head
In the manger where the beasts were fed?
So that the poorest here might cry,
" *My Lord was as lowly born as I.*"

   .   .   .   .   .

Is there no way to Him at last
But that where His bleeding feet have passed?
Did He not to His followers say,
" *I am the Life, the Light, the Way* "?

PHEBE CARY.

THERE are few features in the life of Jesus which impress me more than the way in which His work and His growth, His effective and receptive life went on together. . . . True, there were times when He withdrew Himself, and, leaving all activity behind, lay on the mountain days and nights passive before His Father, waiting to be more completely filled with Him. But those were rare, exceptional occasions. The ordinary dependence upon God was perfectly expressed by those words to His disciples, " My meat is to do the will of Him that sent me!" When He gave the sermon on the mount, when He calmed the tempest on the lake, when He raised Lazarus from the dead, we do not doubt that both processes were going on, enfolded in the completeness of each of those actions. He was saving the world, and He was becoming more perfectly His Father's Son at once. . . .

Rest and action in the experience of the completest soul are not antagonistic; they are hardly distinct from one another. Action is the most refreshing rest, and rest is in some sense the most effective action to the soul that lives on complete dependence and obedience to God.

IV. 240.

But if I face with courage stout
  The labor and the din,
Thou, Lord, wilt let my mind go out,
  My heart with Thee stay in.

GEORGE MACDONALD.

Strengthened with all might, according to His glorious power, unto all patience and long-suffering, with joyfulness.—COL. i. 11.

ONE sufferer cries, "Lord, make me strong;" another sufferer cries, "Lord, let me rest upon Thy strength." Do you say they come to the same thing? Yes, if the doing of the task, the bearing of the pain, is everything. Yes, if the only object is that the ship may not founder and the back may not break; but if, beyond this, there is hope and purpose that the man who does the task or bears the load shall himself become God-like in his doing and suffering, then no mere deposit of the strength of God can do the work—only the ever-open union of his life with God's, which makes the two lives really one, so that the power that is in God is not made the man's by being transferred from God's to him, but is his because it is God's.

III. 126.

God, whom my roads all reach, howe'er they run,
My Father, Friend, Beloved, dear All-One,
Thee in my soul, my soul in Thee, I feel,
Self of myself.

SIDNEY LANIER.

If this counsel or this work be of men, it will come to naught ; but if it be of God, ye cannot over-throw it.—ACTS v. 38, 39.

THAT which is rooted in God must live. There is no hope or peace anywhere in the world if this is not true. Who cares which way the fickle wind is blowing at this minute if there be no purpose which stands behind and governs it, no One who holds the winds in His hands ? But if there be, who will not labour bravely, trying to put himself into the current of the great purpose of the world; begging to be defeated if he mistakes the great purpose and is helping evil when he thinks that he is helping good; ready to wait and work through all delays;—sure of one thing and only one, that in the end, through every hindrance and delay, God must do right ?

III. 262.

I do not dare to pray
For winds to waft me on my way,
But leave it to a higher Will
To stay or speed me, trusting still
That all is well, and sure that He . . .
Will land me—every peril past—
Within the sheltered haven at last.

Then whatsoever wind doth blow,
My heart is glad to have it so;
And blow it east, or blow it west,
The wind that blows, that wind is best.

CAROLINE A. MASON.

LIFE grows healthily from less to more. It does not begin with its best and fade away towards nothingness. It opens with promises which involve incompleteness, and goes forward with a climbing sun toward a rich and radiant noon. . . . If I am travelling through a country which is sure to grow less and less rich as I get farther on, it is inevitable that I shall strive at every step to gather all of its fleeting riches that I can. . . . I shall leave no well untasted and no tree unplucked. I shall burden my shoulders with the load of what I cannot eat. But if I know that, as I pass on from field to field upon my journey, each is to be richer than the last, I shall be calm and patient and serene, seeing to-day in the broader light of to-morrow; asking to-day to give me its appropriate gift, not demanding of it that which it is not ready to bestow nor I to take; and going on with faith, which is the deepest and most precious result of every blessing.

XII. 17.

I will not wrong Thee, O To-day,
  With idle longing for To-morrow;
But patient plow my field and sow
  The seed of faith in every furrow.

Enough for me the loving light
  That melts the cloud's repellent edges,—
The still unfolding, bud by bud,
  Of God's most sweet and holy pledges.

HARRIET McEwen KIMBALL.

THE evening of your abundant prosperity arrived. The darkness gathered in about the radiant luxurious life which you had lived. No longer did it seem as if the sun shone and the flowers bloomed and the seasons came and went for you. You said, " It is all over. I have had my day." To some of you since you said that, there has come a great surprise. What seemed all over has proved to be but just begun. The day which you thought you had had, you can see now that you had hardly touched. Prosperity has come to mean to you another thing. The hours in which it meant plenty of money, plenty of friends, seem now so thin and superficial. To work, to help and to be helped, to learn sympathy by suffering, to learn faith by perplexity, to reach truth through wonder, behold! this is what it is to prosper, this is what it is to live. You did not really begin to live till the darkening of your happiness brought you into the knowledge of a happiness which can never darken. The evening and the morning have been your first day.

VI. 331.

Life's self, the immortal, immutable smile
Of God on the soul, in the deep heart of
    Heaven,
Lives changeless, unchanged; and our morn-
    ing and even
Are earth's alternations, not Heaven's.
OWEN MEREDITH.

He came unto His own. . . . To them He gave power to become the sons of God.

JOHN i. 11, 12.

THE man to whom it seems incredible that God should have been made man is not so likely to have been misled by a peculiar reverence for God as by an unworthy estimate of man. . . . He has taken things as he sees them and lost sight of their ideals. He has seen the mercenariness of friendship, the squalor of home, the animalness of love—everything sunk down out of its nobleness; and he has said, "There is no place for God here. It would degrade Him to become man, man being thus." Ah, brethren, if we could only begin at the other end! God *did* become man, and therefore manhood must be essentially capacious of Divinity. He lived in a human home, and so our homes must be capable of a Divinity they do not have. He entered into friendships, and so friendship must be sacred. He worked, and so work must be honorable. He cared for the body that He lived in, and so the body cannot be so vile as men have called it and as we make it. If *this* could be the way the Incarnation came to us, then surely it must be a constant inspiration to us that it was "His own" to whom Christ came.

VII. 27.

O soul of mine! I tell thee true,
  If Christ indeed be thine,
Not more makes He himself thy kin
  Than makes He thee divine.

DENIS WORTMAN.

JESUS "came unto His own." To men forgetful of their godlike nature He came to tell them that they were the sons of God; and to men who could not do without Him He came because they needed Him. Oh, my dear friends, by what high warrants does the Saviour claim us for His own! Because we are His Father's children, and because we are so needy, therefore our divine Brother comes. He comes to you and says, " You called Me." And you look up out of your worldliness and say, " Oh no! I did not call. I do not know You!" But He says, calmly, "You did, although you do not know it. That power of being godlike which is in you, crushed and unsatisfied—that summoned me; and that need of being forgiven and renewed which you will not own—*that* summoned Me. And here I am! Now wilt thou be made whole? If thou canst believe, all things are possible to him that believeth."

VII. 30.

I did not know that I had called Thee, Lord:
  I knew not half my dearth, my sin, my
    grief;
Yet gladly now I take Thee at Thy word,—
  Lord, I believe; help Thou my unbelief.

JOHN WORDEN.

CHRIST came in answer to a most urgent and pressing *call of need.* That is what it signifies when it is said that "He came *unto His own.*" For in a true sense everything is a man's own which *needs* that man; not everything which he needs, but everything which needs him. Do you not know what that is? Your child is yours not merely by the claim of birth and nature, but by the tie of continual dependence. He is most yours when he needs you most. . . . He came to those who needed Him; most of all to those who from the stricken earth held up to Him the deepest of all needs, the need of sin that craved forgiveness; and that was what made them His. Certainly no level-eyed intercourse of sinless man with sinless Christ could have wrought in us such a profound and precious sense that we belong to Him as this simple knowledge that we *need* Him. Need has its sacred rights. Because we want forgiveness and help, and He only can forgive and help us, therefore we are His.

VII. 28, 29.

My faith burns low, my hope burns low,
　Only my heart's desire cries out in me
By the deep thunder of its want and woe,
　Cries out to Thee.

Lord, Thou art Life though I be dead,
　Love's Fire Thou art however cold I be:
Nor heaven have I, nor place to lay my head,
　Nor home, but Thee.

CHRISTINA G. ROSSETTI.

*He planteth an ash, and the rain doth nourish
it.*—Is. xliv. 14.

LET it not be a group of ash-trees, but a
group of men, . . . a thought of God
entrusted to the earth for its embodiment and
execution.   What are these dreams and visions,
these upward reachings, these certainties of
infinite belongings,—what are they, O thought
of God, but the unbroken tension of the chain
which binds the thinker to His thought forever?   And what are all these earthlinesses,
these tender clingings to the things our senses
understand, . . . these calls of present duties,
this fear of dying, this love of the present,
warm, domestic earth,—what are they all but
the pressure of the warm ground upon the seed
entrusted to it?   The man who does not somehow hold the complete truth about his life—
both of these truths combined in one—does
not live worthily.   The man who has and
holds them both, look, what a life he lives!
Look how substantially his roots are fastened
in the earth.   Look how aspiringly he lifts his
branches to the sky.

V. 282, 283.

Here in Thy great world-garden, Lord, we
stand:
Keep us, for here the blossoms blight so fast!
The fruit is flawed in turning from Thy beams
To the biting east—to folly and to sin.
And let all trees, the wildings of the wood
And grafts of rarest culture, waft Thee praise!

LUCY LARCOM.

THE growth of the tree is a mysterious and spiritual power. It cannot be detected at its labor when with a sudden stroke of the axe you tear the tree's trunk open. Your sight is not keen enough to catch it. And yet how closely, how inextricably it is bound up with the grosser elements, in connection with which alone it does its work. There must be the black earth and the brown seed, or nothing comes. What growth-power ever made manifestation of itself, creating out of nothing, in the air, a tree that had no history and no progenitor? The material is first, and then the spiritual.

And need I even suggest to you how every man has in his bodily constitution the physical basis of the most subtle and transcendent parts of his profoundest life? Out of the very marrow of his bones comes something which his finest affections never outgo, and which gives a color to his soul's loftiest visions. . . . There is a physical correspondent to everything he thinks or fancies. There is a physical basis to his most spiritual life.

Do honor to your bodies. Reverence your physical natures, not simply for themselves. Only as ends they are not worthy of it, but because in health and strength lies the true basis of noble thought and glorious devotion. A man thinks well and loves well and prays well because of the rich running of his blood.

VI. 245, 246, 249.

Health of body with health of soul—
This is the only worthy goal.

The Lord God formed man of the dust of the ground, and breathed into his nostrils the breath of life; and man became a living soul.—GEN. ii. 7.

I DO not know, I cannot guess, what was the nature of the historical event to which that verse refers. But I do know that it is absolutely true to that great order which pervades the universe. Everywhere the earthly conditions offer their opportunities to the celestial miracle. The fuel is cut in the woods of earth; it is piled, hard and lifeless, on the unheeding stone; and then from it the flame arises, a live aspiring column, and lays its fiery tribute at the feet of God. "That is not first which is spiritual, but that which is natural; and afterward that which is spiritual." Would it not be good . . . if these words should be written in golden letters on the walls of every gymnasium and also on the walls of every school of learning and cell of meditation in the world? . . . As they stood on the walls of the gymnasium, what they declared would be the need of a strong body for all best spiritual life. As they stood written on the study wall, they would mean the utter failure of the strongest body unless a spiritual life came down from above and occupied it, came out from within and clothed it with a worthy purpose. VI. 246, 248.

> Let us not always say,
> " 'Spite of this flesh to-day
> I strove, made head, gained ground upon the whole!"
> As the bird wings and sings,
> Let us cry, " All good things
> Are ours, nor soul helps flesh more, now, than flesh helps
> soul." BROWNING.

THERE are men deeply impressed with the infiniteness of life. . . . There comes great happiness to them. That happiness is perfectly hollow unless there is a meaning behind it, unless it tells of intentions somewhere, unless it means love. They know that " Eat, drink, and be merry," is not the end of it all. To love some one who is loving them, that is what they want to do. " Oh, that I could find Him ! Oh, that I could find Him! " is their cry. Great sorrow comes. But to them sorrow cannot rest in broken limbs or lost fortunes. Those again are only symbols. The essential thing lies deeper. . . . Then if any glimpse is offered of a Son of God, a manifestation of the Invisible Deity who sends happiness and sorrow and who can forgive sin, there is no tendency to disbelieve; there is the hunger of the heart leaping with hope, there is the stretching out of the arms as when they told Bartimeus, " Jesus of Nazareth passeth by."

V. 207, 208.

'Neath some shadow oft I wait,
Like blind Bartimeus at the gate,
Assured that when my Lord draws nigh,
Sin, doubt, and darkness all shall fly;
Hence to His cross I cling the more,
Whene'er these shadows touch my door.

JOHN ORDRONAUX.

The Lord is at hand.—PHIL. iv. 5.

OH, my dear friends, if you knew that in the most evident of all ways, which is by death, the Lord were coming to you to-morrow, and if you could be perfectly free from all base feeling, from fear and flurry, from defiance and from dread? . . . what would be the condition which it would make in you? Would it be any elevation, refinement, solemnity, and broadening of life? Would it be the calming of frivolity, the release of charity, the kindling of hope? Would it not be all of these?

Not yet for us does that great, solemn footfall sound outside the door. But none the less is the Lord at hand. He is always at hand. All expectation may be expectation of Him.

IV. 368.

Who shall know the Master's coming?
Whether it be at dawn or sunset,
When night dews weigh down the wheat-ears,
Or while noon rides high in heaven,
   Sleeping lies the yellow field?
Only, may Thy voice, Good Master,
Peal above the reapers' chorus,
And the sound of sheaves slow falling,—
"Gather all into My garner,
   For it is My harvest time!"
DINAH MULOCH CRAIK.

THAT life which we dream of in ourselves
we see in Jesus.   Where was there ever
gentleness so full of energy?   What life as
still as His was ever so pervaded with untiring
and restless power?   Who ever knew the purposes for which he worked to be so sure, and
yet so labored for them as if they were uncertain?   Who ever believed his truths so entirely, and yet believed them so vividly as
Jesus?   Such perfect peace that never grew
listless for a moment; such perfect activity
that never grew restless or excited; these are
the wonders of the life of Him who going up
and down the rugged ways of Palestine, was
spiritually walking on "the sea of glass
mingled with fire."

As more and more we get the victory over
the beast, we too are lifted up to walk where
he walked.   For this all trial, all suffering,
and all struggle are sent.

IV. 126.

Peace, perfect peace, in this dark world of
sin?
The blood of Jesus whispers peace within.

Peace, perfect peace, by thronging duties
pressed?
To do the will of Jesus, this is rest.

Peace, perfect peace, our future all unknown?
Jesus we know, and He is on the throne.

E. H. BICKERSTETH.

WHEN Jesus had risen from the dead, you remember, His disciple refused to believe till with his own hand he had felt the wounds in the hands and feet and side. And Jesus gently rebuking him, compares, as it were, the methods of authority and experience, of faith and science, so to speak, to the advantage of the former when He says, " Thomas, because thou hast seen thou hast believed. Blessed are they that have not seen and yet have believed." And yet when we come to think of it, is not His rebuke really that Thomas had not used the method of experience enough, not that he demands it too much? He rebukes him that in all the years that they had been together he had not observed Him deeply enough to learn His character and understand His words. Is He not pleading, not against science, but for a higher science? . . . " If I do not the works of my Father believe me not," a direct appeal to experience.

VI. 133.

Oh, for a faith more strong and true
Than that which doubting Thomas knew—
    A faith assured and clear,—
To know that He who for us died—
Rejected, scorned, and crucified—
    Lives and is with us here!

PHEBE CARY.

And a little child shall lead them.—Is. xi. 6.

HE who helps a child helps humanity with a distinctness, with an immediateness, which no other help given to human creatures in any other stage of their human life can possibly give again.   He who puts his blessed influence into a river blesses the land through which that river is to flow; but he who puts his influence into the fountain where the river comes out puts his influence everywhere.   No land it may not reach.   No ocean it may not make sweeter.   No bark it may not bear.   No wheel it may not turn.   Sometimes we get at things best by their contraries.   Learn the rich beauty of helping a child by the awfulness of hurting a child,—hurting a child even in his physical frame,—hurting him still more in soul and mind.   The thing that made the Divine Master indignant as He stood there in Jerusalem was that He dreamed of seeing before Him a man who had harmed some of these little ones, and He said of any such ruffian, "It were better for him that he had never been born."   If it is such an awful thing to hurt a child's life, to aid a child's life is beautiful.   X. 506.

Great hearts have largest room to bless the
        small;
Strong natures give the weaker home and rest;
So Christ took little children to His breast,
    And with a reverence more profound we fall
In the majestic presence that can give
Truth's simplest message: "'Tis by love ye
        live."   LUCY LARCOM.

THE first truth is the essential unity of man's life and God's, and so the essential glory of humanity. Christ came not merely to man, but *into* man; and that was possible because the manhood into which He entered was "His own," had original and fundamental unity with His Godhood, was made in the image of God. Here was man, made in God's image, separated from God, trying spasmodically to struggle back, failing and falling so continually that the consciousness that he belonged with God was well-nigh lost. That it might not be lost, that it might be a real and living thing, it must be asserted from the other side. Man and God had the capacity of entrance into each other. Since man would not, and, as it almost seemed now, *could* not enter into God, God would enter into man. Man had failed of being Godlike; God, then, would be manlike, and so the first truth—that God and man belonged together —should not be lost for want of assertion. Is not this a noble and inspiring value of the Incarnation? VII. 26.

Lord, if Thou grant me grace to hear and see
Thy very Self who stoopest thus to me,
    I make but slight account
Of aught beside wherein to sink or mount.
CHRISTINA G. ROSSETTI.

Because there was no room for them in the inn.
LUKE ii. 7.

RELIGION makes us feel the littleness to which we have reduced our lives, and then proclaims, in contrast with that littleness, the great capacity God meant them to have. ''You have cramped your life,'' it seems to say. ''You have made it small and narrow. By long unspirituality you have made its doors so low that none but short or stooping thoughts can enter. You have made its rooms so mean that great truths can not live in them. But never dare to think that this was God's plan for your life. He drew its architecture on a lordly scale. He designed for you great, generous, capacious lives. He built you to be 'temples of the Holy Ghost.' . . . You may make your lives foul and tawdry and meagre; you may diminish and overcrowd them till there is no room for a noble thought or a pure desire; but you do it at your peril. God made them roomy; and there is room for His holy Son to find a nativity within them if you will only set and keep their chambers open.''
VII. 80, 81.

Christ, He requires still, whensoe'er He comes
To feed or lodge, to have the best of rooms:
Give Him the choice; grant Him the nobler
    part
Of all the house:—the best of all's the heart.
HERRICK.

The Word was made flesh, and dwelt among us.
                              JOHN i. 14.

WHO is it that lies once more to-day before the world, the Son of God and Son
of man, at Bethlehem?   Mary bows down and
learns the Incarnation, and feels the solemnity and sublimity of the human life into
which the Divinity has entered.   The wise
men come and find their King in this weak
babe.   The shepherds see the hope of Israel
fulfilled, the Saviour come.   Oh, on this Christmas Day let us be with them all!   Let us feel
thrilling through this humanity which we so
often scorn the glorifying fire of the Incarnation.   Let us give up our lives to Him and beg
that He will rule them.   But, more than all,
let us give our souls, hungry and sinful, a
Christmas leave to go to Him who is their
Saviour, whom they will know for their Saviour
if we let them go to Him.

It is a day of joy and charity.   May God
make you very rich in both by giving you
abundantly the glory of the Incarnation, the
peace of Christ's kingship, and the grace of
Christ's salvation. ·

                              VII. 96.

The heart must ring Thy Christmas bells,
   Thy inward altars raise;
Its faith and hope Thy canticles,
   And its obedience praise!

                              WHITTIER.

Now the God of hope fill you with all joy and peace in believing, that ye may abound in hope by the power of the Holy Ghost.—ROM. xv. 13.

SUCH peace in believing is to be distinctly a peace by Gospel faith. . . . Let me be a thorough believer in Jesus Christ,—let me, that is, have taken Him with all the revelation of humanity that there is in Him, and where is the fellow-man with whom I shall not be at peace? Is it the man who domineers over me and bullies me? The supreme mastery of my Lord adjusts all these lower masteries, and compels them to keep their proper places. When I have learned really to "fear Him who can cast both soul and body into hell," I am able indeed not to "fear them that can kill the body." The martyr seeing Christ standing at the right hand of God is at full peace with his murderers.

VI. 203, 204.

And he [St. Stephen] *kneeled down, and cried with a loud voice: Lord, lay not this sin to their charge. And when he had said this, he fell asleep.*—ACTS vii. 60.

Oh, for the vision that sufficed
That first blest martyr after Christ,
    And gave a peace so deep
That while he saw with raptured eyes
Jesus with God in Paradise,
    He, praying, fell asleep!

PHEBE CARY.

Thou wilt hide them in the secret of Thy presence . . . from the strife of tongues.

Ps. xxxi. 20.

THE very words are full of peace before we hardly touch them to open their meaning. But their meaning is deeper the more we study it. . . . Suppose that St. John should come and talk with you, or be at your side without a word in the midst of the wildest of our social Babels. Would he not bring his peace with him? Would you not let every one else go, and be alone with him, even in all the crowd? And now if it is possible, instead of the great disciple, for God Himself to be with you, so that His presence is real, so that He lets you understand His thoughts and lets you know that He understands yours; and as close to you—nay, infinitely closer—than the men who crowd you round, and whose voices are in your ears, the unseen God is truly with you, what then? . . . He has blinded you to all but Himself. He has hid you in the secret of His presence.

I. 83, 84, 85.

Yet shall I envy blessed John?
  Nay, not so verily,
Now that Thou, Lord, both Man and God,
  Dost dwell in me:
Upbuilding with Thy Manhood's might
  My frail humanity;
Yea, Thy Divinehood pouring forth,
  In fulness filling me.

CHRISTINA G. ROSSETTI.

It is no little thing when a fresh soul,
And ,a fresh heart, with their unmeasured
    scope
For good, not gravitating earthward yet, . . .
Are sent into the world,—no little thing
When this unbounded possibility
Into the outer silence is withdrawn.

JAMES RUSSELL LOWELL.

WHAT is it when a child dies? 'It is the great Head-master calling that child up into His own room, away from all the under-teachers, to finish his education under His own eye. The whole thought of a child's growth and development in heaven is one of the most exalting and bewildering on which the mind can rest. Always the child must be there. Always there must be something in those who died as children to make them different to all eternity from those who grew up to be men here among all the temptations and hindrances of earth. There must forever be something in their perfect trust in the Father, something in the peculiar nearness and innocent familiarity of their life with Jesus, . . . something pure even among all the perfect purity which we shall all have reached, something wiser than the wisest, showing that even there there is a revelation that can be given only to the babes; something more perfectly triumphant and serene to mark forever the perfected life of those who never sinned.

IV. 149.

These are they which follow the Lamb whithersoever He goeth.—REV. xiv. 4.

It doth not yet appear what we shall be, but we know that when He shall appear we shall be like Him.—1 JOHN iii. 2.

IS life decreasing or increasing? Is it growing richer or poorer? The ordinary cheap philosophies assume that life is like a fire which speedily reaches the fulness of its heat, and then fades and fades till it goes out. The high philosophy which gets its light from God believes that life, as it moves deeper and deeper into God, must move from richness into richness always. . . . All that we believe is but the promise of the perfect faith. All that we do is great with its anticipation of the complete obedience. All that we are but gives us suggestions of the richness which our being will attain. Those moments make our real, effective, enthusiastic life. They create the fulfilment of their own hopes and dreams. Oh, cherish them! Oh, believe that no man lives at his best to whom life is not becoming better and better, always aware of greater and greater forces, capable of diviner and diviner deeds and joys! XII. 21, 22.

Oh, sweet to live, to love, and to aspire!
 To know that whatsoever we attain,
Beyond the utmost summit of desire
 Heights upon heights eternally remain,
To humble us, to lift us up, to show
Into what luminous deeps we onward go.

LUCY LARCOM.

It is toward evening, and the day is far spent.
LUKE xxiv. 29.

THE year which came to us twelve months ago, all fresh and young, is old and weary. A new year will come to crowd him from his place. On such a day it is not mere habit, it is a natural and healthy instinct, which makes us stand between the new year and the old, between the living and the dead, and listen to them as they speak to one another. The old year says to the new year, " Take this man and show him greater things than I have been able to show him. You must be for him a fuller, richer day of the Lord than I could be." The new year says to the old, " I will take him and do for him the best that I can do. But all that I can do for him will be possible only in virtue of the preparation which you have made, only because of what you have done for him already."

IV. 357.

I am fading from you,
  But one draweth near,
Called the Angel-guardian
  Of the coming Year.

I brought good desires,—
  Though as yet but seeds,
Let the New Year make them
  Blossom into deeds.

ADELAIDE A. PROCTER.

Then cometh the end.—1 COR. xv. 24.

I will remember the years of the right hand of the most High.—Ps. lxxvii. 10.

IF around this instability of human life is wrapped the great permanence of the life of God . . . if the whole element of time is so lost in His eternity that not the beginning and the ending of experiences but their spiritual relations to our growing characters is everything,—then is there not light upon it all?   To value everything which comes to me, and yet to know that not its form but its spiritual essence is really valuable, therefore to hasten while I have it to get out of it what it has to give me, and to even rejoice that some day in the loss of its formal presence I shall be able to make myself completely sure of the possession of its spirit,—that is the true attitude of the soul toward every good thing that God gives,—health, friends, wealth, learning, *time.*

V. 369.

Why cry so many voices, choked with tears,
" The year is dead! " It rather seems to me
Full of such rich and boundless life to be,
It is a presage of the eternal years.
. . . So let us rather cry:
This year of grace still lives; it cannot die!

MARY G. SLOCUM.

Turn ye even unto Me with all your heart, and with fasting.—JOEL ii. 12.

FASTING is both a symbol and a means. Every kind of abstinence is at once an expression of humility and an opening of the life. What then is Lent? Ah, if our souls are sinful and are shut too close by many worldlinesses against that Lord who is their life and Saviour, what do we need? Let us have the symbols which belong to sin and to repentance. Let us at least for a few weeks, among the many weeks of life, proclaim by soberness and quietude of life that we know our responsibility and how often we have been false to it. Let us not sweep through the whole year in buoyant exultation, as if there were no shame upon us, nothing for us to repent of, nothing for us to fear. By some small symbols let us bear witness that we know something of the solemnity of living, the dreadfulness of sin, the struggle of repentance. . . . Perhaps the symbol may strike in and deepen the solemnity which it expresses. Perhaps as we tell God of what little sorrow for our sins we have, our sorrow for our sins may be increased, and while we stand there in His presence the fasting may gather a truer reality of penitence behind it.

II. 214.

Who goeth in the way that Christ hath gone
Is much more sure to meet with Him than one
    That travelleth byways.

GEORGE HERBERT.

It is finished.—JOHN xix. 30.

OH, what a finishing that was! It is as if eternity were crowded into the heart of Him who spoke. All He had been forever had consummated itself at last. The long yearning to let men know what a love waited for them in the heart of God was satisfied. The light was kindled on the mountain-top, and already the quick ear of Divinity heard the stirring in thousands of valleys, where men, hopeless before, were gathering up their burdens and with the inspiration of an unfamiliar hope were starting to struggle up with them, determined not to rest until they cast them down into the shadow of that unseen cross. What cry like this has the world ever heard? Not even that first utterance of calm creative power, "Let there be light," had greater meaning or sublimity than this last agony of love that burst from the lips of the satisfied Redeemer: "I have been lifted up. I shall draw all men unto Me. Now it is finished."

VII. 265.

Done is the work that saves!
  Once and forever done,
Finished the righteousness
  That clothes the unrighteous one.
The love that blesses us below
Is flowing freely to us now.

HORATIUS BONAR.

That I may know Him, and the power of His resurrection.—PHIL. iii. 10.

THE life of a true Christian seems to me to be full of Easters; to be one perpetual renewal of things from their lower to their higher, from their temporal to their spiritual shape and power. You are called upon to give up a luxury, and you do it. The little piece of comfortable living is quietly buried away underground, . . . undergoes some strange alteration in its burial, and comes out a spiritual quality that blesses and enriches your soul forever. . . . So the partial and imperfect and temporary are always being taken away from us and buried, that the perfect and eternal may arise out of their tombs to bless us. . . . They are not simply taken away to be kept—the child that you saw die, the dream that you saw fade—to be kept in some future state till you shall be fit to come and get them; . . . they are here all the time; not to be had by-and-by, but to be had now. They can be had in their spiritual return to you by-and-by only as you first have them and keep them spiritually now. . . . The power of the future resurrection is all along a power of present regeneration.

What can I do, then, but invite you all to know that power by earnest self-surrender, by patient prayer, and by a childlike faith that willingly takes into its loving life the willing, living, loving Christ of Easter Day?

VII. 277, 278, 285.

He that hath the Son, hath life.—JOHN v. 12.

A cloud received Him out of their sight.

ACTS ii. 9.

FOR a human being to go out from this earth is a dreadful thing if it is only with this earth that humanity has any known relation. . . . But now let us believe in the Ascension. Once a human being—the best and completest of all human beings that have ever lived, the human being whose humanity was perfect by its very union with Divinity—has gone, still human, out of the sight of men,— gone, evidently all alive. We can not trace His course. The cloud received Him. But yet we know that somewhere out beyond the limits of our little earth that true humanity of His has found a home. Humanity can live beyond the earth, can keep broad live relations with the universe. The man who goes to-day, then, goes still into the dark, but the darkness into which he goes is pierced by a path of light, and at its heart there is a home of light to which he goes. The humanity of Jesus has gone before and makes the vast unknown not unfamiliar. Around our thought of it our thoughts of the men we have seen die, our thoughts of our own coming deaths, can gather with confidence and calmness.

VII. 298.

Thou Who wast Centre of all heights on the
    Mount of Beatitudes,
Grant us to sit with Thee in heavenly places.

CHRISTINA G. ROSSETTI.

He saith unto them, Have ye received the Holy Ghost since ye believed?—ACTS xix. 2.

AND what that first Whitsunday was to all the world, one certain day becomes to any man, the day when the Holy Spirit comes to him. God enters into Him and he sees all things with God's vision. Truths which were dead spring into life and are as real to him as they are to God. He is filled with the Spirit and straightway he believes; not as he used to, coldly holding the outsides of things. He has looked right into their hearts. His belief in Jesus is all afire with love. His belief in immortality is eager with anticipation. Can any day in all his life compare with that day? If it were to break forth into flames of fire and tremble with sudden and mysterious wind, would it seem strange to him—the day when he first knew how near God was, and how true truth was, and how deep Christ was? O, have we known that day? O, careless, easy, cold believers! if one should come and ask you, " Have you received the Holy Ghost since you believed ? " dare you, could you, answer him, " Yes " ?

II. 227.

I bow my forehead to the dust,
 I veil mine eyes for shame,
And urge, in trembling self-distrust,
 A prayer without a claim.

 . . . . .

No offering of mine own I have,
 Nor works my faith to prove;
I can but give the gifts He gave,
 And plead His love for love.

WHITTIER.

Through Him we both have access by one Spirit unto the Father.—EPHES. ii. 18.

SEE what Godhood the soul has come to recognize in the world. First, there is the Creative Deity from which it sprang, and to which it is struggling to return—the divine End, God the Father. Then there is the Incarnate Deity, which makes that return possible by the exhibition of God's love,—the divine method, God the Son; and then there is this Infused Deity, this divine energy in the soul itself, taking its capacities and setting them homeward to the Father—the divine Power of Salvation, God the Holy Spirit. To the Father, through the Son, by the Spirit.

Let us keep the faith of the Trinity. . . . Let us seek to come to the highest, through the highest, by the highest. Let the end and the method and the power of our life be all divine. If our hearts are set on that, Jesus will accept us for His disciples; all that He promised to do for those who trusted Him, He will do for us. He will show us the Father; He will send us the Comforter; nay, what can He do, or what can we ask that will outgo the strong and sweet assurance of the promise: Through Him we shall **have** access by one Spirit unto the Father.

I. 243, 246.

We from Thy oneness come,
Beyond it cannot roam,
And in Thy oneness find our one eternal home.

FABER.

PHILLIPS BROOKS'S WRITINGS.

SERMONS. First Series.

30th Thousand. 12mo. 20 Sermons. 380 pages. Cloth, $1.75. Paper, 50 cents.

"Humanity, and not sectarianism, is built up by such sermons as these. Mr. Brooks is a man preaching to men about the struggles and triumphs of men."—*New York Tribune.*

SERMONS. Second Series.

THE CANDLE OF THE LORD, etc. 20th Thousand. 21 Sermons. 378 pages. Cloth, $1.75. Paper, 50 cents.

"Dr. Brooks is wonderfully suggestive in opening men's thoughts in directions which give to life fresh meanings."—*New York Times.*

SERMONS PREACHED IN ENGLISH CHURCHES. Third Series.

12th Thousand. 14 Sermons. 320 pages. Cloth, $1.75. Paper, 50 cents.

"He has a message to deliver, it is from God; he believes in its reality, and he delivers it earnestly and devoutly, and his hearers catch the enthusiasm of his own faith."—*Churchman.*

TWENTY SERMONS. Fourth Series.

12th Thousand. 378 pages. Cloth, $1.75. Paper, 50 cents.

"Mr. Brooks brings to the pulpit the mind of a poet and the devout heart of a Christian, with a very large and generous human personality."—*Independent.*

THE LIGHT OF THE WORLD, AND OTHER SERMONS. Fifth Series.

12th Thousand. 21 Sermons. 382 pages. Cloth, $1.75. Paper, 50 cents.

"Because he reveals to men with force and beauty their true and deeper selves, meant for all good and right things, Dr. Brooks preaches a word which they ever rejoice to hear, and having heard, can never go away unprofited. His larger parish will cordially welcome these twenty-one sermons."—*Literary World.*

SERMONS. Sixth Series.

7th Thousand. 12mo. 20 Sermons. 368 pages. Cloth, $1.75. Paper, 50 cents.

"How shall we describe these twenty sermons? They take the old stories told in the Hebrew narratives and fill them with a life that throbs and glows with the breath and blood of to-day. Simplicity and power seem to be the attributes of this preacher. . . . Gladly we welcome this new vial containing the life-blood of a master spirit."

—*The Critic.*

SERMONS FOR THE CHURCH YEAR.

Advent, Christmas, Lent, Easter, etc. Edited by the Rev. JOHN COTTON BROOKS. 7th Series. 22 Sermons. 360 pages. Cloth, $1.75.

"The principle of selection upon which this volume has been formed gives it a certain unity in that the sermons chosen present the great facts in the life of Christ in their order, so that the entire Christian year is consecutively presented through spiritual interpretation."—*The Outlook.*

PHILLIPS BROOKS'S WRITINGS.

LECTURES ON PREACHING.

Delivered before the Divinity School of Yale College in January and February, 1877. 12th Thousand. 12mo. 281 pages. $1.50.

"The enthusiasm for the profession which this book displays has contagion in it, because it is not expended on that which separates the profession from other occupations, but on that which it shares with them. Throughout the book runs a single thought never lost sight of,—the greater the man the greater the preacher; and again and again, when discoursing of practical methods, the lecturer returns in some form to his golden text, that it is the man behind the sermon which makes the sermon a power. It is because the lecturer, holding this truth firmly, addresses himself to the living facts of a preacher's profession rather than to the mechanism or elaborate organization in which he works, that his words will be life to the living and glittering generalities to the moribund."—*Atlantic Monthly*.

THE INFLUENCE OF JESUS.

The Bohlen Lectures for 1879. 14th Thousand. 16mo. 274 pages. Cloth, $1.25.

Lecture I. The Influence of Jesus on the Moral Life of Man.
" II. The Influence of Jesus on the Social Life of Man.
" III. The Influence of Jesus on the Emotional Life of Man.
" IV. The Influence of Jesus on the Intellectual Life of Man.

"The ringing keynote is the Fatherhood of God to all mankind, the favorite idea of this distinguished preacher, and one which he here develops with all his characteristic energy, eloquence and hopefulness."—*The Literary World*.

TOLERANCE.

Two Lectures addressed to the Students of several of the Divinity Schools of the Protestant Episcopal Church. 4th Thousand. 16mo. 111 pages. Cloth, 75 cents. Paper, 50 cents.

"Mr. Brooks's two lectures in eloquence, sweetness, and literary charm are what he always is when at all equal to himself. For their substance they lay down a doctrine of tolerance which would at a touch bring all sections of Christendom together on the basis of a tolerance which carries in it the promise of spiritual unity."—*Independent*.

BAPTISM AND CONFIRMATION.

15th Thousand. Paper, 10 cents.

THE GOOD WINE AT THE FEAST'S END.

A Sermon on Growing Old. Paper, 25 cents.

A CHRISTMAS SERMON.

Paper, 25 cents.

THE SYMMETRY OF LIFE.

An Address to Young Men. Paper, 25 cents.

THE LIFE HERE AND THE LIFE HEREAFTER.

In attractive paper covers. 25 cents.

AN EASTER SERMON.

Paper, 25 cents.

THE LIVING CHRIST.

An Easter Sermon. Paper, 25 cents

PHILLIPS BROOKS'S WRITINGS.

ESSAYS AND ADDRESSES.

Religious, Literary and Social. Edited by the Rev. JOHN COTTON BROOKS. Large 12mo. 538 pages. Gilt top, $2.00. White cloth, gilt edges, $2.50.

Among the thirty-seven Essays are "Heresy," "The Best Methods of Promoting Spiritual Life," "Authority and Conscience," "A Century of Church Growth in Boston," "The Conditions of Church Growth in Missionary Lands," "Poetry," "The Purposes of Scholarship," "Milton as an Educator," "Courage," "Dean Stanley," "Martin Luther," "Biography," "Literature and Life," etc.

"A welcome memorial of his life and work—another evidence of his widespread sympathies, his intellectual activity, and above all his loving and Catholic Christianity. Every one of these essays and addresses is worth not merely reading, but study, for its own sake; for its clearness and purity of style, its sincerity and suggestiveness, its information, its strength and purpose."—*Churchman*.

"Every essay and address is distinguished by that rich exuberance of thought and noble earnestness of purpose that made Phillips Brooks unique among the religious teachers of this generation."
—*New York Tribune*.

LETTERS OF TRAVEL.

Written to his Family. 14th Thousand. Large 12mo. 302 pages. Cloth, gilt top, $2.00. White cloth, full gilt, with cloth cover, $2.50.

CONTENTS.

First Journey Abroad. 1865-1866.

In the Tyrol and Switzerland. 1870.

Summer in Northern Europe. 1872.

From London to Venice. 1874.

England and the Continent. 1877.

In Paris, England, Scotland, and Ireland. 1880.

A Year in Europe and India. 1882-1883.

England and Europe. 1885.

Across the Continent to San Francisco. 1886.

A Summer in Japan. 1889.

Summer of 1890. Last Journey Abroad.

"They abound in everything which can make such a compilation attractive—pleasing scenes and incident, good company, a light, dignified and vivacious style, and the strong, personal charm of a very unusual man driving the quill."—*The Independent*.

"We owe a debt of gratitude to the family who have consented thus to open the door and let us sit by Phillips Brooks's side and hear him talk in familiar conversation."—*The Outlook*.

Sent by mail, post-paid, on receipt of price.

E. P. DUTTON & CO., Publishers,

31 West 23d Street, New York.

PHILLIPS BROOKS'S WRITINGS.

PHILLIPS BROOKS YEAR BOOK.

Selections by H. L. S. and L. H. S. 31st Thousand. 16mo. 372 pages. Gilt top, $1.25.

"I am so much impressed with its wonderful insight and the spiritual fitness of the quotations that I desire to express my personal gratitude to the editors for the spiritual help which they have given to me and to thousands of others, by the rare discrimination and excellent taste which they have shown in their happy work. No complaint can be made to the effect that this book does not fairly represent Bishop Brooks. It gives us a great many of his best thoughts, his communion with the Master, his spiritual insights, and his highest aspirations."

"One of the richest and most beautiful books of the year in point of contents. . . . It would probably be impossible to find in any volume of this size, drawn from distinctively religious writings, a richer fertility of spiritual resource and intellectual insight than is to be found in these pages."—*The Outlook*.

"Those who have known and loved Phillips Brooks, those who have listened to his glowing words and seen his illumined face, and those who have merely been able to trace his thought in print, will take a tender pleasure in turning the leaves of this "Year Book" compiled by loving hands. It will be a help from day to day ; for the ringing sentences, the wise counsellings and the inciting to a higher life, strong in themselves, seem almost sacred now one feels impelled to heed them."—*Boston Transcript*.

JUST READY.

GOOD CHEER FOR A YEAR.

Selections for every day by W. M. L. Jay. 16mo. 378 pages. Gilt top, $1.25.

THE PHILLIPS BROOKS CALENDAR FOR 1897.

Twelve leaves (8¼ x 10), with illustrations in colors, and selections from last volume of Sermons. In box, $1.00.

THE PHILLIPS BROOKS CALENDAR.

A Block Calendar for 1897, with a leaf to tear off for every day, giving a short selection. 50 cents.

Sent by mail, post-paid, on receipt of price.

E. P. DUTTON & CO., Publishers,
31 West 23d Street, New York.